Bountiful Blessings

Bountiful Blessings

Book Two of Traded for One Hundred Acres

Karen Ayers

Strategic Book Publishing and Rights Co.

Strategic Book Publishing & Rights Co., LLC
USA | Singapore
www.sbpra.net

For information about special discounts for bulk purchases, please contact Strategic Book Publishing and Rights Co., Special Sales at bookorder@sbpra.net.

ISBN: 978-1-68235-353-0

To Jim, my husband, for loving me and allowing me time to write. Thank you for being one of my biggest fans. I love you sweetheart.

*****

To Ken, my investor and friend. Thank you for believing in me and encouraging me with my writing. You believed in my writing way before anyone else did.

*****

To Angela, my daughter. I hope you know I smile each time I think about how much you love our Lord. You have had a hard life from time to time, but you have the most amazing, forgiving heart. I am so glad I made you my daughter. I love you.

*****

To Jennifer, my daughter. I will never forget the night you looked up at me with those tiny eyes on that cold winter's night in January. I had no idea how to be a mother, and I had to learn it all with you. I treasure the bond you and I share and pray that you and your own children will always be as close. You are a terrific mom and hairstylist, and I am so proud of you. I love you.

*****

To Kris, my son. You came into my life at such a young age and called me Mom. Even though I am no longer married to your father, you are no less my son. I loved you then, and I still love you now. Follow your heart, son, for there isn't anything you can't do if you put your heart into it. I love you.

*****

To Mary, my daughter. I think of you often, Mary, even though you may not realize it. If you ever read this, please email me. I will never regret adopting you. I would love to be a part of your life. I love you.

*****

To Heather, my daughter; my sweet baby girl. I have watched you grow into such a well-educated, independent young woman who is beautiful inside and out. I am so proud of the woman, wife and mother you have become and know you are a great teacher that children look up to. I am looking forward to seeing what the future holds for you. I have no doubts it will be amazing. I love the bond we share. I love you.

*****

To Lance, my son, the youngest of the clan. Thank you for being one of my best friends and being a boy who was such a delight to raise. Thank you for doing much of the research for this book; you are so bright. I pray that life gives you all that you hope for. Never let anything keep you from going after your dreams. I love you.

*****

To my children by marriage, Megan, Whitney, Brandon, and Jordan. I hate the word STEP-children. I will just call you my children by marriage if you don't mind. I want you to know I love each of you, and I am so glad you are now in my life. Even though I will never take your mother's place, please know I am here should you ever need me.

*****

To Lorri, my editor. You go above and beyond for me. Please know that I think of you as a dear friend and love you with all my heart.

*****

Thank you to all my fans and friends I haven't mentioned by name. Just because your name isn't here doesn't mean I care for you any less. I have met so many wonderful people along the way with my books and have no idea what I would do without your reading and promoting. Thanks also for all the kind words you have said to me. I love you all.

*****

Thank you, Strategic Book Publishing for all the work and effort you put in to make my books look their best. You have such a professional staff that is a delight to work with.

*****

Thank you, Katie (my sister) who took the cover photo and allowed me to borrow my nephew Russell to play the part of Matthew. And thank you Shannon and Craig (great friends) for allowing me to use your daughter Hadley, to play Catherine. This is just how I pictured Matthew and Catherine.

*****

KAREN AYERS

But most of all, I thank Jesus Christ for wrapping me in His loving arms and loving me even when I didn't deserve to be loved. You saved my soul and forgave me by Your grace and mercy. To You I owe everything, and because of You I have hope and a future.

Chapter One

1842 America

Alice Bowen loved springtime. In fact, it was her favorite time of year, when the warmth took over the colder temperatures, and she could sit on her front porch, soaking in the sunshine and the glorious fragrance of spring.

It wasn't so many years ago she watched her late husband, Mitchell, plow their fields and get ready to plant the seed. But today, she watched Joseph, her seventeen-year-old son, who had been hard at work since daybreak.

Joseph was such a handsome man and made Alice so proud.

Joseph was only eleven at the time his father passed, but he jumped right in and took over as well as any man could have. He worked hard on their farm and never complained.

There was so much on her mind today.

Ten years ago, today, her daughter, Savannah, left them at just sixteen years of age, to embark on a journey west. She traveled by covered wagon to Arkansas with Jonah Bell, a man fourteen years her senior.

She had replayed the days prior to that day so many times in her head. She could remember them as if they were just yesterday, the day Jonah Bell first stepped up on their porch and talked to Mitchell about his plans.

It was a beautiful spring day, and Savannah had gone to the mercantile in Dahlonega. She so loved getting away from the house and never complained when asked to go.

Savannah was a dreamer, and always carried her journal in her skirt pocket in case she was inspired to write a poem or write about her day.

Alice knew, if she were ever running late getting back, that she was probably down at Mill's Pond, writing in her journal and daydreaming.

It had surprised Alice to see Jonah's wagon rounding the corner and heading up the hill to the house.

His wife, Clara, had only been gone three short weeks. She had passed giving birth to their daughter, Rose.

Alice's heart hurt for him each time she thought about all he must be enduring through this painful ordeal.

She observed through the window, not wanting to interfere.

She assumed he was desiring to speak to Mitchell about personal matters, and the truth was she had no idea what to say to a man who must be grieving so.

They had never been very close to the Bells, and now she regretted that.

"Come sit a spell, Mr. Bell," Mitchell called out to Jonah as the wagon come to a halt.

Jonah walked toward the house and up the steps, as he removed his hat. "Thank you, Mr. Bowen, but I cannot stay long; I must get back to Nelly's house. She is keeping Rose for me while I do my errands."

"My wife and I are terribly sorry for your loss, Mr. Bell. If there is anything we can do, please let us know."

Jonah nodded. "Thank you, I appreciate that. There *is* something you can help me with, Mr. Bowen. I am just not sure how to ask. Been pondering on it for a couple days now."

"Might as well spit it out, Mr. Bell; that way we shall discuss whatever it is ye need."

Jonah rubbed his head and grew quiet for a moment.

Alice could tell from watching through the lace curtain that something was weighing heavily on his mind.

"I was wondering if you would be willing to trade your daughter's hand in marriage for my land and cabin?"

Mitchell chuckled. "You want to marry my Savannah, so soon after ye wife passed?"

"It's not what you think, sir. I need someone to take care of my daughter as I travel to Arkansas."

"I see. Are ye planning on staying in Arkansas with my daughter, to live?"

"Yes, sir. I am guessing she is old enough to marry and leave home?"

"She is, indeed."

"There's a right smart bit of land I own, Mr. Bowen, and I am sure with it already adjoining yours, you have thought of the possibility from time to time."

Mitchell smiled and rubbed his hand across the three-day stubble on his face. "That I have, indeed, Mr. Bell. In fact, I'm willing to meet your price and conditions. When do you expect such a transaction to take place?"

"Pardon me, sir, for giving such short notice, but I would like to get started in order to make it in time to build a cabin before winter sets in. Traveling by wagon in cold conditions is not something I wish to endure. If we embark on our journey in the next couple of days, sir, we should make it there by the middle of the summer, which shall give me ample time to erect a small cabin before the harsh winds set in from the north."

"I see, and short notice it is, Mr. Bell. But have no fear; I shall have Savannah ready to go day after tomorrow. Let me say one thing, if I might. If ever I hear of you mistreating my daughter in any way, I shall personally hunt you down like a bear and tear you to shreds." Mitchell smiled slowly and leaned back in his chair.

"I'm an honorable man, Mr. Bowen," Jonah shifted from one foot to the other. "The only reason I asked to marry your daughter in the first place, sir, is because it wouldn't be proper to take her across the land alone and not be married. Truth is, sir, I have no intention of ever consummating the marriage when my heart still belongs to Clara."

Mitchell Bowen laughed, wickedly. "Oh, I suppose that prediction won't last long lying by a girl as sweet as my Savannah. She'll be ye wife, Mr. Bell, and a wife does have her duties to perform for her husband. What I mean was not to harm her. I am only allowing this because she is already sixteen, and you're the only beau around that's single for hundreds of miles that's good enough for my daughter. It's high time I push her outta the nest, so I shall have one less mouth to feed."

Alice couldn't stop thinking about that conversation and how Mitchell had hurt her to the deepest part of her soul on that day, ten long years ago. And how Savannah reacted when she told her the news not long after she came back from the mercantile.

Alice suspected she would be upset, but Savannah was more concerned about taking care of Rose; Mr. Bell's three-week-old daughter, than the fact that she would be hundreds of miles away and would soon become the wife of a man she hardly knew.

It was on that day she realized that her sixteen-year-old daughter carried a crush for Mr. Bell, and she was afraid he would never love her as every woman desired to be loved.

"Can I go and visit Chrissy? We are going to do our homework together." Mary came out on the porch, carrying her book in her arms. She looked so much like Savannah, and now at almost twelve years of age, she was beginning to act like her as well, when it came to her books.

"Did you finish your chores?" Alice asked.

"You know I did, Mother; I always finish before I ask."

Alice nodded her head in agreement and smiled. "Yes, you always do. I should have known better than to ask. Yes, you may, but be home before dark."

"Thank you, Mother, I will." Mary stepped off the porch and headed toward the Adams farm.

"Where is she going?" Joseph asked, wiping the sweat off his brow.

"She's going to Chrissy's to do homework. The field looks great, Joseph. You did a fine job, just as you always do."

Joseph took the ladle and drank some of the cold water sitting in a bucket on the porch step.

"Just doing my job."

"Is something wrong, Joseph?"

"No, Mother." Joseph placed the ladle back into the bucket and sat down.

"You seem a bit distant today. In fact, you have been distant all week. Is something on your mind, son?"

Joseph brushed the dirt from his shirt and looked out toward the newly plowed field. "I was just thinking about Savannah."

"You, too? I can't seem to get her off my mind today."

"Been ten years, Mother. She's almost twenty-seven now, and all we have are a few letters."

"Her life and home are in Arkansas with her husband and three children. I am grateful we have the correspondence between us, and we keep in touch through mail."

"Mary doesn't even remember her; she was too young when she left. And honestly, some days it is hard for me to remember what she looked like."

"Mary knows her from the letters and looks so much like Savannah, you can remember what she looks like by your younger sister."

Joseph sighed. "I sometimes hate Father for what he did."

"Joseph Bowen," Alice scolded. "Do not ever let me hear you talk ill of your father, to say you hate him."

"I'm sorry, Mother, but I do. Father didn't even ask her; he just give her away. What kind of man does that to his own child?"

"It wasn't like that, Joseph. Why are you bringing this up now after all this time? Your father has been gone six years."

"Because I was too young to bring it up when it happened, and I did not understand until years later what actually took place. Father had no right to do that. It's like he didn't care about her at all. She was his oldest daughter."

"Joseph, your father did the best he could. He thought he was doing the right thing for Savannah at the time, and just look how happy she is. She loves being Jonah's wife and the mother to Rose, Matthew and Catherine. If you asked her, she wouldn't trade her life in Arkansas for anything."

"Father was only looking out for Father. He wanted land and another cabin. He never cared about Savannah, nor me. I am not even sure if he loved you, Mother."

Alice stood up in anger. She had never heard Joseph talk ill of his father before, and she did not intend to allow him to disrespect him now. "That's quite enough, Joseph. I will not sit and listen to you disrespect your father."

"I am not a child anymore, Mother. Father is no longer here, and what I speak, you know is the truth; you just don't want to admit it. You don't have to fear him any longer."

"I didn't fear your father."

"Yes, you did, Mother. I am sorry if that upsets you, but you did, and so did I."

Alice sat back down in the rocker and looked again toward the field in silence, not knowing what to say. Maybe she did fear Mitchell, or her daughter would have never been forced to marry a man she hardly knew.

"I miss her, Mother, and I know you do, too."

"I do. There is not a day that goes by I don't miss her, but it helps me to know that she is happy, and I feel blessed that we can communicate."

"Let's move to Arkansas, Mother. There's nothing to keep us here. This farm means nothing to me, because every time I look at it, it just reminds me of Father."

"Oh, Joseph, if it were that easy. We can't just pick up and move. Mary has friends here and she is still in school. And I have a good business of baking and sewing. That business has brought us good income for a long time."

"She can meet new friends, Mother, and you can bake and sew from anywhere. We have the money to go after selling the land that once belonged to Jonah. You don't have to bake and sew any longer; you just choose to."

"It doesn't have anything to do with money, son. There is no school close to Savannah's home. She teaches the children from home. I don't want to pull Mary away from school. Do you have any idea how far it is to Arkansas?"

"Yes, I do. We can take a stagecoach, stopping in several towns and changing coaches and staying the night. It would be a long journey, but the reward at the end would be worth it. I want to see my sister, Mother. I want to meet Jonah and see if he is really the man, she claims he is, and I want to meet my nieces and nephew."

"Sounds like you have been pondering about this for a while."

"I have. I am old enough to go on my own, but I cannot leave you. You need me, and I know that. When I was growing up,

I planned to move to Arkansas as soon as I was grown. I wanted to see Savannah and get away from Father. But when Father passed, I knew the only way I'd ever be able to see her again is if you went with me."

Alice's heart was breaking. Her grown son was so much a man who had every right to venture off on his own, but he felt obligated to stay. And he was right; she needed him, more so now than ever.

"Thank you, son. Thank you for being the man that you are. Mary will be out of school in four years, and we shall talk about this again, I promise."

Joseph looked at his mother in disappointment, without saying a word.

He stood, put on his hat, and headed to the barn.

*****

Jonah stopped his horse under the same tree he and Savannah had stopped their wagon under almost ten years ago. He remembered asking her to look at the land below, and they both decided that this would be where they built their cabin.

Now, with the addition on the cabin, the two barns, John's small cabin, and the fields beyond, he smiled, admiring their hard work.

The valley was certainly beautiful, and the Bell's farm was paradise to him. It was a dream he and Clara, his first wife, originally shared, to move from Dahlonega, Georgia to Arkansas and build a home to settle in and raise their children.

And he had been living that dream, with his wife, Savannah, a woman he intended upon their marriage to never allow himself to fall in love with.

Jonah chuckled to himself, thinking back. Even though he told himself Savannah would never win his heart, his heart had other plans.

It wasn't long after the move to Arkansas that Jonah started to melt toward her a little more day by day, and as much as he fought it, there was no stopping how deeply in love he fell with her.

Jonah could see their children in the distance, playing in the creek. That same creek where Savannah washed their clothes and carried water to bathe and cook with.

Rose, now ten years old and so much like her mother, Clara, acted much older than her age. To Rose, Savannah *was* her mother, for she was all she'd ever known. Even though they both told her about Clara at an early age, she rarely asked about her. Jonah knew it would be just a matter of time and the questions would come.

Matthew, now six, loved following Jonah around and soaking up all he could. Jonah knew that one day he would grow into a fine young man, one that he and Savannah would be so proud of.

And then there was Catherine, their baby girl. She came along just eleven short months after Matthew, a surprise to them, for sure, for they had not expected another baby so soon.

Jonah rode slowly to the cabin and took it all in. He didn't take life for granted, and even though he once was a broken man, he knew he wouldn't change a thing.

Thank You, Father, for so many blessings. And for forgiving me when I blamed you for Clara's death.

Thank you for sending Savannah to not only show me how to love again, but also show me just how much You love me.

You have given me much more than I ever deserved.

****

"Shall I set the table, Momma?" Rose asked, helping Catherine out of her wet clothes.

"Yes, please do, sweet girl. Did your Pa ever make it back?"

"Yes ma'am, he is in the barn putting away Midnight."

"I trust Matthew is with him?" Savannah asked, taking a taste of the rabbit stew.

"Of course," Rose giggled. "He follows him everywhere."

"No harm in that. Your brother must learn all he can, for someday he will be a man with his own farm and family to tend."

"Can I go to the barn with Pa?" Catherine asked.

"No, you may not, little missy. You shall help your sister prepare the table for dinner."

"But Momma, I want to pet Midnight like Matthew."

"Tomorrow you can pet Midnight. As for now, your sister has you cleaned up for dinner. Now set the napkins on the table, please."

"Okay," Catherine grumbled and reluctantly did as she was told.

Savannah giggled to herself. Catherine was her adventurous child and hated to be told no.

After Matthew was born, she never dreamed to have another child so soon, but in less than a year Catherine was born, and had been a fireball ever since.

"I could smell that delicious stew all the way to the cabin," John commented when he walked through the front door.

"Papa John!" Catherine screamed and ran to the elderly man to hug him around his legs.

"Catherine, don't rush up on Papa John like that, you could cause him to fall," Savannah scolded.

John Barge had lived in a cabin on their land for the past seven years. The children thought of him as family and called him Papa John.

John laughed. "It's okay, Sweet Pea, I wouldn't have it any other way. Come let me sit down and give you a proper hug."

"You'd think she'd not seen you in weeks the way she carries on," Rose piped up.

"I have not seen Papa John since yesterday." Catherine crossed her arms and pouted.

"Are you feeling okay today, Papa John?" Savannah was worried about their elderly friend more so lately, as she could tell his time was getting closer, and she hated to think of what they would do without him, especially the children.

"Just a wee bit tired these days."

"You know, Papa John, we can always bring your meals to you, should you desire to stay in your cabin." Savannah knew that time would eventually come and mentally prepared herself. She and Jonah both loved John as if he were their own father.

"Oh no, child, it motivates me knowing I am coming to dinner to eat some of ye delicious food. Gives me something to look forward to all day. As long as these old bones will still allow me to move, then moving is what I will do."

Savannah laughed. "Well, you can always come to breakfast and lunch as well."

"It doesn't take much for me these days. I have plenty of water in the cabin, and as much as I eat for dinner, I am just not hungry until dinner again."

"What do you do all day to occupy your time? Shall I teach you how to sew to keep you from being bored?"

John chuckled. "I am afraid ye can't teach an old dog new tricks. I spend my time resting and reading the Good Book. Always gives me comfort to read God's promises and know that one day I'll be carried over yonder with my Martha."

Savannah finished placing the food on the table and smiled at John. She worried about him, even if she never told him so.

Years ago, John would have been able to eat plenty at every meal, but lately dinner was the only time he ventured toward the house.

His appetite had faded, and he spoke more often of seeing Martha.

"Smells good, Savannah," Jonah complimented, walking through the front door with Matthew on his heels. "Matthew, get out of those wet clothes and get to the table."

"Yes, sir," Matthew took off to his room to do as he was directed.

"Did you have a good ride into town?" Savannah asked, accepting his kiss on the cheek, with a giggle.

"I did; it is such a beautiful day. After dinner, the children can help me unload the supplies from the wagon."

"I'm sorry I wasn't up to going with ye, Jonah," John said.

Until recently, John had always made the trip into the village with Jonah and enjoyed it.

"That's not a problem, John. How are you feeling today?"

"Just tired is all. Seems old age has sapped all my energy. Not much use to anyone round here anymore."

"Now, now, we will have none of that, will we, Savannah?" Jonah looked toward his wife, knowing she was the best at motivating.

"Jonah is right, you are family and you have done way more than your share since we have met you. You deserve a break. Besides, you do help us more than you know. Without you, our children would have no Papa John."

Rose kissed him on the cheek. "We love you, Papa John."

John smiled and nodded. "And I love ye, too, precious child. I love ye all. I know I would not have made it this far had it not been for ye all. I have lived the last part of my life a very blessed man."

Matthew ran back into the room and sat quickly at the table. "I am starving!" he screamed.

Everyone laughed at his eagerness to eat. Matthew was a bottomless pit when it came to food.

"I bet I can eat more than you, Matthew," Catherine boasted. "Bet you can't!"

"All right, children," Jonah scolded. "Dinnertime is not a competition to see who can eat more; besides, it is not good for your belly to eat too much."

"That's right; we will get fat, huh, Pa?" Matthew took a bite of his stew.

"Fat is not a nice word, Matthew, and we have not said grace yet, young man," Savannah looked at her son sternly.

"Papa John, would you do the honors of saying grace for us this evening?"

"I surely will," he said, as he bowed his head. "Father, thank ye kindly for this delicious food that is spread before us and bless the hands that prepared it. Thank ye for all the blessings ye have bestowed upon us, and for loving us the way that only ye can do. Amen."

Jonah loved this time of day, when his family sat down at the dinner table and reflected upon their day. He smiled at Savannah and she winked at him.

Jonah knew that he was a very blessed man.

Chapter Two

Savannah finished hanging out the wash on the line beside the creek bed and walked back toward the house.

What a glorious day it was going to be. She loved listening to the birds sing, knowing they were busy building their nests to lay their eggs.

"Can I make a cake tonight, Momma?" Rose asked, when she entered the cabin.

"What's the special occasion?" Savannah put down her basket and started to peel the potatoes to go with the roast she had been simmering since daylight.

"Must we have a special occasion to bake a cake? Someday I will meet a man like Pa, and I will have to know all these things to please him."

Savannah giggled. She loved her eldest daughter and who she was becoming. There was no doubt she would make some man a wonderful wife someday. "You think cake pleases a man like your pa?"

"It pleases Papa John, and he is a man. His favorite part of the meal each evening is dessert."

"You are right about that, sweet girl, but then anything sweet pleases Papa John. Yes, you may. What kind of cake would you like to bake?"

"Chocolate, that's Papa John's favorite."

"Sounds good. Good thing your Pa brought back some cocoa from the mercantile. I am so glad your Momma Alice sent some new recipes; she is such a good cook."

"Do you think I will ever get to meet Momma Alice?"

"I do hope so, Rose, more than you can imagine."

Savannah often thought back to the last morning she saw her mother and how sad she looked as she was leaving.

"Was my real mother beautiful?"

Savannah looked quickly toward Rose who was standing on a chair reaching up for the flour in the cupboard Jonah had built.

Rose had never asked about her birth mother.

"I only seen Clara a few times, but yes, she was incredibly beautiful. You look just like her."

Rose smiled, as she took down a mixing bowl. "She had blonde hair as I used to?"

"Yes, long and blonde. Yours has now turned a lighter shade of brown, but still just as beautiful. I wish your pa had been able to bring more of your mother's things for you to have when we traveled from Georgia, but there wasn't enough room in the wagon."

"I have her quilt on my bed that she made when she was pregnant with me. Pa told me about it."

"She was an exceptionally good seamstress and great at quilting. I only know half of what she knew."

"You sew wonderfully, Momma, and you keep us in such nice clothes. I hope that someday I can sew as good as you do."

"Thank you, sweet girl, you flatter me. Your Momma Alice taught me the basics and the rest I learned by trial and error."

"How did you meet Pa? I don't think I ever heard that story."

"Why don't you ask your pa that question?" Savannah was not sure how Jonah would like for her to answer. How much did

15

he wish his daughter to know about the truth of him asking her father for her hand in marriage in exchange for his land?

"Why, Momma? Do you not remember?"

"Of course, I remember, silly girl, but I do believe that is a question for your pa; besides, I can't have *all* the answers," she joked.

She and Jonah had been married ten years and never once had Rose been interested in the way they met, and the truth was she did not know where to begin. Did Jonah want Rose knowing he married another woman just three shorts weeks after her birth mother passed?

What would Rose think if she knew that when they left Georgia together with her as an infant, they barely knew each other at all?

Catherine burst through the door soaking wet and laughing.

"Why are you wet, Catherine?" Savannah scolded. "Did you fall in the creek?"

"No, Momma, I jumped in the creek," she laughed. "I wanted to play in the water. I think I shall build a dam like a beaver does."

"Catherine Bell, please do not dam up the creek, and I have told you before, you cannot play in the water unless you come and ask me, and not in your good dress. You told me you were playing around the house."

"I was, Momma, the creek is around the house." Catherine always had a good excuse for everything.

Savannah could not help but giggle; Catherine did have a point. "Go to your room now and change out of those wet clothes and hang your dress on the line to dry."

"That's where I was going," Catherine rolled her eyes, huffed, and headed toward the back of the cabin.

"That child," Savannah commented.

Rose laughed. "Was I like that when I was five? I do remember liking to play in the creek."

"Yes, you loved playing in the creek, but you were hardly like Catherine. I am afraid that Catherine has a mind of her own."

*****

"Steady, son. Hold the gun steady," Jonah whispered to Matthew, helping him sight in a huge ten-point buck standing in the distance eating grass from beyond the field.

"I can't do it, Pa," Matthew whispered back, shaking. "It is too heavy."

"Yes, you can, son," Jonah helped him hold the weight of the rifle.

"One day this is how you will feed your family. Now, take aim just like I taught you and pull back on the trigger."

Matthew pointed the rifle at the huge buck, shaking, and took aim.

A loud boom rang out through the valley as Matthew took his shot. "I got him, Pa! Look, I got him!" Matthew jumped up and down with excitement.

"Yes, you did, son. I told you that you could do it." Jonah ruffled his hair, proud of his son's first deer.

"I don't believe it, Pa; I just don't believe it!"

"Well, believe it, son, you shot your first buck, and a big one at that! Your momma will be so proud of you. Not many six-year-old boys have shot a buck like old Sebastian. Been stalking this bad boy for the past year."

"And you let me take him, Pa? Why didn't you do it?"

"Because son, you deserve it. You did just what I taught you to."

"What now, Pa?" Matthew was still shaking with excitement.

"Take a breath, son; we got work to do. What comes next is not that pleasant but something you must learn, and now is as good a time as any, I reckon."

"Gonna be a lot of good eating, huh, Pa?"

"That's right son, you did good."

"Can we come hunting again tomorrow, Pa?"

Jonah laughed. "No, son, we will have enough meat to last a while. Remember, we don't kill for the sport; we kill to put food on the table. We will come again soon enough."

"Okay, Pa. I can't wait to tell Momma what I did!"

*****

"I heard a shot about a mile from here," John announced as he came into the cabin just before dinner. "Someone must be out hunting."

"I heard it, too," Savannah agreed. "Jonah was taking Matthew hunting today; he had been begging him for weeks. We need some fresh meat in the smokehouse."

"Why can't I go hunting with Pa?" Catherine grumbled. "It's not fair that I was born a girl. Matthew gets to do everything fun, and I don't."

John laughed. "Come here, precious girl, and sit on my lap and let us talk a spell."

Catherine drug her feet across the floor and slowly climbed up on John's lap, sulking.

"Do you know how blessed you were to be born a girl, Catherine?" he asked.

"I don't *feel* blessed," she crossed her arms and pouted. "I wish I had been born a boy, so I can do fun stuff."

18

"Well, ye may not *feel* blessed but ye are. Being a man is hard work. Just look at all ye must do as a man. At times it can be no fun at all."

"But I don't want to sew and cook. I want to ride horses and shoot guns. I want to be a cowgirl."

Savannah and John laughed at the same time, knowing how much of a tomboy Catherine truly was.

"And one day you will be able to do that if you desire, but not at five years old," Savannah added.

"Matthew is only six, and I will be six before long. I am going to shoot better than Matthew and someday have a horse all my own. I am going to call my horse Lightning and it will be the fastest horse in the valley."

Savannah nodded. "I don't doubt it one bit, missy. I have a feeling you will be the very best cowgirl around these parts for miles."

"Did you ever shoot a deer, Papa John?" Catherine asked.

"That, as well as other animals to survive."

"What kind of animals?" Catherine was glued to every word.

"Deer, elk, rabbits, coons, turkeys, squirrels. My Martha could always cook up a tasty meal, just like ye ma does."

"Was Martha your wife?" Catherine was a child of many questions, and Savannah loved seeing John interact with the children. He had been their Papa John ever since they were born, and he treated them all the same, even Catherine, who was sometimes a challenge.

"Yes, ma'am. She and I were married quite a spell when she left to go be with Jesus."

Catherine lay her head on John's shoulder. "I am so sorry, Papa John. I wish I could have met her. Do you think she would have liked me?"

"And I wish the same, and yes, she would have loved ye children as her own, just as I do."

19

"Did you have not any children?" Catherine asked in a sad voice, as if not having children had to be the worst thing in the world.

"No. Maybe that is why the good Lord blessed me with ye," he smiled and hugged her tight. "He knew that one day I would be able to claim all of ye as my own, and He knew that I couldn't handle so many."

"I love you, Papa John. You are the very best."

"And I love ye, too, sweet girl."

*****

"It was huge, Momma," Matthew spoke holding his hands apart, after dinner. "I was afraid I couldn't do it, but I did." Matthew smiled with pride. "Pa helped me hold the rifle, though, 'cause it was so heavy."

Savannah hugged her son tight. "I am so immensely proud of you, son. He is a beauty, and it will be nice having the meat to cook. Looks like all your practicing paid off."

"I was so afraid I was going to miss him, but Pa let me try anyway."

"That I did, son. And you didn't miss at all. You are a very good shot."

"Just like you, huh, Pa? Pa is the best shot around; he can hit his target every single time!"

Savannah loved seeing Matthew so happy and proud of himself. He reminded her of her own brother Joseph, when her father had taken him hunting and he, too, had shot his first deer.

Joseph came home beaming from ear-to-ear and so proud of himself. Of course, her father had been nothing like Jonah. Never bragging on Joseph, the way Jonah did Matthew.

Mitchell Bowen was a man who did not know how to show love, and she hated that Joseph had to live with that, always wondering what he could do to please him. Knowing that no matter what he did, it would never be good enough.

Oh, how she remembered so well.

So many things of the present brought back memories of the past. It seemed that she was missing her family more and more these days. Ten years had been much too long.

"When are you going to take *me* hunting, Pa?" Catherine asked, with chocolate all over her mouth.

Jonah laughed. "When you are big enough to hold a rifle and know about their safety. It isn't like playing cowboys and Indians with sticks. A rifle can be deadly when you don't know how to use it."

"I am just one year younger than Matthew," she stated.

"And that you are. So, let me say it like this. When you are old enough to listen to your Momma and do as she says without getting into trouble."

"I did not get into trouble," Catherine looked across at Savannah, wondering what her Momma had told Pa.

"Was that not your good dress I seen hanging outside on the clothesline, and I know you haven't worn it since your momma washed it last?" Jonah reminded.

Catherine poked out her lips and pouted. "I just wanted to play in the creek."

"The next time you want to play in the creek, young lady, you best ask your momma first and wear the clothes she tells you to play in. Are we clear on that?"

"Yes, sir," Catherine sighed.

Jonah reached over and pulled his daughter's braided pigtail and laughed. "Stop pouting, Catherine. I will take you hunting soon enough."

"Really, Pa? Really?" She smiled big.

"Yes, really." Jonah knew his youngest daughter was the most energetic of the three, and she was definitely going to give them a run for their money.

"Why don't you go get ready for bed and you can play a bit with your doll house before bedtime," Savannah suggested.

"Okay, Momma." Catherine got down from the table and took off to her room.

"The cake was delicious, Rose. You did a great job," Jonah wiped his mouth of chocolate.

"No doubt about that," John said, getting up from the table. "I think I will go home and get ready for bed myself. I'm feeling a bit-tired tonight. Dinner was wonderful, as always, Savannah. And Rose, ye are becoming a great cook as well. Just like ye mother."

"Thank you, Papa John and Pa; I love baking cakes and pies."

"I am so thankful for mother's recipes she keeps sending us. There is so many we still have not tried."

"Well, I shall gladly be the one to try them out," John joked. "Goodnight all." He placed his hat on top of his head and headed out the door.

Usually John would stay for the Bible reading, but lately he tired easily.

Savannah missed the old John but was grateful for the time they still had.

She stood up from the table and started stacking plates.

"Here, let me do that for you, Momma. Why don't you start reading the Bible as always?"

Savannah loved the way Rose took charge more and more these days. She always acted older than her age; it was hard to believe she was only ten.

"Yes, but I always help you do the dishes first."

"I don't mind doing them tonight, Momma."

"Then I shall not complain. Thank you for all you do to help, Rose. You are amazing."

"Just like me, too, right Momma, after killing that big ole buck?" Matthew grinned.

"Yes, just like you, too. All my children are wonderful, and I am a proud momma."

Savannah sat in her rocker and read aloud the book of Acts, Chapter one, when Jesus ascended to Heaven and left the disciples to do His work here on the earth.

So when the apostles were with Jesus, they kept asking Him, "Lord, has the time come for You to free Israel and restore our kingdom?"

He replied, "The Father alone has the authority to set those dates and times, and they are not for you to know. But you will receive power when the Holy Spirit comes upon you. And you will be my witnesses, telling people about Me everywhere – in Jerusalem, throughout Judea, in Samaria, and to the ends of the earth."

After saying this, he was taken up into a cloud while they were watching, and they could no longer see Him. As they strained to see Him rising into heaven, two white-robed men suddenly stood among them. Men of Galilee," they said, "why are you standing here staring into heaven? Jesus has been taken from you into heaven, but someday He will return from heaven in the same way you saw Him go!"

One of her favorite times each evening was reading aloud her mother's old, tattered Bible and then explaining to her children what she read. It brought back memories of days long ago when her mother had read from the same Bible each night when she was a child.

What she would give for just one more hug. There were times when she closed her eyes and could still smell the very scent of her mother and hear her sweet voice. So many things she knew she would never forget for as long as she lived.

23

She ran her finger over the notes her mother had made beside the verses she just read aloud.

Jesus now expects us to be his disciples and go and tell others of Him.

Alice Bowen was one of a kind. Where her father lacked making her feel loved, her mother more than made up for it.

Some days seemed harder than others, wishing she was still in Dahlonega, until she looked around the room at the man she so loved, and their three children, and then knew she would do it all over again in a heartbeat.

"Get to bed, Children. Morning comes early and there is a lot of vegetables to be gathered in the fields. I will need all of you to pitch in," Jonah directed, as he got up from his chair and took the Bible from Savannah's hands, placing it on the table beside her rocker.

"And you, sweet lady, look exhausted. Let us go to bed."

Savannah smiled sweetly, that same smile that Jonah fell in love with. He could tell her mind seemed to be far away tonight.

And it was true, it had been a long day, and Jonah longed to take her in his arms and touch her soft skin next to his.

He took her hand in his and led her to their bedroom. It was the time of day he longed for, just to have some time alone with the woman he loved.

"Have I told you lately that I love you?" she whispered softly.

"Not today," he smiled.

Savannah kissed him tenderly. "Then I am telling you now. I love you, Jonah Bell. I love you more and more with each passing day. I love doing life with you."

"And I love you, my sweet wife," he pulled her close and kissed her passionately. "I am a truly blessed man."

Savannah loved the feel of Jonah's strong arms wrapped tightly around her.

24

It did not matter what went on throughout the day. When the rest of the world was sleeping, and it was just the two of them, it made everything right again.

*****

Savannah awoke sometime before the sun and lay quietly in the darkness of their room, listening to the sound of Jonah breathing peacefully beside her.

This was the time of day she loved to be with her Lord, just to soak in His presence and thank Him for their bountiful blessings.

Father,
Thank You for Your many blessings, for they are more than I could have ever imagined.

Thank You for Jonah, and the way that he loves our children and myself, for I could not have asked for a better husband and father.

The way he loves and shows love is amazing. Bless him, Lord, for he works so hard for us all.

Thank You for seeing so many years ago that I would find myself here today, even when I didn't understand what You were up to. I cannot imagine myself being anywhere else.

Give me peace for the longing I feel for my mother and family back home. It is not that I don't love being a wife and mother to my children; it is just that there are times the pain of missing them is so much to bear.

Maybe one day, Father, You will find a way that we can once again be reunited. I would so love for my children to meet them, and for them to meet my children. What a glorious day that would be.

25

Father, I ask that you continue to allow John to live as pain free as possible. I see him growing older and weary, and it troubles me to see him declining. He is such a kind, gentle soul.

And thank You, Lord, for today, and for all the vegetables You have allowed us to have. I don't take any of it for granted.

In Jesus' Name,

Amen

Chapter Three

The day was smoldering hot as they picked green beans off the vines and placed them in the large wicker baskets Savannah had made each of them for gathering the harvest.

A few ears of corn were already gathered for creamed corn and corn on the cob. The rest would dry on the stalk to be gathered after it dried. Jonah would carry it to the mill to grind and be turned into cornmeal for baking.

John was back at the cabin shucking what was gathered for dinner for the next few days.

The children loved corn on the cob, and it helped him to feel useful.

Jonah knew it would take them several more hours before the beans were all gathered, yet the children never complained, not even Catherine.

The girls were in their summer bonnets, and Matthew was in his straw cap to shield their faces from the hot blistering sun.

They had been taught at an early age that everyone must pitch in to get the job done. Watching his children work made Jonah proud.

Catherine, at the age of five, worked as hard as Matthew, insisting her basket would be full faster than his, always competing with her older brother.

Savannah stood up straight, stretched, and wiped the sweat from her neck with her apron. "Are you all hungry?" Her stomach had been rumbling for the past half-hour.

"I am hungry, Momma," Catherine said. "Can we eat something now?"

Savannah looked toward Jonah. They had been at it since breakfast, and breakfast came around daylight.

"I think a break would be a good idea. Let us all go to the house and get a bite to eat."

The children screamed and ran for the house, excited to be getting out of the field, even for a short while.

Jonah and Savannah laughed as they followed behind.

"I guess we wore them out," he teased.

"Wore me out, too."

"Are you okay?" He knew she was always the last one who seemed to be tired.

"I am fine, just a bit tired. You did keep me up late," she winked.

Jonah chuckled, "It didn't seem like you were complaining."

"Who, me? Never," she giggled.

When they entered the house, John had the table set with bread and butter, homemade jelly, and a boiled ear of corn for each.

"John, what on earth?" Savannah beamed. "What have you been up to?"

"Figured ye all would be coming in for lunch soon, so I got it ready and waiting. It's the least I can do, seeing as I am of no use in the field any longer."

"Thank you so much, John, this is wonderful," said Jonah, washing his hands in the wash basin. "Children, get your hands washed."

"Savannah already had the bread and jelly made; I just boiled the corn. I will do the dishes, too. I know ye all have a long way to go to be finished."

"You mean you know how to wash dishes, Papa John?" Catherine asked, taking her turn washing her hands.

"I do know how, little one, believe it or not. Papa John used to live many years alone and had no one else to do it for him."

"You mean when your Martha went to see Jesus?" she asked, remembering the conversation of the night before.

"That's right, ye are a smart girl and a very good listener. Until then, my Martha washed all the dishes. I didn't realize all she did for me until she wasn't there anymore."

"Thank you so much, John, for doing all this. I appreciate all you do for us." Savannah kissed his cheek as she sat down at the table.

"Are you not going to join us?" Jonah asked.

"Oh, I must confess, I already had a large chunk of that delicious bread and a smear of jelly before ye got here," he laughed. "And, of course, an ear of corn, and I must say it was quite tasty."

"Well, I am glad to see your appetite has picked up some," Savannah teased. "I hope I can expect you for dinner as well."

"Ye know it."

*****

They were lugging their last basket of tomatoes toward the house when Matthew called out. "Look Pa, there comes a man on a horse."

Jonah looked toward the hill to see a man he had never seen before on a white horse riding in their direction.

It was not often they saw strangers. Their only visitors were the Ingalls or the Ayers family, and even that was not often.

29

"Whoa," the man called out and pulled back on the horse's reins, stopping close to the front door of the cabin.

Jonah extended his hand. "Good evening, sir, I am Jonah Bell. How can we help you?"

"Good evening, I am Pastor Corbin Anderson. My wife and I and our three children moved in and built a cabin about two miles back. I wanted to ride over and say hello."

"I thought I heard hammering when I rode into town the other day. Please forgive me, if I had known I would have come to help you; in fact, all the neighbors would have. I just thought it was Noel Ayers making furniture; he is quite a craftsman."

Pastor Anderson climbed down off his horse and extended his hand to Savannah as well. "Ma'am."

"This is my wife, Savannah," Jonah introduced.

"Hello, Pastor Anderson, it is nice to meet you, and these are our children, Rose, Matthew and Catherine."

"Nice to meet you all as well and think nothing of not helping us; my two boys are fourteen and fifteen, and they are strong as an ox."

"Do come in, Pastor Anderson, and have a cup of coffee," Savannah motioned them into the house and headed for the coffee pot.

"Thank you for your hospitality. Sorry it took me this long to ride over. How many neighbors are in close range?"

"There is Tom and Nancy Ingalls, with their daughter Grace, and Noel and Mary Lou Ayers with their seven children, Daniel, Peggy, Jerry, Powell, Glenda, Janice and Ricky. And then there is John Barge who lives in a cabin here by us."

"Sounds like quite a little community you have here, which is what I was hoping. I am sure, as time goes on, there will also be others moving into the territory to settle here."

"Yes, I am guessing the same," Jonah agreed. "We were the first besides John to settle here in the valley, but we were excited to see others move in."

"I know it's picking season, but do you think a community meeting might be arranged soon? I have an idea that might interest you all; at least, I am hoping it does."

"Pardon me for asking, but can you tell me what this meeting is about?" Jonah was curious.

"I am a pastor, Mr. Bell, and there is no church around for ten miles, much too far to travel daily by horse, and no school for the children. From what you just told me there is quite a bit of children around this community. I would love to meet with everyone and discuss the possibility of erecting a church and using it for a school by day."

"Oh Jonah, that sounds wonderful," Savannah exclaimed. "How wonderful it would be to have a place of worship close and a school for the children to attend."

Jonah rubbed his head. "Does sound good. Do you have any idea where this would be built? Or is that something we will discuss?"

"Yes, I would like to put all our heads together and see what we come up with. Since you know them all well, do you think you can arrange such a meeting?"

Jonah shook his head in thought. "I'll make the rounds and invite the Ingalls and Ayers families to attend, and by Friday evening maybe we can all get together. Bring some baskets of food and come here for a picnic by the creek, how does that sound? Our harvest should be in by then-- gives us almost a week."

"That sounds wonderful, Mr. Bell. I thank you both for your kindness."

"Just call me Jonah," he smiled.

"Would you like to stay for dinner?" Savannah invited. "Sorry I don't have anything prepared yet; we have been in the fields all day, but it shall not take me long."

"Thank you for the offer, but Katie is cooking dinner for us and should be finished by the time I get home. How much more do you have to gather?"

"At least a couple more days' worth," answered Jonah. "After that, I will make the rounds to invite everyone to the meeting."

"Then we will see you all bright and early in the morning. I will bring my children and wife and help all we can."

"I am afraid I don't know what to say," Jonah was amazed by his kindness and willingness to help.

"Say nothing at all; it's what neighbors do for each other. I shall see you in the morning then." Pastor Anderson drank the last of his coffee and handed Savannah his cup. "Thank you, ma'am, it hit the spot. Nice meeting you both."

*****

"What do you make of that?" Jonah asked, after Pastor Anderson left.

"I think the valley just got a new pastor who truly understands how to serve people. And just think, Jonah, we may be able to get a church and a school for the children to learn in. Isn't that great?"

"When we first moved here, I always knew that one day others would come, and I know you are excited about the church."

"Aren't you?"

"Of course, I am, but you know the Bible much better than I do."

"And that is what a church is for, to worship and help us learn more. And a school, Jonah. I am beyond excited!"

"Me too, Momma," Rose smiled. "I have always wanted to attend school with others."

"Yes, Rose, what a good way to make close friends. I loved attending my school in Dahlonega when I was your age."

"I want to stay here with you, Momma," Catherine poked out her lips in a pout.

Rose reached down to take her sister's hand. "Catherine, can you not see how exciting going to school would be?"

"She grumbles about everything," Matthew stated.

Savannah set the cornbread she had made the night before on the table and the milk. "Come now and let us eat; we shall all discuss this later. It has been a long day, and I don't know about you, but I am hungry."

*****

Savannah found it a joy to be around Katie Anderson; she was genuine and real, and loved to talk every bit as much as she did.

Their children had been taught to respect and serve in a godly way. They worked hard and were a delight to be around. It was going to be wonderful to have them as close neighbors. Especially Elisa, who was the same age as Rose.

They arrived just after daylight and went straight to work in the field, helping them gather the remainder of the crops.

To Jonah's surprise, they finished a day earlier than expected and had enough to share their bountiful blessings with them as well.

"We never expected you to share your crops with us; that was not why we helped," Pastor Anderson stated, as they all ate the soup Savannah had put on to cook earlier that morning.

"As you can see, we have more than enough. God has been good to us with just enough rain and sun, and we could have never gotten finished this early had it not been for your help."

"That's right, Momma and Pa were killing us," Catherine stated, making everyone laugh.

"What do you children think of having a school close enough you can walk to?" Pastor Anderson asked.

"It would be wonderful," Rose answered, "Don't you think, Elisa?"

Rose and Elisa had become instant friends, just as she had with her neighbor Grace, when they were younger.

"I would love that," Elisa nodded. "I am glad we moved here."

"Thank you, boys, for your help today," Jonah said to Nathaniel and Josiah, the Anderson's sons.

"Yes sir, it was no trouble, sir," Nathaniel smiled and nudged his younger brother to do the same.

"Yes sir, you are welcome," Josiah added, taking a huge spoonful of soup.

Katie laughed. "Looks like we both have some great children, and your little ones work so hard and yet never complain; that is amazing to me."

"Thank you," Savannah smiled. "We are very proud of them."

"I just shot a big buck a few days ago," Matthew bragged.

"Really?" Pastor Anderson smiled. "I thought I heard a gunshot. How big was it?"

"It was this big," Matthew reached his arms as far apart as he could get them.

"Perhaps you can teach Nathaniel and Josiah to hunt, Jonah; I have never been much of a hunter."

"Be my pleasure--we will have to do that."

Katie got up from the table to clear the dishes, but John took them out of her hands. "Ye all have worked hard today, and I already have the wash tub of hot water waiting. I can sit on the stool and do dishes."

"Papa John, there is way too many dishes; I can do them later," Savannah tried to shoo him away.

"Nonsense, I want to and insist."

Savannah clucked her tongue and shook her head, knowing she had lost the battle; besides, she wanted John to feel needed and appreciated. "Okay then, thank you," she kissed his cheek.

"Who wants a piece of Rose's chocolate cake? She is becoming quite a baker."

"That is wonderful, Rose," Katie held her plate out to get a piece that was offered. "Maybe you can share a few of your recipes with Elisa and me."

"My Momma Alice sends us a new recipe each month; I will recopy them for you."

"Thank you, Rose, that will be wonderful. I have never been much of a baker."

Corbin patted his stomach and laughed. "I beg to differ; where do you think this come from?"

*****

By Friday, Jonah had set up two long tables under the oak tree beside the creek to place all the food everyone had prepared.

Blankets were spread out, so everyone could sit and eat.

It was a table fit for a king. It reminded Savannah of picnics back home when her mother prepared a feast.

Jonah had yet to tell them what the meeting was about, and yet they came, just excited to be getting together on such a beautiful summer day.

"What a beautiful day for a picnic," Marylou Ayers beamed, eating a piece of the fried chicken she had brought.

"I just can't wait to see what this is all about," Nancy jumped in. "Jonah told us we were going to be thrilled."

Tom laughed, "Nancy has tried to guess what it is a million times in the past couple of days. We shall see if she guessed right."

"Maybe you should go ahead and fill them all in," Jonah looked toward Pastor Anderson.

"Had you rather me wait until we are finished eating?" he asked.

"No, we are anxious," Nancy laughed. "I cannot stand the suspense. Please fill us all in."

Pastor Anderson got to his feet where everyone could easily see and hear him. "First of all, I want to thank you all for coming today on such short notice, and to all you ladies for cooking such a fine meal. We are truly blessed men to have you all.

"As you know, I am a pastor, and I have been preaching since I was a young man and first met my wife, Katie." He reached down and took his wife's hand.

"We felt God calling us to come here to the valley. At first, we were not sure why, since there was no church to speak of. So, we prayed about it and trusted God that He had a plan.

"A few days ago, we met the Bells and told them of our plans, and of course, when you hear, you will understand why we wanted to include the community."

"I like that," Noel said, "This community." He looked around the long tables at the four families that sat with their children and nodded. "We are growing and eager to hear what you have in mind."

"I propose we all work together, all of us, and erect a building that will provide us a place of worship on Sundays and a school for our many children through the week.

"I feel that a growing community needs a place to worship as a body, for the Bible tells us that where two or three are gathered in My name, there I am in the midst. And I am sure you all agree that a school would surely benefit our many children, so they can learn and thrive and come together to create friendships that will last a lifetime."

"Well, you didn't guess that one," Tom looked at Nancy and chuckled.

"That is wonderful!" Nancy screamed! "I love it. What about you, Marylou?"

"Yes, I think that is a grand idea. Our seven children could really benefit from having a school close by. I always said I didn't feel qualified to teach them what they need to know."

"What do you men think?" Jonah asked, looking at Tom Ingalls and Noel Ayers. It would take them all in agreement to work together to get it built.

"I am all for it. I would love to have a place to worship again. That is one of the things Nancy and I have missed so much, since moving to the valley. We read God's Word together and pray, but there is just something about coming together as a community and worshipping."

"I have been a carpenter for years and I will certainly love to help. I can build the benches and desks that will be needed. I think it's a grand idea," Noel added.

Pastor Anderson smiled. "This makes me genuinely happy. Praise be to Jesus, for opening the door. We have saved some money back, and it should build a building big enough."

"There is enough timber here in the valley. We can build it as we did most of our cabins, stacking the logs together, and maybe even put a steeple, too," Jonah stood to his feet as he spoke. "We can all pitch in and have it built in no time. Does anyone have any ideas on where we might place such a building?"

Pastor Anderson answered, "I was thinking, if you all agree, that we should build it almost dead center from where we all live, so no one will have to go far. We certainly don't want the children walking a long distance in cold temperatures."

"Sounds like a good plan," Tom agreed.

"Are you going to be our children's teacher?" Nancy asked Katie, assuming that was the plan.

Katie's eyes grew wide and she giggled. "I guess we didn't think that part through. I am afraid I quit school at an early age to work on my parent's farm and am not qualified to teach them. My husband is a fine pastor, but I am no teacher."

"Perhaps we can hire a teacher," Marylou suggested.

"What about you, Momma?" Rose jumped in. "You would make a great teacher!"

"What a great idea," Nancy agreed. "What do you say, Savannah? Would you consider teaching all our children like you teach your own? I would feel much more confident if you were teaching Grace instead of me."

"I agree with that," Katie added. "I have not had the pleasure of knowing you long, but from what I know of you, I think you would make a great teacher."

Jonah looked at Savannah and smiled. It was not often she was at a loss for words and he found it very amusing.

Savannah shrugged, "I guess. But I must tell you that I don't feel very qualified, either."

Nancy reached over and took her hand. "Sweetie, as it stands now, none of us do, and yet we all do the best we can with our own children. You know enough that our children would benefit with you teaching them. We have the utmost confidence in you, don't we?" she asked, looking around.

Everyone agreed that it should be Savannah who became the teacher to their children. It was a unanimous vote.

"You are serious, aren't you?" she said, looking around the table at everyone nodding in her direction. "Jonah, what do you think of this? If I were teaching every day, it would take me away from the house and cooking and cleaning."

Jonah smiled at her. "I don't think we could pick a better teacher anywhere. I see you with our children, and I know how gifted and smart you are. They would all benefit from you teaching them."

"But what about the things I do around the house? Teaching fourteen children would require a lot of afterhours time, too, planning, and grading papers."

"We will all pitch in and help, won't we, children?" he looked at his three children who were taking all this in. Even Catherine had yet to say a word so far.

"You know we will, Momma," Rose smiled. "You are already a great teacher to us; why not teach a few more?"

"We could all pitch in, Savannah," Nancy added. "We cannot pay you in cash, but we could trade your time with our children for things we can do for you. I can take on your sewing; you know how I love to sew. I only have one child and would love to be able to make more dresses."

"And I would be happy to come once a week and do your wash and hang it on the line for you," Katie offered.

"Guess that leaves me bringing over a pot of stew or beans a couple times a week to help out," Marylou smiled.

Savannah looked at all the children sitting around the table. Fourteen children, with eyes on her. Could she do this? She had been studying since she was a small child and felt she was more than qualified yet did not want to take away from her own family and the way things were now.

"Well," Nancy shrugged, "Are you going to keep us all in suspense?"

Savannah laughed. "I cannot believe I am saying this..." She nodded her head yes. "Yes, I will teach your children; that is, if you are sure you don't mind, Jonah? Our family must always come first, after God, of course."

Jonah reached and took her hand in his. "I think it is a great idea, Savannah. I don't mind at all; in fact, I think you should. It's time you get out of the house each day and shine in other areas. You are so much more than just a wife and mother."

Nancy jumped to her feet and cheered. "We have ourselves a teacher!"

"Then it's settled; we will start as soon as possible and build The Valley Church and School." Pastor Anderson was thrilled. God always had a plan, even if at first, he did not always understand.

The valley was about to come alive, and as scared as Savannah was, she had never felt so excited. Being a teacher was a dream she had kept hidden, especially after marrying Jonah and moving west.

God truly was a good God. For He knew the plans He had for her all along.

She could not wait to write her mother a letter and tell her all about their upcoming plans.

*****

Dear Mother, Joseph, and Mary,
It feels like it has been forever since I have written to you all, I hope you don't mind that I am sending one letter to be read by each of you. Jonah is traveling into town tomorrow for supplies and I did not have ample time to write each of you separately.

So much is happening here in the valley of Arkansas. New neighbors arrived not long ago; a pastor and his wife; Pastor Corbin Anderson, and his wife Katie, and their three children, two boys and a girl. Elisa is Rose's age, and I am just thrilled for her. Rose needs good friends.

Today the community gathered at our home for a picnic and meeting, and it has been decided that we are going to build a church here to worship in, that will also serve our children as a school.

What I am about to tell you next is the part I have been waiting all day to write you. I am giddy with excitement!

They have asked me to become the teacher, and I said yes. I asked Jonah of course, and he agreed it was a good idea.

The women have offered to help me with my sewing, washing, and cooking in trade for teaching their children. That is something I will have to get used to. I am that much like you, Mother, and very independent.

I still cannot believe it! When Jonah and I first settled here there was no one around except John Barge and even he wasn't close. Now we have three other families that are in walking distance and will soon have a place to worship again and a school!

God truly blessed us this year with our crops. We have been picking and putting things away for the winter all week. There was even enough to share with the Anderson's and also to go to Market tomorrow. What a great season we have had.

Rose tries a new recipe at least once a week. She is becoming quite the baker, I might add. Thank you so much for the recipes, Mother. She looks forward to your letters to see what you have sent. She is writing them in a book she plans to give to Katie Anderson, so your recipes are going to be shared. I knew you would not mind.

I hope you are doing well in school Mary; I am so proud of you and your eagerness to learn.

And Joseph, I thank you for taking over when Father passed. You have done well taking care of Mother and Mary. I hope your crops were also plentiful.

I miss you all, so very much. I pray for you daily, and I will never give up dreaming that one day I will see you all again.

It is getting late and my eyes are growing weary. Tomorrow comes early, as it always does.

I love you all,
Savannah.

Chapter Four

Jonah pulled the wagon close to the Andersons' home, waiting for Pastor Anderson to emerge. They planned to ride into the village together and get most of the hardware that would be needed to build with.

The Anderson home was small and quaint, and Jonah knew by their choice of location deep in the woods that Corbin more than likely did not plan to plant a crop.

Maybe that is what pastors do--lead the flock, and the flock takes care of the shepherd. Jonah was more than willing to share his crops with this family.

"Good morning," Pastor Anderson emerged. "What a lovely day for a ride into town. God is such a wonderful God to give us such a beautiful day for it. I woke up feeling refreshed and ready; how about you?"

"Yes sir," Jonah chuckled. "Savannah had breakfast done and shooed me out the door not long after daylight. She loves the days I travel into town and mail her letter and pick up another from her family."

"Totally understand that. Katie and I are from Alabama, and so we know all about writing letters. We have traveled a lot since she and I have been married but feel the valley will be home to us for the rest of our lives. Unless, of course, God sees otherwise. I have found that we don't always know the plans of God; we just have to be ready and willing when He says, "Let's go.""

"Giddy up," Jonah called out to the horses and put the wagon in motion. "You are right about that. I found that out the hard way myself."

"Oh?" Pastor Anderson looked his way, curious about his story.

He liked Jonah right away and hoped to get to know him better. One of the reasons he was eager to have alone time was so they might talk and get better acquainted.

"I don't normally go around telling people my story. One, I feel it's none of their business, and two, I don't want to remind Savanah how we met. I rather them think we met and fell in love and that's how our story started, but that wasn't the case."

"If you'd rather not tell me, I will understand."

"The only other person I ever told was John, and that was because he became more of a father to me than a friend. I don't mind telling you, if you don't mind listening. It's nice to have a pastor to talk to."

"I'd be happy to listen, Jonah. In fact, it is what I am here for, anytime."

"Rose is not Savannah's by blood. But she is every bit as loved by her as Matthew and Catherine."

"Yes, that is very easy to see."

"I was once married to a woman named Clara. We got married in Savannah, Georgia and soon traveled to Dahlonega in search of gold."

"And did you find any?"

Jonah chuckled. "I found out really quickly that I was not cut out for gold mining."

"Yes, you and I both. I'd rather take my chances on Jesus and not wading in the frigid cold waters of the northeast Georgia mountains, panning for gold."

"Clara and I started dreaming of moving to Arkansas and becoming farmers instead, out in the open valleys and flatter land. It was something we spoke of often, and then she became pregnant."

"With Rose?"

"Yes, with Rose. We decided to wait until Rose was born and then travel west by covered wagon with her feeding Rose along the way. We thought it would be easier to travel after the birth instead of while she was pregnant. It was the perfect time of the year because Rose was to be born in early spring, which would give us time to make it here and build a small cabin before winter."

"Sounds like a good plan."

"It was, until Clara passed during childbirth. It ripped my heart apart, and I vowed to never love another woman again. Franky, I was afraid of loving someone else. To get that close and then risk losing them was more than I could bear."

Pastor Anderson lay his hand on Jonah's shoulder and lightly squeezed it. "I understand; the heart is a powerful thing."

"I had a hundred acres back in Georgia, with a small but nice cabin. I genuinely thought of staying there and raising Rose alone but being there in the home Clara and I built together was unbearable, and the nights were even worse."

"Yes, I imagine it was."

"I knew nothing about taking care of babies and kept running back and forth to Nelly's house who was helping me take care of her. She had recently had a child of her own and thankfully had enough milk for both."

"That was truly a blessing."

"Almost three weeks later I knew I could not go on there in Georgia; it was much too painful. I had only seen Savannah a few times and knew she was old enough to get married and leave home, and honestly she was the only person I could think of that was wasn't already married."

"So, you asked her to marry you?"

"I wish I had. Truth is, I asked her father for her hand in marriage and traded my land and cabin for her."

"Oh, I see. And how did Savannah feel about that?"

"I have thought about it a hundred times, Pastor Anderson, and at that moment I was selfish and didn't think of anyone but myself. I was not sure how she felt about it. Her father quickly agreed without thinking about it at all, which really surprised me. Two days later, Savannah and I officially met, and on that same morning we headed west."

"Wow, that is really something. To see you two together one would never know you two aren't madly in love with one another."

"Oh, we are, now. Took me a lot longer to fall than it did her. She told me later that she had carried a crush for me while I was married, and I purposely pushed her away because my heart belonged to Clara. I felt guilty even thinking Savannah was beautiful. For two years, we slept together and not so much as touched."

"Wow, that had to be hard for any man."

"It was. Fact was, I did think she was beautiful and over time I was starting to fall in love with her and didn't seem to miss Clara as much, and for that, too, I felt guilty. It was John that reminded me of my vows to Clara--till *death* do us part, and that it was okay to love again."

"That is some story. I am sorry you had to go through that, Jonah. Most men would have turned away from God at that time; I am glad you didn't."

"Oh, but I did. It was Savannah that brought me back. She is such a good woman who loves our Father more than anyone I have ever met. Her faith is like no other."

"I can see that about her. Katie thinks she is wonderful, and she is never wrong about people."

"Thanks for listening--feels good to be able to speak freely."

"Think nothing of it. It is a pleasure to have your friendship. A true friend is sometimes hard to acquire and doesn't judge you on your past."

"Thank you, I appreciate that."

"So does Rose know Savannah is not her birth mother?"

"She does. I felt I owed it to Clara to tell her the truth. Clara wanted a baby so bad. She, too, was a good woman who loved our Lord."

"I think you did the right thing by telling her. You are a good man, Jonah. I see the way you treat John as if he were your father, and the way you built him a cabin there beside you. He is a blessed man to have you and your family."

"Thank you, Pastor Anderson, but the truth is, we are the ones that are blessed."

"So how did you all meet?"

Jonah chuckled, remembering. "It was Christmas Eve night, and the snow was starting to fall. By the looks of the signs, we were in for a blizzard. I thought we were the only ones in the valley and up until that time had yet to have company."

"He was out traveling in that?"

"He was on his way back from town with his supplies to do him for winter. He lived further away than we did, and he had waited too late in the season to go after them."

"It's a good thing you were there."

"Yes, he still says today that we saved his life on that cold winter's night. Truth is that the knock at the door scared me to death. There he was, shivering from the cold, and me, pointing my rifle at him."

Pastor Anderson chuckled. "I imagine you thought it might be someone about to cause you harm."

"Yes. I had heard the stories of some of the tribes who did not take kindly to us taking their land, and I thought I was about to run into one head on. I just kept thinking about protecting Savannah and Rose."

"How soon did it take you to realize he was harmless?"

"Not long at all. Even though that was several years ago, he was still an old man, and he assured me that he meant me no harm. He only wanted to know if he could stay in my barn until daylight and the snow had stopped falling."

"Poor man. I am so glad you were there."

"We quickly invited him in to get warm by the fire, and Savannah, being the woman that she is, fixed him a plate of food. And that is how John Barge soon became Papa John."

"That, too, is quite some story. So, did he never go back home?"

"Oh yes, he went back, then come back again to help me build my barn and back again to his home. Savannah and I went to visit and found him sick and near death and Savannah nursed him back to health. I decided to move him here with us. Couldn't bear the thought of him living way out there alone at his age."

Pastor Anderson smiled and nodded. "Yes, just as I said. You are a good man, Jonah. May God bless you and keep you, all the days of your life."

"It's amazing the way God works, isn't it, Pastor Anderson?"

"How do you mean?"

"Even at the times in my life I was at my lowest and was angry at God to the point I stopped believing in Him altogether, He was still there for me, and He still loved me, and took me back the moment I was ready. He doesn't hold grudges; He just loves us as we are."

"Yes. He loves us more than we love our own children. When one of your little ones do something wrong, you still love them."

"There was a time, right after Clara passed that I only held Rose to carry her back and forth to Nelly's. There was no nurturing from me whatsoever. I would even let her cry rather than hold her."

"Did you blame her for Clara's death?"

"I feel bad about it, but I guess I did. Savannah made me realize that and kept pushing me to hold her and bond with her."

"God understands, Jonah. He was human once too, remember? He came to earth in the flesh and died for all of us, so that we could have eternity with Him."

"Not sure what would have happened to me if I had not traded my land for Savannah's hand in marriage. She saved my life, truly she did."

"God had a plan all along. Sometimes we just have to sit back and wait to see what happens next."

"I will never understand why God allowed Clara to die so young."

"We must not question God and His ways. Clara had done what she was put here to do, and I believe that the Holy Spirit placed Savannah on your mind because He knew what the outcome would bring. As much as He loved you, He did not want you to be lonely, so he sent a helpmate."

"Pastor Anderson, can I tell you something that I have never told another soul before?"

"Of course, you can tell me anything, and it will stay between the two of us."

"As I said, I had only seen Savannah a few times before I went to speak to her father, but what I had seen of her I knew she was breathtakingly beautiful. Even though I felt like I would never consummate the marriage, I wanted to be sure that if I ever decided to that it was with someone I was attracted to. Does that make me a bad person?"

Pastor Anderson smiled. "Of course not. You believed marriage was forever, and any man would have done the same thing. I totally understand. I mean why would any man desire to be married to a woman they are not attracted to?"

"For so long I tried telling myself that I didn't want to be attracted to her, that she was too young, and I hated myself for the thoughts I had."

"But she was your wife, and God wants us to desire each other. What you did and the feelings you had were all perfectly natural. After all, you did marry her, which made her your wife."

Jonah shook his head. "I guess I always wanted to talk to someone about that. I would have never cheated on Clara; she was my love."

"And you didn't cheat on her. As you already stated, it took you two years to consummate your marriage to Savannah. If anything, you did more wrong by waiting so long."

"I guess I never thought of it in that way. I know it hurt Savannah the way I pushed her away. She tried so hard, but I ran each time we got too close. We kissed once, and I went weeks and hardly spoke, ashamed of myself for getting that close."

"But just look at the two of you, now! You are a beautiful couple, and it's easy to see that you are both madly in love with the other."

"Yes, we are. It's a great feeling to have that again. To enjoy life, and love, and desire another's company, another's touch."

"Love is an incredibly beautiful thing, Jonah. We are both blessed with godly, beautiful wives. Oh yes, we are blessed men indeed."

*****

The village was bustling with locals and travelers who were stopping for this and that on this hot summer day.

Pastor Anderson took the list and headed for the hardware store while Jonah went to the post office and barber for a haircut.

"Good day to you sir," Dottie called out, running toward him as he made it back to his wagon.

"Good day to you, too, Dottie. So nice to see you today." Jonah reached behind the seat and brought out a jar of homemade jelly to give her.

"Savannah told me to make sure that I did not forget to give you this; she made it not long ago."

"She is the sweetest. I am so glad she and I finally became friends. How are the children doing?"

"They are doing great. Enjoying playing in the creek in this summer heat."

"How's that little darling of yours?" Dottie asked, referring to Catherine.

Jonah laughed. "As bossy as ever."

"Takes after her aunt Dottie, I see," she chuckled. "A woman has a right to speak her mind, I am glad she is making use of that right."

"That she is," Jonah agreed. "And how are you doing, Dottie?"

Dottie looked back toward the saloon and smiled. "Staying busy as always."

"Maybe next time I will bring Savannah with me, and you two can visit a bit."

"Sounds wonderful. Please tell Savannah and the children I said hello?"

"Of course, I will, and you have a wonderful day."

"I sure will," she waved and carried her jelly back across the street to the saloon.

Pastor Anderson watched as Dottie crossed the street, making his way back to the wagon. "I see you gave her a jar of Savannah's homemade jelly?"

"Yes sir, Dottie and Savannah go way back," Jonah laughed.

"Oh, really," Pastor Anderson seemed amazed. "Do tell."

"Savannah used to be jealous of Dottie. Dottie was a bit of a flirt the first time she ever met me, and Savannah thought I was more attracted to her than she. That was back in the days when there was no intimacy between us."

"Yes, then I can see why she might be a bit jealous."

"Later, after Savannah realized that I did love her and only her, they soon became friends more so than enemies. Dottie did apologize."

"Savannah is a good woman to befriend a woman that chooses to please men for money. My Katie is the same way, and they are both right. Jesus died for all of us, not just some of us. Not many people are willing to look beyond the flesh and sin, and love like Jesus."

"So, how did it go at the hardware store?"

"They are getting our order together now. They told me to pull around the back."

"Giddy-up," Jonah put the horses in motion. "Hard to believe we are going to be building a church and school."

"God has mighty plans for our valley, and I am so grateful for wonderful neighbors that love Him the way my family and I do. Nathaniel asked me why I built our cabin before I spoke to you all about erecting a church. What if you decided you did not want a church; what would we have done then?"

"And what did you tell him?"

"I told him that I was just following the Holy Spirit, and that He never steers me wrong."

"We are the ones that are grateful to you for following His voice and bringing us all together."

"How does Savannah *really* feel about becoming a teacher to our children? I feel like she was put on the spot and pushed into it."

Jonah laughed. "Trust me, Savannah is thrilled to take on the task. She told me late last night that she dreamed of becoming a teacher since she was a little girl but had given up that dream long ago."

"Well, would you look at that," Pastor Anderson chuckled. "God knew her dream and He is bringing it to life. Just more proof that He is in control and opens doors for those that love Him."

"Yes, she told me how blessed she feels. She is just worried about neglecting what she feels is her duties around the house. I tell you that woman never stops. She is the backbone of our home."

"The women will help her out with that, and it will make them feel as if they are contributing. I think she will make a great teacher. Katie has done the best she could, teaching the children, but she and I both would like their education to go deeper. Nathaniel is already fifteen, but maybe with a year or two with Savannah as his teacher, he will thrive with his learning."

"If anyone can do it, Savannah can. I haven't a doubt in the world."

Chapter Five

Savannah,

It is hard to believe that ten years have passed since I last seen your face. I think of that morning often and wish I had of had more time to prepare you for being a wife and mother; not that you haven't turned out wonderful, but I often feel guilty for the way we sent you off. I hope you know if I had anything to do with it, I would not have agreed to it. I know you and I have spoken on this many times, but I just wish I could look you in the face and know for sure you do not hate me.

Now, when I read your letters and hear about your family and how happy you sound, I am thrilled that maybe I didn't have anything to do with it, because where would you be now? You may still be here in Dahlonega, but would you truly be as happy as you are at this moment?

I always knew that Jonah would someday fall deeply in love with you. How could he not have? You are so beautiful and kind.

I must tell you though, and please do not worry over this, but your brother Joseph seems so distant lately. He misses you so terribly and says that if he did not feel obligated to stay here and take care of Mary and I, that he would be on his way to Arkansas. I do not know what he says in his letters to you, but please know that I never told your brother he had to stay here. He is a grown man now, of seventeen, and is free to go as he pleases. I would never want to hold any of my children back from following their dreams.

Truth is, he begs me to move to Arkansas, but I feel that Mary is doing so well in school and I know that you teach the children at home. I keep thinking that in four years when Mary is sixteen, maybe that will be a good time to venture out west. You see, Savannah, I want to see you as much as your siblings do. I know four years sounds like a long time, but I feel it will go by as quickly as the last ten have.

I have been keeping busy baking and sewing as usual and sending you another recipe for a lemon pound cake. Hope you and Rose will like it. Please tell her that Momma Alice is so immensely proud of her and give Catherine and Matthew a kiss from me.

I Love you and miss you always
Love Mother

Savannah smiled as she closed the letter. Jonah mailed the letter to her mother that morning, so her mother had no idea about the school that was about to be built, and Savannah wondered if that would change her mind and make her want to venture out west sooner than four years.

Could it be possible that something might be arranged, and her family could move out west, or would they even want to?

Mary was just eighteen months when she left and only knew her through letters. Surely, she had friends there and would not want to leave. Would it be fair to beg them to come and Mary resent her for it?

The valley was not as populated as Dahlonega. She imagined now in 1842 that it was very populated, with more people moving in to pan for gold.

Meeting Savannah for the first time, for Mary, would be like meeting someone who had been your pen pal for years but not your family at all.

Savannah opened the other letter from Joseph, glad her family had gone to bed earlier than usual.

Jonah always knew, on letter night, not to expect her to come to bed early.

Dear Savannah,

The harvest was good this year. I must say I am quite proud of myself. Done fairly good not having any help. Mother is so busy with her sewing and baking business and Mary always has her head in her books.

Not that I am complaining if it sounds that way. As a man, I know it is my responsibility, and mother never goes a day without thanking me. She is a great mother, we were truly blessed when God picked her for ours.

I was only seven when you left us, but I still remember you as if it were yesterday.

Mother gets on to me and says I am disrespecting Father when I get upset over what he did to you that made you leave without even asking, but I can't help it.

I know you and I have spoken on this before, but it seems the more I think about it the more upset I get.

I guess I hold a lot of anger and resentment toward Father about a lot of things.

I want to miss him, Savannah, but I just cannot.

I do not think there was a time I ever heard him tell either of us that he loved us. He was just demanding and mean. I do not even understand how someone like Mother even stayed with him, but then you know Mother, she feels that a woman should not speak up and always allow the man to lead.

I do hope Jonah is as kind to you as you say he is, and you do not just say that to make him look good. I would hate to think you are being forced to be with a man who treats you as Father did Mother because of a few acres of land.

I begged mother to move out west, but she will not even talk to me about it. She is more concerned about Mary getting a good education. If it weren't for knowing they need me, I would be on my way.

I love you Savannah, and I miss you.

One day Mary will be out of school and then there will be no more excuses. I will see you again, I must believe that.

Your brother,

Joseph

Savannah closed the letter and placed it back inside the envelope. She had been corresponding with her brother for the past ten years and had never once heard him talk of a girlfriend. His mind had been on coming out west ever since she left. Maybe he was waiting, thinking this would be the place he would meet that special someone.

Savannah opened the last letter from her sister Mary and started to read.

Savannah,

I hope this letter finds you well.

I have been working on a project for school over minerals. I have been going over Chrissy's every day and looking for different rocks and doing a report.

Miss Turner said we can work with partners and since Chrissy is my best friend, we have been having fun getting to spend more time together to do our homework. I hope we win first place. The winner gets five dollars, and Chrissy and I are going to split it. It was donated by a few of the merchants in town. Everyone is hoping to win.

Mother says you were always good in arithmetic. I am afraid it is my worst subject in school. Joseph has been trying to help me some in the evening, but he is not patient at all and just makes me angry. I wish you lived closer to help me. It would be so nice to learn from you as Rose, Matthew and Catherine do. Mother says I favor you, but I know I did not take after you when it comes to arithmetic.

How is Rose, Matthew and Catherine doing? Makes me sad at times that I have never met them. Still do not understand why you had to move so far away. I have asked Mother, but all she tells me is that's where Jonah wanted to live.

I never did tell you thank you for leaving your porcelain doll for me. I still have her and keep her on my bed. Mother told me how much you loved her, so it means a lot to me. I have always cherished it.

I know this has been a short letter, but I have been getting up earlier for school to get my chores finished so I can come home and not have to worry about them. And Mother never seems to mind me going to Chrissy's if my chores are finished.

Wish me luck on my project. I cannot imagine what I will do with 2.50, but I am sure I am going to feel rich.

Your sister,

Mary

Savannah placed all three letters inside the beautiful box Jonah had made her several years ago, for her to house them in. She treasured all her letters and took them out often to reread.

She wondered what Mary would think if she knew her sister was about to be a teacher and could help her with her arithmetic?

Would it make a difference, or would she still not want to leave her best friend, Chrissy?

Savannah sat back down in the rocker to pray a bit before going to bed. There was so much she needed to thank God for, and even as tired as she was, she could not imagine falling to sleep before she did so.

Thank You, Father, for all You have brought to the valley.

Thank You for guiding the Andersons here and leading them to build a church, Your house, where we will gather and sing praises to Your name.

Father, please keep my family back home safe and in Your loving care.

And Father, thank You for the opportunity to live out the dream of teaching.

I ask that you help me to never step in front of You and that I always allow You to lead, at home, with my children and in the classroom.

Amen

*****

Everyone gathered around the place for the new building for the ground-breaking.

The sunrise had beautiful streaks of oranges and yellows, as if God were painting them a picture, saying He was well pleased.

"Let us all join hands and say a prayer before we begin," Pastor Anderson said, as he bowed his head.

"Thank you, Father, for every life that is represented here today, all twenty-three of us. This community is growing and thriving, and I know more and more will continue to come to this beautiful valley. Only You know what was and is and is to come, for You are the holder of all things, and always have our best interest at heart.

59

"Father, we ask that You bless this ground and this building and bless each of the hands that hold the planks and drive the nails, and those hands that prepare food and bring us water. Let this day in 1842, be a day to remember, a day that this church, Your church, was born.

"Let this be a place that many souls come to You and a place that children grow and learn, not only Your word, but how to read and write so they will prosper and go forth into the world sharing Your love and thriving themselves.

"May they never forget the knowledge they learn in this building and bless Savannah as she so graciously invests her time in our children. In Jesus' name we pray, Amen."

"Amen," everyone said together.

"So, what do you say men, are you ready to get started?" Pastor Anderson asked.

*****

For the next two months, they worked hard. Everyone pitched in, from the oldest, where John sorted and handed nails, to the youngest, where Catherine carried water.

The women cooked and kept the children and men fed and helped carry lumber and cleaned up.

Noel worked on building the benches and desks that would serve the church on Sundays and the children through the week. He also made a desk for Savannah and a pulpit for Pastor Anderson.

It was a busy time for the valley, all working together and becoming a family, a community, where unity was contagious, each learning from the other.

Savannah was thrilled about becoming the children's teacher because she cared about them all, seven boys and seven girls. Her mind constantly went to different things she could teach them to make learning fun and not a chore.

"Mrs. Bell?"

"Yes," she turned to find Daniel, the Ayers' oldest son, bleeding.

"Oh goodness, Daniel, what have you done?"

"I cut my finger, and I was wondering if you could patch it for me."

"Yes, yes, come here quickly." Savannah took him to the first aid supplies Pastor Anderson insisted they have on hand and took a closer look at his wound.

"Doesn't look like you need stiches, thank God. Let us get this cleaned and patch you right up."

"I am sorry I was so clumsy."

"No need to apologize, Daniel; accidents happen. We all tend to be clumsy from time to time."

"What did you do, Daniel?" his mother, Marylou, asked.

"He cut his finger," Savannah answered, "but he will be good as new in no time."

"You are as good a nurse as you are a teacher," Nancy laughed, realizing what was going on.

"Oh no, you don't," Savannah teased. "You are the nurse, remember? Anyone can patch a finger."

"Just look at it, ladies," Nancy said, pointing to the almost-complete building. "Isn't she a beauty? Who would have ever guessed this would happen?"

Katie put her arm around Nancy's shoulders. "I have to agree with you; she's a beauty. Our men have done well."

"Our children, too," Marylou added. "I think they want the school as bad as we want the church."

"I agree with you on that," Savannah said, putting the last touch to Daniel's finger. "You can run along now, as good as new, just keep that bandage on a few days so dirt doesn't get inside."

"Thank you, Mrs. Bell." Daniel said, and ran off to help the other boys.

"Feels weird being called Mrs. Bell."

"Why is that?" Nancy asked. "That's who you are, and our children have to respect that."

"I know; it just feels strange. I am going to count on you ladies to help me come up with ideas to make learning fun. I mean, it cannot just be all books and homework. I was thinking we can have a dance once a year, and let the children get involved with the decorating. Maybe a Christmas dance, like a celebration of Christ's birth."

"What a lovely idea," Katie commented. "I will help any way I can."

Catherine came running to Savannah, out of breath. "Momma, tell Matthew to let me help carry the wood pieces to the stack for winter; he says I am a girl and I am too little, but I can do as much as he can. I am only one year younger, and he is just being mean," Catherine pouted.

"Matthew, let your sister help, too. There are enough scraps that both of you should have plenty to do," Savannah called out. "Are you ladies sure you want me teaching your children, when I can't seem to keep mine in line?"

The women laughed, for they knew that Catherine had a mind of her own and was truly a handful.

*****

Eight weeks passed, working several hours a day, and now they stood, outside the church--all four families on Sunday morning, ready to go inside to worship.

"Can you come up here, Savannah?" Pastor Anderson asked, standing in front of the doorway.

Savannah climbed the six steps and took her place by Pastor Anderson.

"As the new teacher at this school, I wanted to give you the honors of entering first. Also, from this day forth, I shall refer to you as Mrs. Bell, as our children shall."

"Thank you. Let us go inside and worship, everyone!" she motioned them in and went inside to take a seat.

Pastor Anderson walked to the head of the church. "It does my heart good to see each of you here this morning. I never dreamed this would all come together so quickly, but God is good, and His blessings are plentiful with each new day.

"I would like to let you all know that because you were all so generous in helping build the church and allowing us to use the supplies you had as well, Katie and I were left with extra money we planned to use to build with. Because of that, we rode into town yesterday and ordered a chalk board, two dozen slates and a dozen hymnal books."

Tom stood up. "Pastor Anderson, I think I can speak for my wife and myself. We want to thank you for all you have brought to this community."

Nancy nodded her head in agreement.

"Marylou and I thank you, also," Noel stated.

"Noel, the furniture you built here is top quality. You did an excellent job, and I thank you for that," Pastor Anderson smiled. "All of you have worked so hard. We are a team here, and truly, you do not have to thank me for anything. It was God who gave me the idea; I just brought it to you, and together we all brought it to life."

Pastor Anderson looked toward Savannah. "Mrs. Bell, I did not prepare a sermon today; I wanted rather to just leave the floor open to speak freely. However, I do intend to have a sermon prepared for next Sunday, so I expect you all back," he laughed.

"With that being said, would you like to say anything and tell us of some of the ideas you may be thinking about as our new teacher here in the valley?"

Savannah stood and walked to the front. "First of all, I would like to thank you for trusting me with these precious children. I know some are of the age you wish not to be called children, so forgive me," she looked toward some of the older children and smiled.

"We are fast approaching winter, and as you all know, sometimes it can be bad. I know you each have two to three miles to walk, so please, if you see snow falling, stay home. It's easy to get lost out there and turned around in the snow and wind, and I don't wish for any of you to take a chance.

"School will be Monday through Thursday, from nine until three. That will give you plenty of time to do your chores and have Friday off to help around your home. I know you each have responsibilities at home, also.

"Come ready to learn and bring your lunch. We will take lunch and recess at noon for half an hour. That will give us five-and-a-half hours of study time each day, twenty-two hours per week.

"We will learn writing, reading, spelling, history, and arithmetic. There will be lots of discussion, and I do hope you join in and ask questions."

Peggy Ayers, the Ayers' thirteen-year-old daughter raised her hand.

"Yes, Peggy, do you have a question?"

"Is there a dress code, Mrs. Bell?"

Savannah smiled. "What you usually wear is fine, Peggy; you are always beautiful."

Peggy blushed and dropped her head.

"Are there any more questions?" Savannah asked.

"You will let us know when you need us, right?" Nancy asked.

"Yes, I certainly will; you can count on it. If there are no more questions, I am finished, Pastor Anderson."

"Thank you, Mrs. Bell. Does this mean school starts tomorrow, or had you rather wait a couple of weeks when the slates come in?"

Savannah looked around the room at the children. "What do you think, Children? Shall we start tomorrow?"

All the children screamed yes at once, and everyone laughed at their excitement.

"Tomorrow it is, then, Pastor Anderson. I guess I will see you children at nine in the morning."

*****

"Ye did a good job, Savannah," John stated that evening at dinner. "Ye acted like ye knew exactly what ye were doing. I am very proud of ye."

She chuckled. "Thank you, Papa John. Could you not see my knees shaking? I have never been particularly good at public speaking."

"Well, you couldn't prove it by me," Jonah winked, taking a bite of his cornbread. "I was so proud of you today. Those children all love you."

"That is right, Momma, they do. They have all told me so," Rose said.

"What is a teacher's pet?" Matthew looked puzzled.

"Why do you ask that, son?" Savannah asked.

"Because Powell Ayers told me that I was going to be the teacher's pet, because I was your son, and that it wasn't fair."

"You are not going to be the teacher's pet," Catherine scolded, "because I am going to be the teacher's pet."

Savannah laughed. "Simmer down, Children. There is going to be *no* teacher's pet. I will care about each of you, and when we are at school, I want you to refer to me as Mrs. Bell, like the other children must. At school, I will be your teacher; is that understood? And I will treat you as I do all the other children that will be there. I will not have favorites."

Catherine crossed her arms and pouted. "That will not be easy, Momma."

"You will get used to it, just as the other children will, also. You will see; now go and get ready for bed and come back for the Bible lesson. We will have to start doing it right after dinner. School comes early, and you must go to bed early. A rested mind can learn much better than a tired one."

"But we always played a while after dinner," Catherine grumbled.

"And you can again, on Thursday and Friday nights, but not tonight. Not on a school night, so run along missy and do as I tell you."

Catherine got down from the table and stomped all the way to her room.

Jonah shook his head. "I see why God stopped giving us children after Catherine; He knew she would be all we could handle. Matthew, you heard your momma, go and get ready for bed."

"What about Rose? She has to go to school, too," he stated.

"Then Rose can go, and you can stay and help your momma with the dishes, as she usually does."

"Never mind, I am going."

Rose laughed, stacking plates, and carrying them to the washtub. "I am happy you were chosen for our teacher. I am so excited about tomorrow. I know I won't sleep at all."

"You and me both," Savannah agreed.

"I wish I could say that," Papa John said. "I can hardly hold my eyes open. I hope ye do not mind if I miss the Bible reading again tonight, Mrs. Bell. I promise to read it on my own tomorrow."

Savannah laughed. "Papa John, don't you dare start calling me Mrs. Bell! I will always be Savannah to you."

John stood up slowly and kissed her on the cheek. "Good, because I do believe it will be as hard for me as it's going to be for that little munchkin," he laughed.

Chapter Six

Alice finished frosting the chocolate cake and took the apple pie out of the oven. Mrs. Durham would be arriving soon to pick up her order.

She thanked God daily for her baking and sewing; without it, she knew she would go stir-crazy. She had never been the kind of person that could sit still for a long period of time, and with the orders coming in daily, it kept her busy.

Looking out the kitchen window, she saw Joseph take the horses into the barn. He had gone to the mercantile earlier to pick up supplies and drop Mary off at school. His younger sister always got a ride whenever he was willing to oblige.

How many times had she watched from that same window as Mitchell walked in and out of the barn, a barn he had built when they first married, four years before Savannah was born.

The old barn held so many memories, but like a person, they grew old. The planks were faded, and she could see places where Joseph had patched a hole here and there on the rooftop, yet season after season it served their two horses, and even they had grown older.

The kitchen was in bad need of repairs, and even though the money was there to do so, there was something in her that felt the need to keep it as is.

Maybe it was because it had been this way since Mitchell built their home, or maybe everywhere she looked she could remember Savannah standing at the counter mixing up a batch of sugar cookies or helping her make bread.

Savannah was always such a huge help to her, especially when Joseph and Mary were younger, and Alice knew she never really realized how much until she was gone. She missed her company something terrible.

Alice held the memories close and replayed them from time to time, in her mind. It seemed that it was the only thing that had kept her from going crazy right after she saw her oldest daughter, who had become her best friend, riding off on Jonah's wagon that early morning at sunrise, so many years ago.

"Do you think I will ever get married someday, Mother?" Savannah asked, mixing up a batch of sugar cookies. The cookies were Joseph's favorite, and Savannah loved to bake them for him. Her little brother followed her everywhere she went.

"Of course, you will, and probably have a dozen children," Alice joked. She loved the way her thirteen-year-old daughter asked questions, so grown for her age.

"Mother, I hardly think I want a dozen; I would never be able to bake that many cookies."

"At least you would never be bored."

"I hope that someday I am able to cook as good as you do. What if my husband does not like my cooking? Maybe we can build a house right next door and come over here to eat."

Alice chuckled, "I would love that, keeping you close to me."

"I will just have to tell him that I will only marry him if he promises not to go farther than walking distance of you."

"That sounds like a good plan; I just hope he agrees," Alice finished rolling out the biscuits and placing them in the pan to bake for dinner. They would go good with the fried chicken and gravy.

"Do you think he will be like Father?"

Alice looked at her daughter for a moment and thought about what she asked. She never said a bad word about her father.

Alice would never say this out loud to Savannah, but she certainly hoped her husband was nothing like her father at all. Instead, she prayed her daughter would meet a man who doted on her and was loving and kind, a man who adored her and thanked God for her daily.

"Only God knows what he will be like, Savannah. What sort of man are you praying for?"

"Praying for, Mother? Whatever do you mean?"

"Well, I know you pray and talk to God. There is no harm in telling God what you hope for."

"You mean like putting in an order with God?"

Alice giggled. "I guess you might say that. You see, right at this very moment he is out there somewhere, and you want him to be a man you will fall deeply in love with, one that will love God and honor Him and treat you with kindness and affection. A man that will console you when you are sad and laugh with you over silly things. A man that will be a good father to your children and never once make you or them doubt his love."

Savannah nodded and smiled. "I understand, Mother, and that is a good idea. I will start praying for that very thing today. After all, I am thirteen and I am sure God will send him before long."

Alice picked up the mixing bowl Savannah had been using that morning, so many years ago, and wiped away a tear.

Thank You, God, for the memories.

Alice sighed and sat down in a kitchen chair beside the window and watched as Joseph fed the chickens and slopped the pigs.

Her very tall, handsome son worked so hard and yet never complained. His only complaint was wanting them to pick up and leave it all behind and head west to live near his sister, and it sometimes broke her heart, for he had no idea how much she truly wanted that, also.

Alice got up and walked slowly from the kitchen to the parlor, where she spent so much of her time, rocking, and reading from her Bible.

How hard would it be to leave it all behind, and with a few clothes, set out and start a whole new life?

The letter she read just that morning told of a church and school being built, and Savannah was soon to be the new schoolteacher. It did her heart good, knowing how thrilled her oldest daughter was to become a teacher to the children in the community.

Not having a school close was the main reason she would never talk about the move to Joseph, and now there would be no excuse left, except for the fact that it would be painful to leave the past behind her and set out to a territory unknown, not knowing what they would face along the way, or where they would live when they arrived.

But isn't that just the way life is? Each day a present from God that we unwrap daily. If we place our trust in Him, then no matter what comes our way, we trust that He is with us, and for that reason, we are okay. He is a good God, who always loves us and wants the best for us.

"I miss you, Mother," Savannah said, walking into the parlor where she had spent so much of her childhood, sitting on the floor while Alice read from her old, tattered Bible.

"I miss you, too, so very much," Alice smiled.

"Do you remember the morning I left?"

"How could I ever forget it? I think about that morning every day of my life. I watched and cried until Jonah's wagon rounded the bend, and I could not see you anymore. I felt in my heart that it would be the last time I ever saw you on this side of Heaven."

"But it does not have to be that way, Mother. Come to Arkansas. Come and let us bake sugar cookies for your grandchildren. Oh, Mother, you are going to love them all."

Alice smiled. "I already do. You describe them so well in your letters it's like I can see them in my mind."

"But you need to hold them and talk to them and teach them all the things you taught me. Tell them stories of long ago, and about the life you had with Grandma and Grandpa. Tell them about the time you were a little girl and how your favorite thing was catching fish out of the pond."

"You remember all those stories, Savannah? That was so long ago when I told you that."

"Yes, of course, Mother. I remember them all. In fact, I wrote about each of them in my journal so I wouldn't forget as I got older."

"You have always been a good daughter."

Savannah took her hand and smiled, "and you, Mother, have always been the best mother a girl could ask for."

"I want to come, Savannah, but I am just not sure how. There is so many memories here."

"Yes, I understand, but you will make new memories. You always taught me growing up that things are just things, and the most important thing is family."

"Yes, I remember."

"Then come, Mother. Come to Arkansas and start a new life with Jonah and the children and I."

Alice awoke abruptly, as Joseph slammed the front door.

"I am sorry, Mother; I did not know you were sleeping."

"Goodness, I must have dozed off. I sat down in my rocker just a moment to rest. I guess I was wearier than I thought. I was having such a wonderful dream."

"About me, I am guessing?" Joseph joked.

"No, it was about your sister, Savannah. It was so real, as if she were standing right here."

"You must have gotten a letter from her."

"We did, she wrote one to all of us. It's on the kitchen table."

Joseph took off to the kitchen to find the letter. He loved receiving letters every bit as much as she did, and it pleased Alice to see his excitement. Although this letter would change things as Joseph learned that the excuse she always used could be used no more.

Within minutes, Joseph was back in the parlor and pulled a chair close to her. "You were waiting here, weren't you? You knew I'd be back to talk about this." He lifted the letter.

"Yes, I knew."

"Mother, I have begged you since Father passed six years ago to move out west, but you always said there was no school there. First, it was school for Mary and me, and then just Mary, but that excuse can be no more. What will it be now, Mother? What will the reason be now that we can't move?"

"It's not that simple. We have a farm here and livestock. Mary has a best friend, Chrissy. How would that affect her?"

Joseph stared a moment at his mother. "It was never really about school, was it, Mother? You are scared. You fear picking up and starting over, because you have no idea what is on the other side. Moving out west scares you to death."

Alice closed her eyes as the tears fell. "Maybe you are right, son. I feel safe here, like I have everything under control. I am just not sure how to start over."

"Think of the adventure, Mother. You only live once. If you take Mary and me with you, and we get out west where Savannah and the children are, then you will really leave nothing behind but a few rusty things. Our family will be complete again."

"I know, son."

"Father is no longer here to direct your life and tell you what to do. You are free to go and live your life the way you wish."

Alice wiped her eyes with her apron and smiled. "This is what you truly want, isn't it, son?"

"Yes, Mother. Moving to Arkansas is what I want. Why do you think I could care less about meeting a girl yet? Because deep in my heart, I always knew the woman for me is out there. That is where I want to make a life, not here. Not where the memories for me is not good at all. Those memories of the good ended for me ten years ago when Savannah left us."

Alice let out a deep breath she had been holding. "I had no idea your life had been that bad."

"I'm sorry, Mother, but as much as you hate for me to talk ill of Father, he wasn't the kindest man, and you know that. Savannah was the peacemaker between Father and us, and when she left, there was nothing but anger."

"But your father has been gone now six years, Joseph."

"Yes, and for six years I have begged you to move. With Father gone, there was nothing that should have stood in our way, but you always said you wanted us to have an education, and now Mary can get her education in the school they are building with her sister as her teacher. Don't you see, Mother, don't you see how God truly is in control, just as you have always said?"

"What shall we do with the farm, Joseph? The tractor, the livestock?"

"Sell it all, Mother," he laughed. "Sell it all."

"Can we at least let Mary finish out the school year? We have a lot to do to get ready. I have to let Savannah know so they can be prepared for three more people."

Joseph jumped up and pulled his mother in an embrace. "Oh Mother, I don't think I have ever felt happier than I have at this moment!"

Alice laughed at her son's excitement.

"Don't worry, Mother, I will take care of everything. You just decide what you cannot live without, and we shall ship it out ahead of us, if we must. I have been studying this move for several years."

"I must tell you, son, that I truly am frightened. The thought of just picking up and leaving everything behind and starting over is such a frightening thought."

"But you won't be leaving everything behind. You will take what truly matters with you, and once we arrive, then everything will be just as it should."

"I shall speak to your sister about this alone when she arrives home from school. You must remember that she only knows Savannah from the letters she is sent. I am afraid she shall not be as excited about the move as you are."

"I understand, and you must remember that *you* are her mother and that means you are *not* asking her permission to leave, but rather telling her what to expect."

"She will not want to leave Chrissy, I am sure."

"Just as I did not want Savannah to leave us. We do not always get the things we want, Mother. She can write Chrissy letters just like we have Savannah the past ten years. She will adjust and meet new friends. Savannah says the valley is full of children her age, and I know she and Rose will become the best of friends."

"You have so much wisdom for your age, son. I am not sure what I would do without you," she said, kissing his cheek.

"Which is why I never left. I love you, Mother, and you shall see how happy you are once we get out west and wish you had made the move much sooner."

*****

Mary let the screen door slam on her way in from school, out of breath as always, rushing to get home. "May I go to Chrissy's, Mother? I did my chores before school this morning."

"I thought the project was complete."

"It is. We lost to Tommy Tanner and Gabe Butler. I just want to go visit a while. I promise to be back before dinner."

"Not today, Mary, there is something I must speak to you about. I also would like for you to *help* me with dinner. You learn a lot by watching and doing."

"Do I have to today, Mother? Chrissy will be expecting me."

"Yes, you must today, Mary. You should not have told Chrissy you were coming before you asked."

"I am sorry, Mother, but you always say yes. I did not think you would mind."

"A letter came from your sister today; it is on the kitchen table. She wrote a letter for all of us together."

"I shall read it soon," Mary started for her room. Alice could tell she was not happy about not being allowed to go to Chrissy's house.

Mary was never excited like Joseph was each time a letter arrived. Perhaps she was too easy on her and had been all these years.

Alice knew she hardly had any chores at all, only half of the chores Joseph had, or there would be no way she would be able to get them all finished so quickly.

Yes, Alice knew she did way too much for Mary. Perhaps she was trying to make up for what she could no longer do for Savannah.

"Come to the kitchen when you lay your books down; I am about to start dinner," she called out loud enough for Mary to hear.

Mary walked into the kitchen and picked up the letter. "Savannah never writes just one letter to all of us."

"When you read the letter, you will understand. She is a wife and mother of three, and do not always have time to write each of us a letter. I am only glad she sent that one. Go ahead and read it; I think you will find it quite interesting."

Mary sat down at the table and began to read the letter.

"My sister is becoming a teacher?"

"Yes, they are constructing a church that will become a school through the week. There are fourteen children in the valley now, and several of them your age. Savannah's daughter, Rose, is just a bit younger than you, and from what I hear she acts much older than her age. Do you know she takes all the recipes I send and does the baking? She even writes them out to share with the neighbors."

"I know Savannah will make a great teacher. Maybe I should become a teacher someday, too. I still have no idea what I want to do, but I know I don't want to just get married and have babies."

"Sounds to me as if you have thought this through."

"I have. Well, at least I know what I don't wish to do."

"There is no harm in just getting married and having babies. That is what I did, and I have enjoyed every bit of my life with you children."

"But I want to make a difference in the world, Mother."

Alice had never heard her daughter speak of this until now. It was the first she had ever spoken of it. How would she feel when she told her they would be moving west as soon as school was out?

"I have no doubt that you are brave enough and smart enough to become anything you desire. Would you please peel the potatoes while I make the biscuits?"

Mary got a few potatoes, a knife and a bowl and sat back down at the table. "Why do I feel as if there is something you want to tell me, Mother?"

"Maybe because there is. You have been running off to Chrissy's every day for some time now, and I would also like to spend some time with you."

"I knew there was another reason you kept me home besides just peeling potatoes. Is everything all right?"

"Yes, Mary, everything is all right. I have thought about this all day, how I would tell you, but there is just no easy way. After this school term, Mary, we are moving to Arkansas to live close to your sister and her family."

Mary froze, looking toward her mother. "In six months?"

"Yes, in six months. That shall give us ample time to sell the things here and the farm and close all the loose ends. We can decide what we want to take and move them ahead of us in crates. We will go by stagecoach. Your brother has been looking into the route and has made a plan for us to follow."

"Joseph has been begging you for years to move out west; how did he ever talk you into it?"

"I, too, have been wanting to see Savannah. I know you don't remember her, but she was with us for sixteen years and I miss her terribly."

"Then we shall go visit this summer and come back before the next school term, Mother. Why do we have to live there?"

Alice reached over and took Mary's hand in hers. She knew Mary would not be thrilled with the move and telling her would prove to be the hardest thing since the day she told Savannah she was to become Jonah Bell's wife. She lived her life trying to do the best for her children and wanted to see them happy.

"Mary, I knew you wouldn't be thrilled about the move, because to you, your sister is merely a pen-pal, but this is what we are going to do, Mary. I have not gone before now, because I did not want to pull you out of school. I thought you deserved the best education. But now there is going to be a school, and your sister shall become your teacher. You shall meet new friends and you shall see, in no time at all, you shall come to love Arkansas, just as you love our little town of Dahlonega."

Mary's eyes grew wet. "I know I just turned thirteen, and too young to have a say so in the matter. But I truly do not wish to leave, Mother. Please do not move me away. I shall never get to see Chrissy again. She is my best friend."

"I know you don't wish to move, Mary. There are things in life that happen that do not always please us, but they are for our good. There is really nothing to keep us here, except Chrissy, and you can write her letters, just as you do your sister now."

"As you wish, Mother. I trust you. My heart breaks just thinking about it, but I shall go and not complain, and trust that it is God's will, because I know that you are a woman of God and you must feel that it is His will, don't you, Mother?"

"I do. And thank you, Mary, for being so grown up about this. Think of all you will get to see on the stagecoach. You have never ridden a stagecoach before, just as I have never ridden one. Savannah says Arkansas is beautiful."

"Thank you for letting me at least finish out this school year."

"That will give you time also to prepare yourself and tell Chrissy goodbye, and Joseph and I time to tie loose ends and sell the farm."

"Don't you hate selling the farm, Mother? It has been your home since you married Father."

"There is a part of me that is sad, but a bigger part of me that is ready for the adventure and the chance to see Savannah again and my grandchildren. We shall start over, Mary, in a new home, and I shall have my family back together once more."

"I understand, Mother."

"I will write Savannah a letter tonight and tell her to expect us."

Chapter Seven

"How would you like for me to hitch the wagon up and ride you and the children to your first day of school?" Jonah asked, pulling Savannah into a tight embrace just before the sun came up over the horizon.

Savannah giggled. "It's just two miles; the Ayers children are having to walk almost three. I used to walk three miles to the mercantile when I used to spy on you behind that big oak tree at Mills' Pond."

"And just what were you thinking?" he grinned, loving the feel of her warm skin next to his.

"Oh, I just bet you would like to know. Maybe tonight I shall tell you all about it, but as for now, I have children to awaken and breakfast to cook. But I do thank you for your kind offer to take us. You are a wonderful man, but the walk will do us all good and wake us to be ready to learn."

"Then I will wake the children, and you can start breakfast. I love you, my sweet wife, and I am so enormously proud of you. Those children are going to love you."

Savannah was grateful she had prepared the biscuits the night before, leaving her only the meat to fry and lunch to make. Anything to make her life easier was always in the back of her mind.

Savannah knew the life of a teacher would be challenging, she had no doubt, but she was more than willing to take on the challenge.

She had been preparing for this day the past two months, planning lessons and projects and how she would go about keeping the children's lessons by their age group. With nothing to go by, she could only rely on prayer and guidance from the Holy Spirit, and, so far, He had never steered her wrong.

Dear Father, please help me feel your presence this morning.

Please wrap Your arms tightly around me and calm my shakiness. For I realize there is no need for me to fear.

Please help me to be the kind of teacher that shall honor you and that can make a difference in these children's lives, always being willing, and patient, and listening as much as I speak. Help me remember that my ears are as valuable as my mouth.

I trust Father, that this is Your will, and that it was in Your plan all along.

Thank you for Your many blessings on my life,

Amen.

*****

"I'll race you to the school, Matthew," Catherine started to run.

"You are not as fast as I am!" he took off behind her.

"Those two, always in a competition. Are you excited, Rose, to be going to your first day of school?" Savannah was enjoying the walk and to be able to get out of the house. It was a beautiful morning for a walk.

"Honestly, Momma, you have had me in school at our table since I can remember, but yes, I am excited to be going to a building with other children, and some of them my age. I will be able to see Grace daily now, and Elisa, and get to know the others better."

"And I am excited for you. I know you get bored with only Matthew and Catherine every day."

"Not really bored, Momma, because I always can bake or help you around the house, but it shall be nice to have another girl my age to talk to."

"I understand; I remember very well what it was like to have younger siblings and not have anyone but my mother to talk to about personal things."

"Did you not have any friends back in Georgia?"

"A few at school, but none I really got close to. I was more of a loner and pretty much stayed to myself.

The church came into view and Savannah smiled. "That didn't take as long as I thought it would."

Rose laughed. "I trust you won't say that on mornings it's cold or raining."

Savannah built the fire in the stove at the back of the building upon arriving. She planned to get there half an hour earlier each morning to start a fire and break the chill in the building, before the children arrived.

The men agreed to take turns splitting the wood and filling the wood box to have enough for a week at a time, and Savannah was grateful for all the help and how much everyone wanted to pitch in, so she could spend her time teaching and planning.

"It isn't fair that we have to walk in early and it's cold when we get here," Catherine grumbled, crossing her arms, and plopping down on a bench in the back of the classroom.

"That's one of the advantages of having your Momma as the teacher," Rose laughed. "Besides, Catherine, you should be plenty warm enough after running the whole way."

"She does nothing but complain," Matthew pouted and folded his arms to his chest, mocking his younger sister. "And I told you that I was faster than you. Maybe next time you will believe me."

Catherine stuck out her tongue toward her brother.

"It doesn't seem that you are that chipper this morning yourself, young man." Savannah added. "Now, remember children, you are to call me Mrs. Bell while we are at school. I do not want the other children to think I am playing favorites. I will be as tough on you as I am them, but I will love you just as I do now, so don't ever forget that."

"You are going to do fine, Momma," Rose nodded, "I mean Mrs. Bell."

The door flung open and Jerry Ayers walked in, smiling from ear-to-ear. "I brought you an apple, Mrs. Bell."

"Thank you, Jerry, I will eat it for lunch. Please come in and take a seat."

Within the next half-hour, all fourteen children sat on the beautiful benches with desks that Noel Ayers had hand-crafted and chatted quietly with each other.

Savannah looked at the children and silently asked God again to be with her.

"Everyone, can I have your attention, please?" Savannah said loudly.

"I know I have met you all, but I am going to call the roll, and when I call your name, I want you to tell me your age. Then I shall seat you by your age, because even though we shall be working on the same subjects, our work will be by age group, so don't get too comfortable with your seats."

Savannah chuckled when she heard low grumbles around the room, knowing the children sat down where they wanted to be.

"Rose Bell."

"Ten," Rose called out, knowing her momma knew her age, but as she said, she did not want to treat them any differently while at school.

"Matthew Bell."

"Six," Matthew sat up straight, proud to be at school.

"Catherine Bell."

"Five, I am just a year younger than Matthew," she stated proudly.

"Grace Ingalls."

"Eleven," Grace spoke quietly.

"Daniel Ayers."

"Fifteen."

"Peggy Ayers."

"Fourteen."

"Jerry Ayers."

"Eleven."

"Powell Ayers."

"Ten." Powell reached to tug his sister's ponytail, making her yell.

"Mrs. Bell, Powell pulled my hair," Glenda pouted.

"Powell, please do not pull your sister's hair. This is not only a school, but a house of God, and we are to act respectful. Besides, that is very rude," Savannah scolded.

"I am sorry, Mrs. Bell," he apologized.

"Thank you, now I shall continue. Glenda Ayers."

"Nine," she said, turning to stick out her tongue at Powell.

"Ricky Ayers."

"Seven."

"Janice Ayers."

"Five," she spoke so quietly Savannah could barely hear her.

"Please speak up, Janice."

"Five," she yelled louder.

"Thank you. Nathaniel Anderson."

"Fifteen."

"Josiah Anderson."

"Fourteen."

"Elisa Anderson."

"Twelve."

"Thank you all for your patience. Now I want the girls on the left side of me and the boys on the right.

"Janice, Catherine, Matthew and Ricky, I want in the front.

"Rose, Grace, Elisa, Jerry, Powell and Glenda, I want in the middle section.

"Daniel, Nathaniel, Josiah and Peggy, I want in the back."

Everyone moved to the section they were told, grumbling quietly to each other.

"As you know, our slates will be in soon, and it will be much easier, as well as a chalkboard. Fortunately, I have a bit of paper until then, and Mr. Bell purchased each of you a writing pencil. I want each of you to act like family here, and don't be afraid to speak up if you don't understand something or have a question by raising your hand first. No question is a crazy question. They are all important. We do not learn by not asking."

Catherine raised her hand.

"Yes, Catherine?"

"I don't know how to read but a few words yet."

Savannah smiled. "Yes, I am aware of that. As I said, we will work by your age group. There may be several of you that do not know how to read that well yet, and no matter what age, that is okay. That is why we are here.

"Also, I don't ever want to hear of any of you picking on someone else. Even if it is your sibling, and that is the way you carry on in your own home. This is school, and we are to act respectful. Do I make myself clear?"

"Yes, Mrs. Bell," the children said in unison.

"Daniel, Nathaniel, and Josiah, do you think you can take turns making sure the heater has wood and put in a few more sticks when needed? Daniel, your turn can be first."

"Yes, ma'am," he answered and got up to check the heater.

"Peggy, I would like for you to make sure the water jug is filled in the back, and when it is almost empty gather more water from the spring each morning. I have already made sure it was filled today."

"Yes, ma'am," Peggy nodded.

"Rose, Grace, Elisa and Glenda, I want you to take turns sweeping the floor each day when class is over. Rose, you will have your turn today."

"Yes, Mrs. Bell," Rose smiled.

"Jerry and Powell, I want you two to take turns washing down the chalkboard each day after it arrives. Jerry, you will go first."

Jerry nodded his head.

"Janice and Catherine, you two shall clean the slates each morning and pass them out."

"That's a fun job," Catherine cheered and looked at Janice, who politely nodded.

"And finally, Matthew and Ricky, you two shall take turns taking the erasers outside and cleaning the chalk dust off, by beating them on a tree. Matthew, you will go first."

"Yes, Mrs. Bell," Matthew grinned. He thought it was funny calling his momma, Mrs. Bell.

"Janice, would you please pass everyone a piece of paper," Savannah handed Janice the stack of paper. "Please do not doodle on your paper. We are going to utilize every bit of it, front and back. We are not going to waste any of it. Hang on to it until I tell you what to do next."

Janice shyly gave a piece of paper to everyone.

"Ricky, I want you to give everyone a writing pencil, please."

Ricky got up and did as he was told.

"Now, I want each of you to write your full name in the top right-hand corner. If you do not know how to write your full name, do the best you can. I need to know who I need to help. Remember, there is no judgement here.

"Now I want you to write your alphabet, writing small, please, to save space.

"And under that I want you to write your numbers one through one hundred. Do the best you can. This is not a test that will be graded; it is just to allow me to see how much you already know and who may need help in certain areas." Savannah knew all too well that Jonah was a grown man and yet never learned to read or write, and she fully intended to make sure none of these children went through life not knowing.

*****

The day went by faster than Savannah imagined it would. There was still so much she wished she had time for, but tomorrow was another day.

She worked them hard, trying to find each of their strengths and weaknesses, so she would know how to instruct them.

Without knowing the basics, it was hard to move forward, and knowing which ones knew them would allow her to know which needed extra help.

Savannah enjoyed the walk home. It had warmed up, and the leaves on the trees were the brilliant colors of fall and falling with the slight breeze.

Catherine and Matthew ran ahead, eager to get home and play a bit before dinner and bedtime, leaving Rose to help carry home the papers that Savannah would go over after the Bible reading.

"You did great today, Momma."

"Do you really think so? Could you tell how nervous I was?"

"Not at all, you seemed well organized and knew what you were doing."

Savannah laughed. "Would you believe me if I told you I haven't a clue? I never went to college. I have spent most of my life reading, and before I left Georgia, I studied hard in school and paid attention. Mrs. Rogers always told me secretly that I was the smartest girl in class, and that I should be a teacher someday. Mother always taught me at home, too, in the evenings."

"Did you ever want to be a teacher?" Rose asked.

"Yes, I always thought it would be fun. I guess Mrs. Rogers planted that dream inside of me because she believed in me."

"And was it fun?"

Savannah giggled. "Why yes, yes, it was quite fun. I enjoy being a mother and wife and working at our home, but I am looking forward to doing this journey and using my mind for other things."

"Good, because I love having a school, and I love having you as my teacher."

Savannah put her arm around Rose and pulled her closer as they walk. "I love you, Rose; you make this momma proud.

*****

"A penny for your thoughts?" Jonah asked, lying beside Savannah in bed.

She had been staring up at the ceiling for the past fifteen minutes and had not heard a word he said.

"Oh, please forgive me. I was deep in thought."

"I gather that," he chuckled. "Would you like to share?"

"A couple of the older children are struggling to read and write as much as the younger ones. I am trying to figure out exactly how to help them without making it obvious. The last thing I wish to do is embarrass them."

"Are they in the same family?"

"Yes, it's the Anderson boys. Yet Elisa seems to be above her age in reading and writing."

"Maybe that is why Pastor Anderson wanted a school in the valley also."

"Possibly. I mean, I am sure he knows. Why do you think Elisa knows more than they do, and she is younger?"

"Pastor Anderson said they have traveled around a lot. I am sure the boys were always helping out around the house, and Elisa went to school."

"Yes, possibly. I just wish I had some readers."

"Readers?"

"Books for young children that make it easy for them to learn to read. I was fortunate enough to have a reader when I was learning."

"How can we get these readers?" Jonah asked.

"They will have to be ordered in the school supply catalog. Surely the mercantile has a catalog. But I am sure they are quite costly."

"Why don't you take a ride into town with me on Saturday and go through the catalog and place an order? We have a bit of savings. God has blessed us with great crops the past four seasons. We have sold them at market, along with the eggs, fried pies, and your crochet crafts. That is your money as much as mine, and it would help the children."

"Really, Jonah? I had no idea."

Jonah smiled and kissed her tenderly. "Yes, really. Now why don't you tell me what it was you were thinking about me behind that big oak tree at Mills' Pond?"

Savannah giggled. "Oh Jonah, have you literally thought about that all day?"

"All day long; it has about drove me nuts."

Savannah laughed aloud. "I love you, my dear husband."

"And why is that?"

"Because you have so much work to do here on the farm, yet your thoughts are on me."

"I am great at doing more than one thing at a time, and yes, my thoughts are *always* on you."

She kissed him again, more tenderly, and heard him moan. "You are great at a lot of things, Mr. Bell."

"So, does that mean you are going to tell me what you were thinking all those years ago?"

"I have a better idea. Why don't I just show you?" Savannah reached and turned down the wick in the oil lamp. Tomorrow she would teach fourteen children, but tonight it was time to please her husband.

Chapter Eight

Dearest Savannah,
My hand is shaking as I write this. I am filled with excitement
yet beyond nervous for what we are about to do. In better
words, I am quite sure I have never been this frightened in
my life.

I was born in Lumpkin County, Georgia, as you know,
back in the late 1700's around the turn of the century. We
called this town Talonega back then, and there was not much
around anywhere, except my Pa and Ma, and a few other
relatives and friends. I guess in short, I am trying to say, I
have never ventured far from my roots. I have always felt
safe here, on familiar ground.

As you know, we sold the land Jonah left your father, shortly
after he passed. And Joseph and Mary and I have decided that
within the next six months we shall also sell our homestead
here in Dahlonega. We are just waiting for the school term to be
over, which also gives us ample time to tie up loose ends.

We shall decide what to sell and what to place into crates
for the journey west.

Yes, Savannah, we are coming to Arkansas to live, all
three of us.

Ten years is much too long to be apart, and truly, just as
Joseph says, there is nothing to keep us here when the other
half of us lives there.

I have no idea where we shall live or what we shall do, but whatever that is I am hoping it is close to you.

I want to meet and get to know my three grandchildren and I want us to bake sugar cookies together again as we used to.

I only hope they shall love their grandma as much as I know I shall love them and already do.

I am also looking forward to getting to know Jonah. I feel like I know him from your letters, but I mean really know him and see you and he together, in love, the way it should be. Then maybe I shall feel better about you leaving the way you did.

You were once my best friend, Savannah, and I have no doubt that when we embrace it shall feel just like yesterday and that bond shall still be there, as if we have been held by glue all these years.

Joseph is beside himself with excitement. He swears that this is a God thing and that the woman of his dreams is there in Arkansas. It shall be so good to see him happy again. I truly do not think he has been happy since the morning he awoke and found you gone.

Mary, I am afraid is not as enthusiastic because she does not want to leave her best friend, Chrissy. I have assured her they can correspond through mail, just as we have. She is, however, excited about you becoming her teacher, and she hopes you can help her with arithmetic.

I hate having to sell the livestock, but we certainly cannot bring them with us by stagecoach, and Joseph says he has already spoken to Mr. Grizzle next door and he is going to purchase them. He has a large pasture and barn, and they shall fit in nicely with what he already has.

Please do not think I am coming there broke, expecting you and Jonah to take care of us. God has truly blessed us with the sale of Jonah's land and cabin and all these years of baking and sewing. Also, I am sure we will get a good price for the farm and tractor, along with the livestock.

I should have plenty to build a cabin for us. Perhaps there is land close by I might purchase, that is in walking distance of the school for Mary and close enough that I can see you, my sweet daughter every day for the rest of my life. We have a lot of catching up to do.

Your brother, of course finished school last year, so he can help Jonah around the farm. He is young, but he is strong, and very smart, just like his older sister.

I love you my sweet daughter. I hope you are not wishing you had never invited us, because here we come very soon, like it or not.

Mother

Alice smiled as she placed the letter inside the envelope. She asked Joseph to let her mail her letter first so she could be the one to tell Savannah of their arrival.

She was still having a hard time believing that it was going to be a reality.

They were picking up and journeying west to Arkansas in just a few months.

There was so much she needed to do to get caught up and ready for the trip, but as for now, she needed to make a three-mile journey to Dahlonega to mail Savannah's letter.

*****

"It has been way too long since you and I rode to the village together, just the two of us," Savannah reminded, placing her hand under Jonah's arm and sliding closer to him in the seat.

"Yes, it has. It was kind of John to oversee the children today. Rose is old enough to watch out for Matthew and Catherine, but it makes me feel better knowing he is there, and it also makes him feel needed."

"I am worried about John. He has not been himself lately. He only ventures down for dinner and he never stays for the Bible reading. I am afraid he may have gone into a depression."

"He has declined a lot lately, but then he is an old man, Savannah. I don't think he is depressed; I just think he is wearing out. I have tried to take him with me the last couple of times I rode for supplies, to see the doctor, but he insists he is not up for the trip, saying he is ready to meet Martha whenever God sees fit."

"And I have no doubt about that; John is such a godly man. I am sure it will be a happy reunion when he sees his Martha again."

"Yes, I am sure of it. I know I would be if you had left me. I cannot imagine that."

"I am so glad he stumbled upon our home many years ago. He is a pleasure to have as our children's Papa John."

"He is a good man, that is for sure. He has been more of a father to me; I shall miss him when he goes."

"It's just too dreary to think about, Jonah. Let us try to stay positive today."

"Sounds like a plan. Guess what we are going to do when we get to the village?"

"I hope you are going to take me to Annie's Restaurant to eat lunch," Savannah grinned. "I remember when I was pregnant with Matthew and you surprised me. It was the very first time I had ever eaten in a restaurant in my entire life."

Jonah laughed. "I do remember that. You had the meatloaf, mashed potatoes, and green beans. And I do remember the peach cobbler for dessert, with ice cream."

"Oh, Jonah, you remembered that? And it was also the very first time I ever tried ice cream."

"There was a lot of firsts that day."

"Yes, and a lot of surprises. You tricked me by making me go to the doctor for a checkup."

"And I would do it all over again," he grinned. "I'm sorry I have put you through so much, Savannah."

"Whatever do you mean? You only did it because you cared about me."

"I am not talking about the trip to Doctor Murphey's office. I was talking about in general, the past ten years."

Savannah clucked her tongue. "Now, now, remember, this is a day to be positive. We have had this talk a hundred times and I love you. We cannot go back and change the past, and if we could, I would not change a thing. Everything that happened, has brought us to where we are today."

"I would. I would change some things."

"Oh really? Tell me Jonah, what would you change?"

"I would love you sooner. I wasted two whole years by pushing you away."

Savannah squeezed his arm and kissed him on the cheek. "It doesn't matter when you loved me, it just matters *that* you love me now."

"Does it ever bother you that I enjoy making love to you? Is that something you enjoy, too, or do you feel obliged, thinking you have to fulfill your wifely duties?"

Savannah giggled. "Jonah, I enjoy our children, Papa John, our neighbors, being a teacher in the valley, but nothing, and I mean nothing, compares to the enjoyment I get when you take me in your arms and our bodies become one."

"Thank you for saying that. I get afraid at times that maybe you do not feel the same way I do. I know I am fourteen years older than you. Does our age difference ever bother you?"

"There is no age difference when it comes to love, Jonah, you should know that."

"As long as you don't mind being married to a forty-year-old man," he laughed.

"Maybe I would if it was just any old forty-year-old man, but not a sexy forty-year-old man, as you are."

"I love the fact that you find me sexy," he laughed."

"Sexiest man in the valley. But then I have told you this before."

"That you have. And you, my sweet wife, are the most beautiful. When I look at you, you still take my breath away."

*****

"Savannah!" Dottie screamed out, running to meet her as she walked out of the mercantile.

"Hello Dottie, how have you been doing?" She embraced the older lady she was once so jealous of.

"What brings you to the village today? It is so good to see you, and I might say you are looking very pretty today, as always."

Savannah chuckled, "I am sure you don't find my homemade skirt and blouse that attractive compared to your velvet and lace."

Dottie was dressed in a green velvet and silk dress that fit her snugly around the bosom.

"On the contrary, my sweet friend; if I could make a living wearing the clothes you wear, I would. I am sure it is much comfier. So where is that handsome husband of yours? Don't tell me you rode here alone."

"Now, Dottie, you know better than that. There is no telling where I would end up if I were driving the team," she laughed. "Jonah is getting a haircut. I have just come from the mercantile where I have ordered readers for my class."

"Your class?"

"The community has gotten together and built a church in the valley that serves as a school through the week. I have become the teacher."

"Well, my goodness, I had no idea the valley was getting that populated, and who better to be the teacher but you, my friend? I don't know a smarter woman anywhere."

"Thank you, but it can be quite challenging, I am afraid, when you have a classroom full of different ages. I am hoping the readers help me teach the children to read better."

"I can see how that would be a challenge. I still say you are the luckiest woman on earth."

"Why is that?"

"Because you are married to a man that only has eyes for you. He loves you, Savannah, and for that, you are blessed. You have three beautiful children, and I adore them all. And just where are they today? It has been a while since I have seen them."

"Papa John is watching over them so Jonah and I could have some time alone. We are going to Annie's to eat lunch in a bit. It is nice to have someone cook for me for a change."

"I am sure you two don't get a lot of alone time. I am glad you both were able to get away. How is John doing these days? He used to ride into town, but we never see him anymore. I guess he is getting on up there in age."

"Yes, he is not so good. I am afraid he is aging fast."

"I hate to hear that. He is a good man; that is for sure. Another man that was only devoted to one woman for life; so sad his woman left him so long ago."

"It looks like there is a lot of building going on," Savannah looked at the new buildings being erected at the end of the street. "But at least you now have the band playing music. Do they play here daily?"

"Yes, the mayor hired them to play at the gazebo for several hours a day. Thought it would be nice instead of all the noise, and I must say it has been."

"That is wonderful; I wish I knew how to play. I miss hearing music."

"We are also getting a new dress shop, which I am just thrilled about, and the saloon is expanding, with a hotel on the top floor."

"That should bring in more travelers, and more business."

"There is a new doctor that has also come to town. Doc Murphey is about ready to retire, and Doctor Wesley will take his place. And there is talk of a new sawmill coming."

"So much happening."

"Trust me, Savannah, you aren't missing anything. With the expansion and all the noise, even with the nice music, it is still enough to drive a person crazy. You are blessed to live in the valley where it is peaceful."

"Yes, I do love it there."

"Have you heard from your family lately? How are they doing?"

"I was just about to walk to the post office and see if I have a letter. I keep praying that they will move here someday."

"Well, just keep praying; I know if anyone's prayers are heard, it is yours. By the way, thank you for the jelly you sent a few months back; it was unbelievably delicious. I am afraid I cannot return you the same favor, as my cooking skills are minimal. If it weren't for Annie's and an occasional chili from the saloon, I would starve to death."

"How are you today, Dottie?" Jonah asked, walking up from behind them.

"Doing great, thank you for asking, and how are you?"

"Doing wonderful. It is a beautiful cool day for traveling, but I am afraid that winter will arrive sooner than later."

Dottie looked up at the cloud-covered sky and tightened the shawl around her. "Yes, been feeling it now for several days. Well, it was good talking to you both; I need to get back to the saloon. I hope you enjoy your lunch at Annie's."

"Thank you, Dottie, take care of yourself," Savannah called out, watching her cross the street.

"It amazes me that you two are friends," Jonah chuckled. "You hated her for so long."

"Hate is such a harsh word; dislike is more like it. Ten years is an awfully long time to have an enemy."

"Yes, it is, indeed. So, what made you finally cave?"

"I realized Jesus loved her as much as me. And that you never looked her way. I stopped being jealous, which I should have never been in the first place. You know, she still asks where my handsome husband is?"

"She does, does she?"

"She does," Savannah smiled, "At least she has good taste."

"So, are you ready for lunch, my sweet wife?" Jonah held out his arm to escort her to the cafe.

"I am. I am starving, and I can't wait to look at the menu."

*****

Savannah snuggled closer on the ride back home and was grateful she brought a blanket for them to share.

"I know you can't wait to read your mother's letter. I will try to get the children to bed earlier tonight."

"It's okay, Jonah, they go to bed early enough. It is you I thank each time I get a letter for going to bed alone. I know how you hate that."

"As you said earlier, hate is such a strong word," he smiled. "At least, I know you are coming to bed later. I don't think I could bear it if I knew I had to sleep in that bed alone the rest of my life."

"Well, you don't have to worry about that; I am not going anywhere."

"You know, Savannah, it might be wrong, but I pray that when we grow older God allows me to go first."

"Why, Jonah? I don't think I could bear to be alone either."

"You are much stronger emotionally than I am. You would adjust better without me than the other way around."

"What a dreary subject you have us on. I thought we were being positive today!"

"I guess that isn't very positive. Just something I had thought about. So, what shall we talk about, sweet wife?"

"Let's talk about your daughter."

"Who, Rose?"

"No, Catherine, the one that acts just like you," Savannah smiled.

"Just like me. However, do you mean?"

"You know what I mean, so strong-willed. I swear, that child," Savannah joked.

"Is she giving you trouble in school?"

"Not trouble, really, she's just very bold and keeps me hopping with a thousand questions."

"Did you tell them to ask questions?"

Savannah rolled her eyes, "That I did."

"Isn't it funny how all our children are so different."

"They each have their own personalities," Savannah agreed. "You know it wasn't long ago Rose asked me how you and I met. I told her to ask her pa. Did she ever ask you?"

"No, she hasn't. Why did you tell her to ask me?"

"I wasn't sure how to answer."

"Maybe she will never ask. But if she does, I will tell her the truth; I think she is old enough to handle that."

"She is a grown woman in a ten-year-old body. You do know that I love her every bit as much as I love Matthew and Catherine, right?"

"Yes," he smiled. "You prove that every day. I could not have picked a better mother for her. Clara would be proud of how you raised her."

"Do you really think so? I often wonder what Clara would think."

"Trust me, she would have loved you. You have done a great job with Rose, and Clara could not have done any better."

"Thank you, Jonah, that means the world to me." Savannah pulled the blanket higher and enjoyed the rest of the ride home.

*****

"Jonah, Jonah, wake up!" Savannah lit the oil lamp beside the bed.

Jonah jumped from a dead sleep. "Is something wrong with one of the children?"

"No, of course not, I have to read you the letter that mother sent me. Please, get up and listen; it is extremely important!"

"Well, this is a first; you never read me your mother's letters." Jonah sat up in bed to listen contently as Savannah read about how her mother, Joseph and Mary's plans to move to Arkansas and cried with every word.

"Oh, Jonah, my family is coming out west," Savannah cried. "In just a few months, I will get to see them all again."

Jonah hugged her tightly. "I am so happy for you; I know what this means to you. I know how much you have prayed for this."

"Where will we put them, Joseph? Is there land that my mother can purchase?"

Jonah laughed. "You know that we will all figure this out together once they get here. Now that I built on to the cabin, there is plenty of room for them to stay with us while we decide together where to build them a cabin of their own."

"My mother has never been out of Georgia before, none of them have. They are going to love it here in the valley! Oh, Jonah, I am beside myself with excitement. I shall not sleep a wink tonight."

"Come, my sweet wife, and lay down. I am sure when you get still, you shall be able to sleep. Perhaps you shall dream of glorious days to come, baking sugar cookies for the children."

"My mother is going to love the children, and they shall adore her. I never thought they would get to meet her. I was so worried that it may never be possible."

"But you see how God always works things out for those that love Him."

"That is so right, Jonah. Oh, how I have prayed for this day ever since Father died."

"Do you think you will be able to get through the next few months, or will you wear us all out with your excitement?"

Savannah laughed. "I am sorry, Jonah." Savannah turned off the oil lamp and lay down beside him. "I shall try to carry on with life as usual, but I just don't see how it is going to be an easy task at all."

Jonah chuckled to himself, knowing Catherine was not like him at all. If anything, she was more like Savannah with her fiery spirit.

But then, Jonah knew, he would not change a single thing.

Chapter Nine

"Catherine, help your sister set the table for dinner," Savannah asked.

"But she does not need any help; there is not that much to do, Momma. I am playing with my dollhouse."

"Catherine Bell, I asked you to help your sister set the table, now!" Savannah commanded.

Catherine grumbled and got off the floor to do as she was told.

"Rose, have you saw Papa John since we have been home from school?"

"No, Momma, I haven't."

"What about you, Matthew? Did you see Papa John outside anywhere?"

Matthew walked in the door from helping Jonah and was taking off his shoes. "No, Momma."

Savannah guessed he was taking a nap and would be in shortly. In all the years she had known him, he never missed dinner. So many times he had told her it was his favorite time of the day, and he always came in early before she was finished preparing it, to talk and play with the children.

"Sure smells good, what's for dinner?" Jonah asked, hanging his hat on the rack beside the door.

"Momma is making pinto beans, cornbread and mashed potatoes," answered Rose. "And I made an apple cobbler."

"Papa John is going to love that; he loves apple cobbler."

"Speaking of Papa John, would you mind going to fetch him and tell him dinner is ready? No one has seen him today," Savannah was getting concerned.

"That's not unusual. Papa John rarely comes out before dinner, unless we are busy doing something and he wants to help."

"But he is usually here before now," Savannah set the cornbread on the table, "and we are ready to eat."

"Give me a moment, and I shall fetch him. Why don't you go ahead and get started and we shall be right back? I am sure he has just lost track of time."

Darkness was falling upon the valley, and Jonah thought it strange there was no light coming from John's cabin. Savannah was right; he was always at the house by now. Jonah hoped he had not turned ill.

Jonah knocked on the door, "John, are you awake? Savannah has dinner cooked, and Rose made one of your favorite dishes, apple cobbler."

There was no answer from the other side, just deathly silence.

"John," Jonah pushed opened the door slowly. "Are you awake, Buddy? Dinner is ready."

Jonah could see from the little bit of daylight remaining that he was laying on the bed. "John, dinner is ready," he said again, and shook his body slightly to awaken him.

John did not move.

Jonah placed his hand on John's cold skin, and horror filled him. "John, John, wake up!"

Still no movement. Jonah lit the oil lamp beside the bed, and the room came alive with light.

John had passed away, and rigor mortise had set in. From the looks of it, John had passed sometime during the night before.

"Oh John!" Jonah cried out, falling to his knees. "I am sure gonna miss you, old buddy. I am not sure what we would have done without you all these years."

Jonah sat in the quietness of John's cabin for a while, broken-hearted, remembering all the things John had taught him, like how to love Savannah and not to feel guilty. He had been a father to him and had shown him and his family real love.

"Who will I share my thoughts with now?" he whispered.

He knew he must get Savannah. The next few days would not be easy on them, especially the children, and he dreaded what was to come.

John Barge *was* their Papa John, and he knew this would be extremely painful for them.

Jonah composed himself the best he could and opened the front door to their home. "Savannah, could you come here a moment, please?"

Savannah got up from the table and headed toward the door. "Children, keep eating, I will be right back."

Savannah closed the door behind her, feeling in the pit of her stomach that something was terribly wrong; Jonah was taking too long to come back.

"What is it, Jonah? Is something wrong with John? Is he not feeling well?"

Jonah took her hand and led her to John's cabin, not saying a word. As they entered the cabin, he embraced her in his arms. "He died last night, Savannah. Papa John is with Martha now."

"Oh, Jonah," she cried, "What shall the children do without Papa John? This is going to hurt them so badly. They have never experienced death before."

"Death is a part of life, and we will get through this together, as a family."

Savannah walked over to John's body and touched him. She had never felt a dead body. "He is so cold, Jonah."

"He has been gone a long while. I wish I had checked on him this morning, but I am so used to him not venturing out anymore until dinner."

Savannah wiped her eyes with her apron. "I guess we must go tell the children."

"Savannah, I need you to tell the children; you are so good at consoling them, and I am going to saddle my horse and make my rounds, first to Pastor Anderson's to tell him there will be a funeral tomorrow, and then to the Ayers' and Ingalls."

"Yes, school must be cancelled. What about a casket, Jonah?"

"I will work tonight constructing something sufficient. When I know what time Pastor Anderson wants to have the funeral, I shall tell the others."

"Jonah," Savannah took his hand. "You are a good man. Do you need me to come help anyway I can, to construct a casket? I know you shall be tired come morning."

"No. This is something I need to do alone. John was like a father to me, and I need this time to make my peace with this. It's the last thing I shall ever be able to do for him."

"I understand. I shall go tell the children, and I shall place you a plate in the warmer for later."

*****

When Savannah entered the house, she found that the children were finished eating, and Rose was washing their dishes.

"Thank you, Rose. You are such a big help. Children, please come back to the table; I have something we must talk about."

"Is something wrong, Momma? Where is Pa and Papa John?" Rose asked, drying her hands on a drying cloth Savannah had made from a flour sack.

"Come, come sit down a moment, all of you," she motioned.

The children came back to the table and sat down, curious as to what was going on.

Savannah looked into all their eyes and knew that what she was about to tell them would hurt, but as Jonah said, death is a part of life, and sooner or later, we all must come face-to-face with it.

"What's wrong, Momma? You look like you have been crying," Matthew asked.

"I have been, Matthew. Do you all remember me telling you that Papa John's wife Martha went to be with the Lord?"

They all nodded their heads yes, because they had been told that story many times since their birth. Papa John, himself, had talked often about his late wife and how special she was. The children loved sitting around him, listening to him tell them stories of long ago.

"Well, Papa John went, also. He passed sometime last night. He is with Martha now."

"No, not my Papa John! why did he leave me?" Catherine cried out. "I don't want Papa John to leave me. Make him come back, Momma. Martha don't need him like we do."

Matthew's lip started to quiver. "He's gone, Momma? Papa John is dead?"

"Yes, son, Papa John is gone."

"So, he's not coming back?"

"No, he's not coming back."

Rose lay her head over on Savannah's shoulder and started to cry. She had been with Papa John longer than the others, and Savannah knew she would take it the hardest. "It's okay to cry, children, it's okay."

Savannah held each of them for the longest and let them cry. She too, felt their pain and shared their tears.

The valley had lost an exceptionally good man when John Barge crossed over, but she knew that he was happier at this moment than he had been since Martha left him. For once again, he was reunited with the love of his life.

*****

Jonah sanded on the casket he had crafted out of pine and hoped John would have liked it.

Noel Ayers had graciously offered to help him, but he knew this was something he must do alone, just as he had told Savannah.

When Jonah thought back over the past ten years, John was always there when he needed someone most.

From when he built the barn and dug every post for his fence, to the night they stood just beyond the house and John assured him it was okay to love Savannah and desire her, after his wife Clara passed.

It was John that noticed something wasn't right between him and Savannah, and John was the first person he ever told about his late wife, Clara, and why he couldn't allow himself to get close to Savannah.

He trusted John. For John was the father he never had. That one person he knew always had his back and was always there when he needed him.

Season after season John helped him with the livestock and the harvest, until age got the best of him.

"Fly high, my old friend," Jonah whispered, and wiped at his tears.

The casket was the last thing he would be able to do for him, and he wanted to make sure he had something nice to rest in.

He knew that it was the hardest thing he had had to do since he buried his first wife, Clara.

"It is beautiful," Savannah whispered, coming into the barn.

"I didn't know you were still awake."

"I wasn't. I awoke and you were still gone, so I brought you your dinner. I know you must be hungry." Savannah set his plate on a piece of plywood and pulled over a chair. "Take a moment, Jonah, and eat a bite; you need nourishment."

"Thank you, I am quite hungry." Jonah sat down and started to eat.

"It truly is beautiful, Jonah. John would have loved it."

"I have a confession. I was hiding the wood to make you a new chest of drawers for Christmas, and I used it to build this instead."

Savannah smiled. "I can't think of anything better I'd rather you use it for. I was thinking that I will put him in that new Sunday shirt I just made for him; he would have liked that. I was planning to give it to him for Christmas, but…" her voice trailed off.

"Yes, he would have. How did the children take it?"

"Not good. Catherine is a mess. Matthew isn't saying much, just went to bed crying, and poor Rose is taking it the hardest of all."

Jonah shook his head. "He has been her papa a very long time."

"It looks like you are about finished here?"

"I am, was just putting the final touch when you walked in."

"You must be exhausted."

"I am, but this had to be done. He will have to be buried tomorrow. Pastor Anderson said we would do the funeral at eleven o'clock. Tom and Noel are coming to help me get the casket in the wagon and place John's body inside. I know it will be hard for you, but could you get him ready in the morning?"

"I will. Will be the hardest thing I have ever done so far, but I will. I will do anything for Papa John. Come, and let us go to bed; it will be daybreak soon."

"I am not sure I can sleep, but I will try for a little bit, at least."

*****

Savannah washed John's body and placed the new shirt on him, cutting it up the back so she could get it on. She had never worked on a dead body before, and John was already starting to smell.

"I am sorry, John. I know you would never have wanted me to see you this way, but I had rather me do this than anyone else. I am going to make you look nice for your funeral. The children will want to say goodbye. They all loved you so. Everyone in the valley loved you."

"Are you ready?" Jonah asked, opening the door to John's cabin.

"Yes, he is ready."

"Okay, I told the children to stay in the house, that you were coming to get them ready for the funeral. Noel and Tom are here to help me with his body, and then we are going on to the church with the casket and dig the hole to have it ready. Pastor Anderson will be by just before to pick you up and bring you."

"Jonah, that isn't necessary; we walk to that building every day."

"I know, but not today, Savannah."

Savannah nodded and walked outside to find Noel and Tom standing in silence, waiting. "Thank you both," she nodded, and headed toward the house.

*****

There was an unusual quietness in the church. It was the first time Savannah could remember that everyone was at a loss for words, especially Nancy, but then, she loved John as well.

John was loved by all, and all the children called him Papa John, not just theirs.

The casket sat in front of the church with the top off so everyone could pay their last respects and say goodbye. Savannah had no doubt, it was the most beautiful thing Jonah had ever constructed.

Pastor Anderson stood up and looked out at the gloomy faces sitting around the room.

"We gather here today to honor a man who lived many years on this earth, brother John Barge. He lived many years without his beloved wife, Martha. But two nights ago, they were reunited again.

"I can just imagine old John's face when he got to see his Martha, after so many years of being apart. She was the love of his life.

"John isn't suffering with that withered old body any longer, for now he has a new glorified body. No more pain and sickness, no more heartache.

"The Bible tells us in John 3:16, For God so loved the world, that He gave his only begotten Son, that whosoever believeth in Him should not perish, but have everlasting life.

"And John believed in Christ and loved Him with all his heart, and I believe that he is not only with his beloved Martha, but also with Jesus.

"In Psalms it assures us of a home beyond the sky. The Lord is my shepherd; I shall not want. He maketh me to lie down in green pastures: he leadeth me beside the still waters. He restoreth my soul: He leadeth me in the paths of righteousness for His name's sake. Yea, though I walk through the valley of the shadow of death, I will fear no evil: for thou art with me; thy rod and thy staff they comfort me. Thou preparest a table before me in the presence of mine enemies: thou anointest my head with oil; my cup runneth over. Surely goodness and mercy shall follow me all the days of my life: and I will dwell in the house of the Lord forever.

"Savannah, would you please come now and share a few words with us?"

Savannah walked to the front of the church slowly with tears in her eyes and spoke softly.

"I think we can all agree that John Barge was more than just a kind man." She wiped a tear from her cheek.

"He was a true friend to everyone, and a papa to every child he met. He loved children, even though he never had any of his own. For years John Barge has lived without his true love, Martha. But yesterday morning, before dawn, he was reunited with her again." Savannah smiled.

"I am sure it was a happy reunion. And even though he will be greatly missed by all, if he has the chance, he would never want to come back, for now not only is He with Martha, but also with Jesus.

"He will continue to live in our hearts and in our memories for as long as we live. He has been a part of our family for many years, since that cold December Christmas, and he will always be a part of us, for death is not final for those that believe." Savannah quietly took her place again beside Jonah.

"Let us sing." Pastor Anderson started singing Amazing Grace and everyone joined in. One at a time they passed by John's casket and paid their respects, with Jonah holding Matthew, and Savannah holding Catherine.

Rose followed close behind, with tears in her eyes.

The men and oldest boys carried the casket, and lowering it with ropes, placed it in the ground that was prepared that morning.

Savannah and the women watched as the men and boys took turns filling the grave in with dirt, and Jonah placed a cross he had made to serve as a marker at the head of the grave.

"Let us pray," Pastor Anderson said, bowing his head.

"Thank you, Father, for John Barge's life. We thank you that he made a difference to everyone he met. He was a good man, and we know he is with You now.

"Father, I ask that You send comfort among these people, especially the Bells, for death is a part of life, and grief is very real. Help us to remember the good things about John and bless these little ones with peace and comfort that only You can. In Jesus' name we pray, Amen."

*****

Savannah asked Jonah to take the children back home in the wagon; she needed to be alone for a bit and decided to walk. He had nodded and done as he was asked, gathering the children and starting home, knowing that she needed the closure as he had the night before.

She pulled her shawl up around her for more warmth and admired the beautiful cold day. Yes, it was getting colder now, but the sky was clear, and she thanked God for that.

There were things Savannah had kept secret and not shared with anyone, not even Jonah. Like resenting her father for the way he treated them and for feeling guilty for loving John more.

Jonah said many times that John was a father he never had, but she *had* a father who was there up until the time she left, yet until John passed and she went through all the emotions one would feel when they lost their father, she discovered she never felt any of those things when she got the news her real father had passed.

Today she realized it had been more of a relief than sadness. A relief because she knew he no longer had a hold on her mother, and maybe then her mother would get the courage to come to Arkansas.

She always resented her father for the man that he truly was and remembered praying that she would never marry a man like her father. She knew that even though her mother would have never admitted it, she hoped for the same.

How sad it was to live your life, and no one care when you pass. It made her wonder if her mother was also relieved deep down, and maybe felt a new sense of freedom that she never experienced with her father alive.

She was happy her family was moving to Arkansas and knew that would never be happening if her father was still alive. She dared to think what would have become of her siblings had their mother gone first.

Funny how it took John's death to realize the anger she was still harboring toward her father. She tried to love him the best she could, but it was nothing like the way she loved John Barge, a man who started out a total stranger to her.

Forgive me, Father, forgive me for holding on to anger.

Father, I am asking you to help me release my anger. I want to get rid of it and lay it at the foot of Your cross, never to pick it up again.

Thank You, Father, for forgiving me, Amen.

Chapter Ten

"Well, hello, Mrs. Bell," Katie smiled, as she opened her front door to find Savannah. "What brings you out on this cold day?"

"I thought I would ride over and visit with you a bit. I wanted to speak to you about Nathaniel and Josiah."

"Sure, come on in and let me get you a cup of hot coffee, and we can sit at the table. The boys are out chopping firewood, and Corbin is at the church going over tomorrow's sermon. Are the boys in trouble? I do hope they have been behaving themselves."

Savannah smiled and took a sip of her coffee. "Oh no, ma'am, they are perfect gentlemen and such a huge help to have around the school."

"Do you feel they are too old to learn?"

"On the contrary, we are never too old to learn something new. I was wondering if you could perhaps spare them another hour after school each day for few weeks. They are behind on their reading and writing, and I would like to give them some extra time after the other children leave for the day. Rose is very capable of walking Matthew and Catherine home, and that would give me some one-on-one time with them."

"Of course, they can stay an extra hour, but goodness, I know you want to get home, too."

"It's okay, it shouldn't take long to have them at the level they need to be, and I will send home study words for them to work together on each night. Just a half hour before bedtime should not take them away from their chores, and I feel it will truly help them."

"Oh dear, I feel like such a terrible mother that has failed her boys."

Savannah placed her hand on top of Katie's and smiled. "You shouldn't feel that way. It is not that they cannot read nor write; they can. It is just that they are a little behind. With a little work, they will be doing much better."

"We have traveled so much, Mrs. Bell, and I am afraid the boys always had so much to do to help out that they missed so much school time, whereas Elisa, being the girl and the baby was able to attend."

"No reason to explain; I totally understand."

"I tried to work with them myself, but as I said before, I quit school at a very young age to help my own Pa and Ma on our farm, and I am afraid I am no teacher. And, of course, Corbin was always too busy with the church and the community wherever we lived that he wasn't able to spend the time that the boys truly needed."

"Well, it is never too late, so don't worry. Give me a few weeks with them, and I know you will see a difference."

Katie patted her hand and smiled. "Thank you for all you do for the children."

"It is my pleasure."

"Tell me how the school year is going so far. I am surprised that we have not gotten a heavy snow yet."

"It is going better than I ever expected, and the new readers and slates are wonderful. It makes it so much easier to teach. And yes, I agree with you about the snow. Usually by this time around Christmas, it has already started. Of course, I am not complaining any, as I know that would keep us from school a bit, and I feel the children truly need to be in school, as well as I."

"So, you really like teaching then?" Katie nodded.

"Oh, yes, I truly love it, but that isn't the only reason. It helps me pass the time. My family is moving out west the end of spring, and I am beside myself with excitement."

"Oh, how wonderful. How many will be moving to the valley?"

"My mother, Alice, my brother, Joseph, and my sister, Mary."

"I am so excited for you, and I cannot wait to meet them all. The valley is big enough for several more families, and I pray that the good Lord sends us some good neighbors."

"They have never met the children, so I can hardly wait." Savannah stood and started for the door. "Thank you for your time, but I must be going, I have my own chores I must attend to before the day is over. And thank you so much for doing my wash once a week; I truly do appreciate it."

"Think nothing of it. It is my pleasure. Do come back anytime, Mrs. Bell, you are always welcome, and thanks again for helping the boys."

Savannah climbed on Midnight and started home.

It felt great having the freedom to ride and visit the neighbors when she needed to. She could remember not so long ago, before others moved to the valley, that Jonah would never allow her to venture off alone, for fear that it would be too dangerous.

She loved living in the valley, and with her family coming soon, she felt such joy. God had heard her prayers and answered.

It wasn't easy each night at dinnertime not having John come and eat with them, but she knew that time would heal all wounds, and maybe with her family coming, the children would be able to let him go and stop the gloominess that seemed to linger at the dinner table.

*****

Dearest Mother,

I still cannot believe you all shall be journeying out west come late spring. It is hard for me to even think when all I think about is you arriving. As you know I have prayed about this since Father passed and I am so glad you finally decided to do so. I truly feel that you shall not be disappointed, and I know you are going to love the valley and the people here. They are excited you are coming and cannot wait to meet you all.

Please forgive me for not writing to you sooner, but there is so much going on here that there are just not enough hours in the day. I truly need two of me.

Papa John passed away not long ago. He was the first to be buried at the new church, and since I go there every day to teach, the children place flowers and little things upon his grave and it gives Catherine peace.

His passing was very hard on the children; especially Rose, but she is the quiet type and won't talk about it much.

Teaching has also been keeping me busy, as all fourteen children are different ages and at different levels, but with much prayer and preparation it is all coming together. The children's mothers help me with sewing, cooking, and my wash, and I am so grateful for that. They insist, they say, because I am devoting my time to their children. There is a lot of good people that live here in the valley, so for that I am blessed and grateful.

I received Joseph's letter and it did my heart good to see how his attitude has changed because he knows now you all will be arriving here soon. It is so good to see him happy.

I would not worry too much about Mary not being excited. It is very understandable, as she truly never knew me. But Mother, I can assure you that once she gets here and

*meets Rose and some of the other girls, she is going to be okay
and fall in love with living here, please trust me on that.*

*I do hate that you must sell so much of your things that I
know you hold dear to your heart. Do try to bring your cooking
ware if you can as I know some of it was my grandmas and
how much it means to you. That is what crates are for, and if
you must pay extra for it, then do so, you will be glad you did
later.*

*I love you so very much Mother and cannot wait to see
you.*

I hope you all have a wonderful Christmas,
Savannah

*****

"Yes, Glenda?"

"Mrs. Bell, could you please tell Powell to stop looking at
me."

"I didn't do nothing," Powell yelled out.

"Powell, there will be no yelling, the other children are trying
to work. Powell and Glenda, please come up here and talk to me
quietly."

Powell and Glenda got out of their seats and walked to the
front.

"Now, quietly tell me what is going on. Glenda, you go first."

"Powell keeps looking at me."

Powell rolled his eyes and sighed. "Mrs. Bell, I just glanced
her way. Tell her to stop being a little tattletale."

"Glenda, did he make a face at you?"

"No ma'am, but I do not like him to look at me when I am
trying to work."

"How do you know he was looking at you?"

"Because I saw him. He stares at me all the time."

"I look around at everyone, Mrs. Bell, I wasn't making a face or nothing; she just wants to get me in trouble."

"Glenda, you could not possibly know your brother was looking at you, unless you were looking at him. Does that make sense? Now I want you to both go back to your seats and stop this. If Powell is not making a face at you or talking to you, then there is no harm in glancing at someone."

"Yes, ma'am," Glenda said quietly and went back to her seat.

Savannah glanced at Rose and saw her smile about what had taken place.

It was good to see Rose smile again. For the past month, she had done nothing but mope around the house and had not even wanted to bake a dessert as she used to, knowing that one of the main reasons for baking was for Papa John.

Papa John passing had taken a toll on her, and Savannah longed to see her get back to her old self again.

"Mrs. Bell," Grace called her name.

"Yes, Grace, and please raise your hand when you need to ask a question."

"I am sorry. Can I please go to the outhouse?"

"Yes, you may, and hurry back."

The children were taking an important test that Savannah had designed according to their reading level, covering the first two stories in their readers.

Nathaniel and Josiah had had a couple weeks' worth of one-on-one time and studying at home, and Savannah could already see an improvement. She was so proud of their hunger to learn and hated that, up until this time, they had never had much opportunity.

"Okay class, when you are finished, turn your slates upside down and put down your chalk so I can tell when everyone is finished. Also, make sure you have your name at the top right-hand corner, so I will know which one is yours.

"Peggy, will you please take them up and place them on my desk?"

"Yes, ma'am."

Peggy was the oldest daughter of the Ayers children and such a big help to her. She always took pride in keeping the water container filled each morning and never once caused a problem.

"Josiah, don't worry about putting any more wood in the heater; I am going to let you all leave a bit early today."

There was a rustle of cheers around the room, and Savannah smiled.

Truth was she had a lot to do at home to finish up Christmas presents and a tree to decorate.

"Remember, children, today starts Christmas break, so I will see you back here January second, the day after New Year's, ready to learn again. And the rule is, if it is snowing hard, stay home. I don't want anyone to get turned around out there and lost."

"What if there is snow on the ground, but it has stopped snowing?" Nathaniel asked from the back of the room. "Oh, sorry, Mrs. Bell, I forgot to raise my hand."

"It's okay this time, Nathaniel," Savannah smiled. "If it is less than 6 inches, which is like this," Savannah showed them with her fingers, "then come on to school. If it comes up way over the tops of your shoes, like this," she showed them again, "then stay home. Does everyone understand?"

The children nodded their heads yes.

"But remember, that is only if it is not snowing. If it is snowing heavily, we have no way of knowing when it is going to stop, so stay home.

"I am proud of each of you and how hard you have been working. You are all doing very well. Please be careful on your walk home today, as every day, and please have a very Merry Christmas. And do not forget your coats, hats and gloves. Class dismissed."

Savannah sat down to quickly go over the slates as the children headed out the door. "Jerry and Powell, you may go ahead also, and you too, Ricky, the erasers can wait. You all go home together."

"Would you like for me to help you?" Rose asked.

"If you will please sweep the floor for me, that would be wonderful. Catherine and Matthew, please have a seat and give me half an hour and we will all walk home together today."

Catherine and Matthew sat back down, and Rose went to get the broom.

Savannah was impressed at how well the children did on their reading test. Many got all the questions right, and the ones who did not were still way above passing; even Nathaniel and Josiah passed. Maybe she was doing something right after all.

"Thank you, Rose, for sweeping. I appreciate you more than you know, and thank you, Matthew and Catherine, for sitting quietly and allowing me to concentrate. Because you did so well, I was able to finish in no time. Are you all ready now to walk home?"

"Yes Momma, can I play with my doll house since we are going home earlier today?" Catherine asked.

"Yes, you may, and if you are good through the holidays, I might even allow you to sit up an hour later."

"Yay," Catherine screamed. "I am glad we are out of school."

"Oh really?" Savannah asked. "I thought you liked school."

"I do, but I like days off, too, and I can't wait for Santa Claus to come!"

"Me either," Matthew stated, putting on his hat and gloves.

"What about you, Rose? Are you excited for Santa Claus to come?" Savannah asked.

Rose smiled, having known who Santa really was the past two years but still loved pretending that a fat jolly man, dressed in red was coming to see all the children of the world on that one magical night.

"Yes, you know I am," she giggled.

"Good, because he will be here soon enough. Now let us get home and decorate that tree."

*****

"Can I help make the Christmas chain?" asked Matthew.

"Of course you can. I am counting on you and Catherine to color all the pieces Rose cut out; you know how to put them together and glue each one. Your pa will be here soon with the tree, and we will be ready."

"Are you and Rose going to make sugar cookies?" Catherine licked at her lips, indicating how much she loved them.

"Yes, we are, aren't we, Rose?"

"It's one of my favorite things to make," stated Rose, getting down the mixing bowl.

"It was one of mine also when I was your age. My mother and I used to bake them a lot because they were my younger brother's favorite. I cannot wait until late spring for you all to meet your Momma Alice and your uncle and aunt. You are going to love them, and I know you and Mary will become the best of friends, Rose. You are pretty close in age."

Catherine looked up from her coloring, "Where will they live, Momma?"

"We have not figured that out yet, but I am sure it will be somewhere awfully close. Mary will be going to school with us."

"Does your brother go to school too, Momma?" Matthew was hoping for someone to play with.

"No, son, Joseph will be going on eighteen when they arrive, and he will be working around the farm helping Pa."

"Oh," Matthew grumbled, making Savannah laugh.

"Don't worry, son, if I know my brother, you will have a good time with him and love Uncle Joseph very much. He loves to hunt too, so you both should get along fine."

"Do you think he has ever shot a huge buck like I did?"

"I guess you can ask him that when he arrives."

"It's getting cold out there," Jonah announced, coming through the door with the tree.

"Yay, Pa is home, and look at the tree!" Catherine exclaimed with excitement.

"Where do you want it?" he asked.

Savannah pointed to the corner of the room beside the window. "Over there would be nice, and it really is a beautiful tree."

"I have been watching this tree grow for two years, and it is finally ready to glorify our home for Christmas. I see you two are hard at work making the Christmas chain."

"Yes, Pa, Matthew and I are coloring the pieces Rose cut out, but I am much faster at coloring them."

Matthew looked angrily at his younger sister. "Why do you always think you have to be better than me?"

"Because I am," she stuck out her tongue.

Jonah laughed. "Okay, you two, that's enough. Catherine, no one is better than the other. You both are amazing children."

"You never shot a big buck before," Matthew reminded.

"That's only 'cause Pa has not taken me hunting yet!" She stuck out her tongue again. "When are you going to take me, Pa? You said you would."

"And I will as soon as I go again, but right now we have a right smart bit of meat on hand. Now hurry up, you two, and finish that chain and stop your bickering."

Savannah giggled at the two of them, always at each other, trying to compete. She guessed that was the way it was with children born close in age.

Savannah always loved Christmas time. Such a magical time of year, with decorations and Christmas cookies and candy canes.

She loved thinking back to the days she lived in Dahlonega, and her mother made Christmas special for all of them each year. They did not have a lot of money, but the love from her mother was plentiful.

And now that she had three children of her own, it was even more special. She was busy each night after the children went to bed, making new dresses and yarn dolls, scarves, and hats.

Jonah had a few surprises hidden in the barn, just waiting for Christmas Eve night to place them under the tree.

Savannah smiled, watching Rose place the cookies on the pan to bake; with each passing day she was getting closer to being the Rose she knew before Papa John died.

This was the last Christmas she ever had to be away from her family back in Dahlonega, for next year they would all once again be together, just as it should be.

Jonah looked at her from across the room and winked, drinking a sip of his hot coffee. Life was good in the valley, and Savannah felt blessed.

Chapter Eleven

"Pa, Ma, get up, Santa come last night!" Catherine screamed throughout the house.

Savannah mumbled, rolling over in bed to nudge Jonah. "Do you hear that? Your daughter is calling us."

"Didn't we just go to bed? It isn't even daylight yet."

"Ma, Pa, get up, get up!" she screamed again.

"Go get up your brother and sister," Jonah called out, "Momma and I will be there in a minute."

Jonah sat up in bed and put his pants and shoes on. "I was hoping for at least another hour of sleep."

Savannah sat up in bed and yawned. "Come on, Santa, the children are waiting."

"Can we open our stockings now, Ma?" asked Matthew.

"Yes, you may."

"Look at all this candy!" Catherine licked at her lips. "I can eat candy every day for a whole week!"

"A sling shot!" Matthew screamed out. "Do you think I can kill a big buck with this, Pa?"

"Well, David did kill a giant with one of those. I want you to be careful with that and not aim it at anything like your sisters or the windows."

"Yes, sir. I will practice and get really good, you will see."

"I have never had a journal of my own." Rose seemed thrilled when she found her new journal and feather pen with ink. "I have always wanted one."

"I guess you have been a good young lady this year and Santa was extra nice to you," Savannah winked.

"What are those under the tree?" Matthew was dying to know all that Santa had brought them.

Jonah handed each child a wrapped package and watched Matthew and Catherine tear into theirs.

"Oh Pa, look, a wooden gun, now I can play cowboys and Indians."

"I guess Santa's elves carved it themselves," Jonah looked toward Savannah, knowing she had no idea he knew how to carve, and smiled, seeing the amazed look on her face.

"I bet you are right, and it goes well with my slingshot."

"I love it, a new dolly. She is so pretty!" Catherine screamed. "I will name her Catherine."

"That's stupid," Matthew grumbled, "that is *your* name."

"I know, and that's the best name around. Then we shall both be named Catherine."

"Open yours, Rose," Jonah encouraged.

Rose opened the package slowly and pulled out a snow dome of a ballerina. "It is beautiful; I love it!"

"That really is beautiful, Rose," Savannah agreed. "It was the first time she was seeing what Jonah had brought the children from the village, herself.

"Here, Savannah, I think there is one here for you." Jonah handed her a beautifully wrapped package.

Savannah smiled as she unwrapped the package and pulled out a beautiful yellow dress. "Oh, Jonah, it is so pretty, and you know I love yellow."

"I thought you would like a new dress for church, and something new for school."

"I really love it, thank you. I especially love that I did not have to make it. Did you buy it at the new dress shop?"

"You are very welcome, my sweet wife. And yes, I did. I hope you do not mind, but Dottie helped me pick it out. I am not good at things like that."

"She did very well; I will have to thank her for her choice in dresses. It's like she knows what I like."

"Did Santa not bring you your dress?" Catherine asked.

"No, Santa only brings things to children; your Pa got me the dress."

"That makes sense," Matthew nodded. "I mean, there is no way he could put everyone something in just one sleigh, right, Pa?"

Jonah chuckled and nodded. "Sounds about right, son."

Savannah pulled a gift from behind the tree and handed it to Jonah. "Open yours. I hope you like it."

Jonah looked at her in wonder. It was much too big to be a new hat and scarf or a new shirt.

"What is this?"

"Why don't you open it and find out?"

He opened the box and stared at it for the longest, without saying a word.

Inside was the new Harper's Ferry Rifled Musket that he wanted but did not want to spend money on himself. They had just come out that year.

"Savannah, how did you know? I never told anyone about this but John."

"I am so glad you told him, because he told me a week before he passed that it was what you told him you wanted."

"I told him I'd love to buy me one someday. I said nothing about wanting it for Christmas."

"Well, I am glad I could surprise you then."

"I don't remember you going into the village alone. I know you saddle the horse and visit the neighbors, but did you ride all the way to the village? That is not a good idea, Savannah, and you know it."

"No Jonah, have no worries. I asked Tom Ingalls to pick it up for me, and he happily obliged. I think he was a bit jealous 'cause he said he wanted one himself and that I should tell Nancy."

"It's special, Savannah, I just love it." He took it out of the box and admired it more closely.

"I am sure you thought you were getting the usual scarf and hat and new shirt?"

Jonah nodded. "I did, and there was nothing wrong with that. I was actually looking forward to the new shirt."

"Good," she said, as she threw him another package and the children one as well.

It was one of the best Christmases she could remember in years. The only thing missing was Papa John, and it made her heart ache, but at least he was able to wear his new shirt.

"Do you think Papa John and Martha are having Christmas in Heaven?" Catherine asked.

Savannah was just thinking the same thing. "I am sure of it, and I can only imagine the huge party they are having there with it being Jesus' birthday."

"Do you think they eat cake, too, Momma?" asked Matthew.

"I am sure they can eat anything they want and never gain a pound."

Jonah pulled Savannah into an embrace. "I love you, my sweet wife. You and these children make me the happiest man on earth.

*****

"Can I walk to Chrissy's, Mother?" Mary asked, looking out at the newly fallen snow.

"You want to walk a mile in this?"

"It's not that deep, and I want to show her what I got for Christmas and see what she got as well. I know we will be leaving in a few months, and I want to see her all I can."

"Okay, you can go, but bundle up good; it's cold out there."

"You aren't kidding," Joseph agreed, entering the kitchen door, passing Mary on the way out. "Here's the milk and eggs."

"I am going to miss Betsy and the chickens."

"I am sure Jonah and Savannah have livestock as well, and we can always get a new cow and chickens. I will miss the horses most."

"If they weren't so old, we would tie them to the stagecoach."

"Yes, but they are, and they would never be able to make a trip like that; it would be too hard on them."

"Are you still as excited as you were about the move?" Alice wanted to make sure he was not getting cold feet.

"Seriously? I am more so. I wish we were leaving tomorrow. Three months to go, and it seems like an eternity."

"Three months will be here before you know it. Have you found a buyer for the farm? And are we getting a good price for it?"

"Yes, and we shall get a great price for it. D.L. Butler is bringing us cash the day before we leave. He is a good honest man and true to his word."

"Yes, he is. I am glad it will go to someone like that."

"So, in the next couple of months we can crate the things we can live without, but want to keep, and send them on ahead to be waiting on us. We can only carry so much on the stagecoach we ride on, because we shall be changing coaches several times."

"It looks like you have this all planned out. You are such a smart boy, Joseph."

"Been planning this for years, Mother, I am simply happy you finally agreed. Where was Mary going?"

"Where do you think? She is at Chrissy's more than she is at home."

"No harm in that, at least for the next three months."

*****

The day was cold, and a light snow was starting to fall.

Jonah could tell by the signs it probably would not be any more than a few inches, but you just never knew in Arkansas.

"May I talk to you about something?" Rose asked Jonah, as he was stacking the last of the wood just outside the front door.

"Sure, you can, follow me to the barn where it's a bit less windy; I have some work to do in there."

Rose followed along beside him, pulling her new crocheted cap down over her cold ears.

"So, tell me, what's on your mind?"

"Can you tell me about my real mother and why she died?"

Jonah knew this day would finally come; he just did not expect it so soon. "Come, let us have a seat for a bit. I'll throw another log or two in the heater."

Rose sat down on a handmade stool, and Jonah sat beside her.

"Back in 1832, the year you were born, it was hard for a woman to have a baby, especially when there were no doctors living close enough to help out. Your mother had a hard time delivering you, and her poor tired body just give out."

"So, I am the reason my real mother died?"

"No, of course not. Many women have babies and do fine. Just look at Savannah, she gave birth to Matthew and Catherine. Some women are just not strong enough; it has nothing to do with the baby, but with their body itself."

"Did you love my real mother the way you love Momma?"

132

Jonah smiled. "I loved Clara with all of my heart. I never knew a woman or love before Clara. I thought I would never be able to love again when she died."

"But you did, I mean you love Momma a lot."

"Yes, I do, I love your momma very much."

"So how did you meet Momma? I asked her but she told me to ask you."

Jonah rolled a piece of straw between his teeth and looked at her for what seemed like the longest.

"Right after your mother died, I felt lost. I knew nothing about taking care of babies, and you were just a wee little thing. I never even held a baby before, and I took you to Nelly's, who was our neighbor during the day for her to help me out."

"Did she teach you about babies?"

"Yes, I guess, sort of speak. You see your real mother and I had planned to come out west to live right after you were born, and I decided that I would keep the promise to Clara and do as we planned."

"But she was no longer there," Rose seemed confused.

"Right, yet you and I were, and I still wanted to come to Arkansas and start over, with a new life."

"So, you knew Momma and asked her to come with you?"

"I knew of your momma, yes, and I asked her father if I could marry her, so she could take care of you while we were on our journey here. It was an awfully long journey, and I could not do it alone."

"So, you did not love her then?"

Jonah knew his daughter was smarter than her age, and this was something she had been pondering a long time. She was so beautiful, just like Clara, and sat looking at him, glued to every word.

"No, Rose, not at that moment. The truth is, we barely knew each other."

"But you both fell in love with one another?"

"Yes, we both did. And we still do love each other very much."

"Do I look like my real mother? I think Catherine looks like Momma, and Matthew looks like you."

"Yes, you do. I think of her each time I look at you."

"Do you think my real mother would be proud of me?"

"Oh, Rose, you are one of the smartest children in the valley. I am certain your real mother would have been immensely proud of you, just as Savannah and I are."

"I am glad you chose Momma to come to Arkansas with you. I don't think I would want to have anyone else as a momma."

"I would have to agree with you. I don't think I would want to have anyone else as a wife; she's the best."

Rose nodded and smiled. "Thank you, pa, for telling me the truth. I always wondered."

"No problem. So, tell me, how do you like having your momma as your schoolteacher?"

"She's always been my teacher, but I love going to school with her and seeing her teach others; she is wonderful at it, and all the students love her."

"As I would if I were a student. In fact, I might have a crush on my teacher."

Rose giggled. "Oh, Pa, you are funny."

"Can I ask you something?"

"Sure, Pa, what do you need to know?"

"You have seemed quieter than normal since Papa John died. Do you want to talk about that?"

Rose shrugged her shoulders. "It really hurt me."

"I understand; it hurt all of us."

"Papa John had always been there, ever since I can remember. I just could not imagine living life without him. I don't understand why people have to die and leave us."

"When your real mother, Clara, died, I felt the same way. It was hard for me to be a good pa to you because I could not stop thinking about Clara and missing her. For a time there, I even blamed God for taking her away from me."

Rose shook her head. "I asked God why He took Papa John, too, and I still don't understand."

"Some things just aren't meant for us to understand, Rose. All I know is that death is a part of life, and that we all must die someday. No one is promised tomorrow. But the good news is that with Jesus, and having Him as your Savior, we do not have to worry about dying, because we know we will be with Him."

"I know Papa John knew Him because he spoke about Him often, but did my real mother know Him, too? Do you think she is with Him now?"

"Oh, yes, that is something you can be sure of."

"So, one day when I die, I am going to get to see my real mother and Papa John again, because I believe too, right, Pa?"

"That is absolutely right, Rose. But you are not going to die for an exceptionally long time. You are going to meet a wonderful man someday and have a home and babies of your own, and he is going to love you baking him all those desserts."

Rose laughed. "I bet he will. And I hope he is just like you, Pa."

"Thank you. I am sure it won't be long, and I shall have to beat the boys off with a stick; you are a very pretty young lady."

Rose blushed. "Thank you, Pa. Unless it is a good boy; then you won't beat him."

Jonah laughed. "I guess that all depends *just* how good."

*****

Savannah screamed as Jonah grabbed her from behind. "Jonah Bell, I did not hear you come in."

"You were deep into peeling those potatoes," he laughed.

"That I was. I am making potato soup and cornbread for dinner."

"And it will be as good as always. Can you take a break for about fifteen minutes?"

"Go on, Momma, I will finish the potatoes," Rose offered, taking the knife from her hand.

"Okay then, fifteen minutes, what's up?"

Jonah took her by the hand and led her outside toward John's cabin.

"I haven't been in there since the day I got him ready for burial," she pulled back slowly.

"Well, you cannot stay out of there forever; besides, it looks nothing like it did the day you were there."

"What do you mean?"

"Come and take a look." Jonah led her in the front door, and Savannah gasped. The room that was once John's bedroom was now a beautiful kitchen, complete with a table and chairs.

"Oh Jonah, it's beautiful, but I am confused; we already have a kitchen."

"Why are you confused? I am going to build onto this side and make three small bedrooms and open up this wall and make a living area for your mother's evening Bible readings."

Savannah gasped. "You are making my family a home of their own, before they even get here, right here beside us? Oh, Jonah, you are wonderful!"

"It's the least I could do; after all, it was I that took you away from them ten years ago. This is as close as I could get them, unless they live with us, of course, and I am sure your mother would be more comfortable in a home of her own."

136

"Why didn't I think of this?"

"Because when you thought of this tiny cabin, you thought of Papa John, but it's time to let Papa John go and get on with the life that is to come."

"You are right. Every time I looked toward this cabin, I only thought of Papa John. I am so glad you are doing this. Are you sure, though, that you want my family right at your door? What if you don't like them?"

"If they are anything like you, my sweet wife, I am going to love them."

"And they are going to love you and our children."

"So now you can write your mother and tell her there will be a cabin waiting on her when she arrives."

"You know what, Jonah? I think I am not going to say a word about this. I would rather surprise her, like the way we surprised John."

"Sounds like a plan; I really like that idea."

"But do you think you can have this finished before they arrive late spring? There is a lot of work to be done."

"I am certain of it. I will get started on the addition in the morning."

"You are going to work through the winter?"

"Maybe it will be mild. At least I will not have to work in the heat of summer. I do my best when I am under pressure to finish something, and I am happiest when I'm busy."

"True." Savannah wrapped her arms around him and kissed him passionately. "I do believe I am the luckiest woman on earth."

"Wow, to what do I owe that?"

"For just being you."

*****

It makes my heart happy to see where my life has come thus far.

God has certainly been with me every step of the way, from the early years back home in Dahlonega to the valley here in Arkansas.

It has been way too long since I have written in my journal, and much has happened.

It is now 1843 and I know it is going to be a glorious year, because it will be the year I get to see my mother again and see how much my siblings have grown.

I wonder what they will think when they see me. I am no longer sixteen, but a woman of almost twenty-seven and I have given birth to two children. My figure isn't what it used to be, but Jonah doesn't seem to mind. If he calls me beautiful, then I am happy.

Jonah shows me his love daily, and makes me feel beautiful and desired, I truly am the luckiest woman on earth, just as Dottie says.

I miss Papa John with each passing day. Even though we had the most wonderful Christmas, it just was not the same without him. He always made everything complete. Just knowing he is with his Martha makes me happy.

Jonah told me that he and Rose finally spoke about her birth mother and the way he and I met, and she seemed to be okay with it. He did not mention the trading of the land for my hand. He did not feel that part was necessary, and neither do I. Honestly, I just as soon to forget it.

I know that it does not really matter how we met; I will always feel that God had his hand in it.

Jonah has started the additions on to John's cabin and I must say he is quite a builder. I am so proud of him and all he knows. I do not think there is anything he can't do.

My family is going to be so excited when they see their new home. I know my mother will because it will be nicer than the home she is leaving.

138

They will be shipping their things on ahead and I will set it all up and have it ready and waiting. I just cannot wait until that stagecoach rides into the village and we pick them up.

My prayers, my dreams, are finally coming true. Sometimes I wonder what all I did to deserve this.

Chapter Twelve

Savannah felt giddy walking home from school. The birds singing and the warmer weather proved it was the first day of spring, her favorite time of the year. A time of new beginnings and fresh new growth.

Nathaniel and Josiah no longer stayed the extra hour. A couple of months had served them well and they were now at the reading level for their age. She was able to help them without any of the other children knowing, except Rose, who walked Catherine and Matthew home each day to give her the time needed.

Matthew and Catherine were always in a race to get home, leaving her and Rose to walk alone.

It was the time of day that Savannah loved. Rose had always been a special part of her life, and she knew they had the same kind of relationship that she and her own mother had.

"It's not much longer now, Momma, and I will be able to meet Mary. I am almost eleven; do you think she will think I am too young to be her friend?"

"Well, of course not, Rose, you may be almost two years younger, but you act far older than your age. I do not think she will care how old you are at all; you are going to be the best of friends, and you can introduce her to the other girls. I think she will be incredibly happy here in the valley."

"Do you think she will be sad that she had to leave her old home? I know I would be sad if I had to leave here and move far away."

"She may be a little sad for a while. That is understandable, but I am sure with you as her friend she will start loving it here in no time at all. Anyone that ever meets you loves you. You always treat people kindly, and I am proud of you for that. Just give her time and you will see that what I am saying is true."

"Do you think she will like Jerry Ayers? I mean, as a boyfriend?"

Savannah smiled. "Why do you ask that, Rose?"

Rose shrugged her shoulders. "I was just curious."

"Do you like Jerry, Rose?"

Rose smiled. "I think he is the most handsome boy in class, and he is the nicest, too. He never gets into trouble, and he always smiles at me during recess."

"Yes, Jerry is a nice young boy. I am sure with seven boys in the class you two probably won't have a crush on the same one, and as friends you will be able to talk about it, and you can tell her that you like Jerry."

"I have never had someone I can talk to like that, except, of course, for Grace and we don't really get to spend that much time together anymore. We see each other at school, but not to go to each other's house and talk like we used to."

"Yes, we have all been busy, that's for sure. Does Grace know you like Jerry?"

"No one does, not even Jerry," she giggled.

"I see."

"I write about it in my new journal. I write about a lot of things."

"I understand; I write a lot of things in my journal as well."

"Do you think I am too young to have a boyfriend?" Rose was curious what her momma really thought about it.

"Well technically, right now it is just a crush since he doesn't know, and I think I can remember when I was your age starting to notice boys."

"Did you ever have a crush on a boy at school, Momma?"

"No, I thought all the boys at my school was childish, but I did have a crush on a man one time, but unfortunately, he was married. I kept it a secret from everyone and never told a soul, because I felt guilty that he was married."

"You mean you didn't even tell your mother? I thought you and your mother was very close like you and I are."

"No, not even my mother. I felt that she would scold me if she knew and tell me it was wrong."

"Why, because he was married?"

"Yes, because he was married. He was also much older than I was, and I was afraid of what she might say."

"Why did you have a crush on this man?"

"Because I thought he was the most handsome man in Dahlonega and was fourteen years older than me. I used to hide and watch him plow in his fields and sneak around in the mercantile and watch him buy his supplies. He never knew I was there, because I was very sneaky and would hide."

"Does Pa know you once had a crush on another man?" Rose was finding this conversation very intriguing.

Savannah giggled. "He does because I told him about it."

"What ever happened to that older married man, Momma? Do you know?"

"I do know, Rose. I ended up marrying him after his wife passed away."

Rose gasped, "Oh, Momma, you mean the older married man was Pa?"

"It was, and so when he asked my father for my hand in marriage, I didn't mind one bit to become his wife."

"That makes me so happy, Momma."

"Why is that?"

"Because I thought you were forced by your father and maybe you didn't want to leave your family. I mean, I know you love Pa, but I did not know you loved him even before he loved you. That is a really good story."

"And Rose, just so you know, I fell in love with you from the moment I met you. You were just three weeks old, and I was so scared that I would not be a good enough momma for you. You were so tiny and fragile, but you thrived quickly and latched on to me, as if I was your real mother. God looked down on both of us when he brought us together."

"Thank you for saying that Momma, but I always knew you loved me. I have never doubted that at all."

Savannah stopped at the top of the hill, looking down at their home. "Just look at it, Rose, your Pa almost has the cabin complete. Isn't God good to us, with all our bountiful blessings? And look, Mrs. Anderson has done our wash."

"It is beautiful, Momma. I have always loved living here. I wouldn't want to live anywhere else in the world."

"Come on, Rose, let us go see what your Pa has completed today and start dinner. I feel in the mood for some fried apple pies, and you can help me if you want."

"I'd love to, Momma, you know how much I love cooking."

*****

Savannah,

I hope this letter finds you well. We were sorry to hear about your children's papa John. I know from your letters he was a very good man, and I am sorry I never got the chance to meet him in person.

I wanted to let you know that I am about to ship ten crates that is supposed to arrive at your post office by the end of May, so I am hoping this letter arrives before they do.

There were so many things Mother did not want to part with, and I wasn't going to argue with her, as I know it means so much to her, like dishes and cooking ware, and quilts for the beds and such, along with her sewing supplies and a few other things.

Please tell Jonah so he can take the wagon into town and pick them up. Tell him I promise to make it up to him, as I plan to help around the farm as much as possible.

I am a fairly good hunter too, and maybe I can carry some of the load he carries and let him rest more. I cannot wait to meet him and get to know him, from your letters he sounds like a wonderful man, and after living with Father it will be refreshing to meet someone like that.

We are supposed to arrive in your town you call the Village the last Saturday in June. They say we will arrive by noon, but you know how that goes. Hopefully, we will not be delayed.

I cannot wait to see you and meet everyone. I still cannot believe this is happening, it still feels surreal. I know it will not really hit me until I step off that stagecoach and give you a hug.

I love you, and will see you soon,
Your brother,
Joseph

Not much longer and her family would finally be whole again.

*****

Savannah was busy, sweeping out the completed cabin and getting it ready to pick up the crates in the next few days, when she heard a wagon heading their way.

"Momma, look, it's Mrs. Ingalls and Grace," Rose called out from the house.

Savannah stepped outside the cabin door and waved. It had been a long time since she had had a visit from her best friend.

"Looks really nice," Nancy yelled out, jumping off the wagon. "Grace, you go on in and visit with Rose, while I go talk to Mrs. Bell."

"Come on up and look." Savannah motioned. "What brings you out today?"

"I brought you a couple dresses each for the girls and some new trousers for Matthew, just as I agreed to."

"Oh, Nancy, you really didn't have to do that. You have enough to do for your own family."

"Yes, I did. You spend your time with my Grace all day, and I must do my part. Grace's reading and arithmetic has much improved. I don't know what you are doing at that school but keep it up."

"Well, thank you so much; they are beautiful," Savannah took the dresses from her and looked them over. "They are going to love having something new."

"So, what is this? I had no idea Jonah was building onto John's cabin, or Tom would have come over to help. He should have said something to us at church."

"It wasn't like he was in a rush; he started it at the first of winter, and my family from Dahlonega won't be here until the last Saturday in June."

"That is right, your family is coming, Grace told us that. I am so happy for you, and I know you are thrilled."

"I am just so excited, Nancy--beside myself, really. The time is getting closer and I still cannot believe it. It has been over ten years since I saw them."

"Oh, Savannah, that is wonderful. They will love it here in the valley, and thankfully now have a place of worship and a school to attend."

"Yes, I know that was the deciding factor for my mother, that Mary have a place to go to school. So, how have you been?"

"Been good, thank you. Just missing my best friend. We need to get together more often."

"I know, since I started teaching, I don't have time for anything, but I would not change a thing. I absolutely love being the children's teacher."

"And we are all so blessed to have you teach them. Katie was telling me the other day how you taught her boys to read better. We are all thrilled at how you are just whipping these children into shape. They will each be equipped to go out and accomplish anything they desire."

Savannah laughed. "Well, they were all great children to begin with. If truth be known, my Catherine is the one who gives me the most grief. That child keeps me hopping."

Nancy chuckled. "Yes, Grace tells me about her. She laughs and thinks she is so funny. She comes home daily telling me of another story."

"I am not sure *funny* is the word I would call her."

Nancy looked around the cabin and whistled. "Man, oh man, Jonah did a fine job here. Your mother is going to be so thrilled. Does she know that her home is waiting on her?"

"No, we have chosen to keep it a secret. I want to surprise her."

"Well, she will certainly be surprised, that's for sure."

"Do you really think she will like it? It is nothing like her home back in Dahlonega, but I think it is exceptionally beautiful."

"Are you kidding? Why would you have any doubts? I mean, who would not like it? Jonah outdid himself."

Savannah smiled. "When we pick up the crates, I plan to unpack them and put everything away. I am sure I will find a lot of memories in those crates."

"Yes, I am sure you will. Do you need me to come and help you?"

"No, thank you. It is something I want to do myself if you can understand that. I am just going to take my time and might have a few minor emotional breakdowns," she laughed.

"I do. It makes perfect sense."

"Thank you for understanding. I know it will be like Christmas time all over again, opening those crates. If I know my mother, she still has the things from when I lived at home, and I know I shall remember them all."

"Oh, I am sure, and I am so happy for you. By the way, my Tom has not stopped talking about Jonah's new rifle he got for Christmas; did he like it? I meant to ask him at church but keep forgetting."

"He was thrilled. Tom was so sweet to go purchase it for me."

"Yes, he tells me all about it," she rolled her eyes, making Savannah laugh.

"You will have to buy him one this next Christmas."

"Maybe I will. I will have to get Jonah to return the favor and pick one up for me."

"You know he would. He goes to the village now a couple of times a month."

"Do you need me to help you do anything more here? I would love to help you any way I can."

"No, I was finished, just waiting now to pick up the crates, and you have already done way more than you should have," Savannah held up the dress outfits for the children.

147

"Then let's go inside, have a cup of coffee and get caught up on the gossip," Nancy joked.

*****

It felt nice to come home from school two days a week and find her wash out on the line. Katie was so good to do that for her. She had not done her own wash since she started teaching, and it almost made her feel guilty.

"Marylou and Noel brought over a pot of stew and a pone of cornbread," Jonah called out from the barn. "I set it on the table."

The house smelled good when she entered, of rabbit stew and cornbread. There were also cookies for dessert.

She would have to remember to take her dishes back to school in the morning, so the children could take them home. It was their routine twice a week.

Everyone was living up to what they agreed. How could she not love teaching their children?

The school year was coming to an end, with just a few more days left to go before summer. As much as Savannah loved teaching, she welcomed the summer break. The very end of spring, beginning of summer is when her family was set to arrive, and she did not want to take any time away from them for several weeks. They had *much* catching up to do.

*****

"It was very nice of Marylou to send the rabbit stew," Jonah said, later that night, while they were in bed alone.

"Yes, it is nice to come home a couple nights a week and not have to cook."

"Her stew is not as good as yours, nor her cornbread."

148

Savannah chuckled. "You just love me, and are used to my cooking, and I thank you. But I am grateful."

"Yes, I too, am grateful. I am grateful she only cooks a couple times a week."

Savannah laughed aloud. "Jonah Bell, you are terrible."

"Why does telling the truth make me terrible?"

"Please never say that in front of the children; I would not want that to get back to her."

"Why do you think I waited until now to say it? I am a smarter man than that."

Savannah kissed him and giggled. "That you are."

"Would it upset you if I asked Tom to go with me to get the crates? With ten crates, the back of the wagon will be filled to capacity, and I may need him to help me load them. I have no idea what is inside nor how heavy they are."

"I understand, and I don't mind. Tom is a good man; I am sure he will not mind helping you. Just as long as you understand that when they arrive, I want them placed in the cabin and left alone to open them and unpack."

Jonah hugged her close. "I do totally understand, my sweet wife. Just as long as you know that if you need me, I won't be that far away. I am sure there is many memories inside those crates."

"I feel like my childhood is hidden there, and I can't wait to open them. Truth is, not all my childhood was pleasant when it came to my father, so I am a bit nervous, also."

"Are you glad school is coming to an end for a while?"

"Yes, I am excited to have the summer with my family. I feel there is so much catching up to do. But I am incredibly nervous, I must confess."

"What makes you nervous?"

"What if all this anticipation my family feels goes away not long after they arrive, and they wish they never moved? What if they do not like it here, like I hope they will? They are selling their farm and their livestock. They can't just go back to the way it was."

Jonah clucked his tongue. "Now, now, look at you. You are letting bad thoughts and the enemy steal your joy. You are the very one who always tells me to be positive. I cannot think of any reason at all that they would not love it here."

"I know it's going to take time for them to adjust. I am glad they are sending ahead so many of their things, so I can make the cabin really feel like home, you know?"

"I know you will do a great job, and I know your mother will be happy."

"I'm just so excited, Jonah."

I know," he smiled. "It shows."

"I am sorry if I have neglected you during this process. I just have so much on my mind, with them coming and the children at school, and John passing. I hope you still love me as much as you always have."

"I love you more today than I did yesterday, and I will love you even more tomorrow. I am proud to be your husband."

Savannah lay her head on his shoulder and snuggled closer. "And I am proud to be your wife. I love you."

"I love you more."

Chapter Thirteen

"Will there be enough room to carry all this back?" Tom laughed, looking at the mass of crates waiting for them at the post office.

Jonah chuckled, "I guess my mother-in-law had a lot she couldn't part with. I just hope the cabin is big enough to house it all."

"Thank you both for coming so quickly. We have never had this much shipped at once and hardly any space left," the postmaster seemed eager to have it removed.

Jonah and Tom worked almost an hour carrying each crate and loading it into the wagon for the ride home.

It was the first time Jonah could remember he did not have a letter to mail. There would not be enough time for it to get to them before they were already headed this way.

"Do you think there is enough room for me to get a bit of supplies since we are here?" Tom scratched his head and looked at the full wagon.

"Go ahead, we will make room. I am going across for a haircut and will meet you back."

Tom nodded and walked toward the mercantile.

The day was beautiful in the village, and Jonah could not believe the number of people everywhere. Not only was their valley coming more alive with settlers moving in, but the village was more active than he could ever remember.

Jonah loved the band that was playing music under the gazebo; it was a nice added touch to such a busy place.

"Mr. Bell," the barber smiled and greeted him, as he walked into the shop. "I suppose ye have come for the usual?"

"That is right, Norman, you know how I like it. And for as long as you have been cutting my hair, you know you can call me Jonah."

"Yes, sir, Mr. Bell, but I am a respectful man to my customers, and ye, my good friend, is one of my best."

Jonah chuckled and took a seat on the red leather barber chair.

"Where is that fine young man today, Mr. Bell? Did he not need a haircut?"

"Yes sir, Matthew is in much need of a haircut, but today we did not have room to bring him. The wagon is filled with crates. Savannah's mother and siblings are moving west, and they shipped their things on ahead of them."

"I see; I am sure Mrs. Bell is thrilled to have her family on their way."

"You are right, she hardly talks of anything else," Jonah grinned.

"And how do ye feel about that, Mr. Bell? Are ye also as excited?"

"I know it will be different, but I am happy, yes, because I know how much Savannah has missed them. I took her away from them over ten years ago when I brought her to settle here in Arkansas."

"Ahh, so ye feel guilty a wee bit, do ye, Mr. Bell?"

"You might say that, Norman. Felt bad about that for years."

"Then I am glad for ye, that they are coming, so ye no longer have to feel that way. I am sure that is not a good feeling."

"The village seems to be growing in size, much so the past ten years. I cannot believe how much it has expanded and seems to have grown bigger each time I am here."

"Yes sir, seems like more and more settlers are coming this way every day. Of course, I shall not complain because it brings me more customers. Would ye like a shave too, Mr. Bell?"

"Yes please, I am starting to look scruffy."

Norman laughed and lathered his face with shaving cream. "That ye are, Mr. Bell, that ye are."

*****

"Thanks for waiting on me and letting me gather a few supplies." Tom shifted his weight a bit to allow more room for the sack of flour that was sharing his seat.

"No problem at all; I was in need of a haircut and shave."

Tom looked at him as if inspecting the results. "Nice," he chuckled. "Nancy has been cutting my hair and shaving me for years. Maybe I need to come here also and release her of that duty."

"You would like Norman, I am sure."

"How is Savannah liking being voted in as the valley teacher? I felt sort of bad for her as she had not much of a choice. I hope she did not feel obligated."

"On the contrary, she loves teaching the children. She is a natural at it, too."

"Yes, she is. I was filling the wood box right before school was out for the summer and could not help but overhear for a bit. I was quite blown away by the way she taught. She is gifted when it comes to teaching."

"She always said she would teach me to read and write, but I told her I had her to do it for me, so there was no need."

"So, you can't read nor write, either?"

"You too, huh?"

Tom nodded. "Too busy on my parents' farm growing up to stop long enough to learn. My Nancy can read though, and Grace is something else. That child is so smart."

"My Rose is like that, too. I am so glad they are getting the education we never got."

"I overheard Grace telling her mother that she wanted to become a doctor someday."

"A doctor? Really?"

"Yes. I guess I better start saving for college. Grace has not thought it through, though. She would have to go away to school. There is nothing like that anywhere in these parts to teach someone how to be a doctor. Not to mention the hardships she would face. Who ever heard of a woman doctor?"

"Her mind could change a hundred times before she gets old enough," Jonah reminded him.

"Yes, I suppose you are right. I am proud of her, but to be honest, I hope she changes her mind. Do not know what Nancy would do if that child went far from the nest. God didn't see fit to give us more than one, and they are pretty close."

"You should borrow Catherine a few days, and maybe then you shall be glad you only have Grace," Jonah laughed.

Tom laughed out loud. "She's a sight."

"Yes, she certainly is. She has been begging me to take her hunting. She is always competing with her brother, wanting to be tougher than he is."

"I guess, only having one child, we don't have to worry about sibling arguments. I sometimes feel bad for Grace, though, having no one to play with. I was thrilled when the school opened because she gets to interact each day with other children."

"You should let her come over sometime and spend the night with Rose during the summer. I am sure Rose would love the company of someone other than her much younger brother and sister."

"That's a good idea; I will ask her."

"I do thank you for riding into town with me and helping me with these crates. I know it would have been hard trying to load them alone."

"No problem at all. I was needing to go for supplies, and I enjoy the company. Nice to have another man to talk to occasionally."

"I hate to ask, but would you mind helping me carry them all into the cabin?"

"Of course not; I had planned to. I guess you all will be busy the next few days unpacking."

"Savannah has already made it clear that she wants to do all that on her own, and we are to get out of her way and leave her to herself."

"Really? I wonder why she wouldn't want the help?"

"Memories. I am sure it will be emotional for her when she pulls out so many of the things she remembers."

"I didn't think about it that way. At least she has time now, with school being out for the summer. How long does she have until her family arrives?"

"One month, to be exact. That will give her enough time to prepare."

"So, they are coming the last of June, then?"

"Yes, and she shall have a couple months with them before school starts back. I am trusting, by that time, they shall be well into a routine and have started feeling comfortable here."

"You have done a wonderful job adding on to John's cabin. You should have let me know, so I could help you."

"Nah, you have enough to do around your own farm. I didn't have to rush, I had plenty of time."

"I am sure they will love it. I do believe you have the nicest farm of any of us. You have worked hard."

"That's only because I have been here the longest and had more time. Truth is, John Barge helped build my farm up as much as I did. I sure do miss him."

"Yes, I am sorry about your loss. He was a good man. He helped build my barn, too, I remember well."

Jonah enjoyed the ride to and from the village with Tom. It was nice to get out with an old friend and talk. He missed those conversations with John and welcomed it.

It would not be much longer, he knew, that things as he knew it would change, and he also welcomed that.

Ten years is a long time to carry guilt, seeing how your wife is in pain over losing her family each time she received a letter, holding on to it until you went to bed, so she could read it alone. Hearing her cry softly in the next room and knowing there was nothing you could do about it. Knowing it was your fault there was such a distance between her and her family.

Sure, she had said she would not change a thing and that she would do it all over again, yet still, it was his actions that took her away, and he knew that.

Just one more month, and they would be reunited.

Jonah could not wait for that day to arrive.

*****

After the crates were unloaded and Tom had left, Jonah opened the top of each crate.

"Are you sure you do not need my help?"

Savannah smiled and kissed him on the cheek. "No, you have done so much already. Thank you for riding into town and retrieving the crates. I really want to do this alone."

156

"As you wish, my sweet wife. Let me know if you change your mind."

After Jonah left, Savannah stood looking at the massive number of crates and felt the excitement a small child would feel on Christmas morning, wondering what could be inside. Each crate was an unwrapped gift that she had no idea what could be inside.

Jonah was so kind to shoo everyone out of the cabin and promise to look after things for a while to give her time alone. This was something she had looked forward to for weeks, unpacking her childhood and putting it away in its rightful place inside its new home.

Savannah knew her mother would expect to find the crates stacked neatly in the barn, expecting to only unpack them after they figured out where they would reside.

It made her giddy with excitement to know what would really take place and how happy that would make her mother, who expected to live with them in their home with just minimal clothes for a while.

Trembling, she opened the crate closest to her and dug through the straw used for packing and felt the coldness of a cast iron pot.

She smiled as she pulled out the heavy pot her mother used for so much of her cooking. It had hung often over the roaring fire and held stews and soups. It was a pot that had been her grandma's, and her mother had taken it after her grandma passed away.

"Be careful when you lift that, Savannah, and use the poker to lift it off. Never use your hands or they will be severely burnt," Alice said.

"I won't, mother. The stew smells so good. I hope I can cook half as good as you someday."

"You will cook much better than me, someday, Savannah. Cooking just takes practice and time. We learn by doing."

Savannah wiped a tear with her sleeve, remembering, and held the pot in a tight embrace. "Where shall I place you?" She softly spoke aloud and looked toward the fireplace. Even though Jonah had bought a wood cook stove, Savannah knew where the pot had to be, and hung it on the hanger above the split pine that was neatly stacked, just waiting to be lit when her mother arrived.

"Yes, that will be your perfect home for now; I could not imagine you anywhere else."

Next, she pulled out an old tin mixing bowl that had made hundreds of batches of cookies for her younger brother. "Oh, I was hoping Mother had not forgotten you. You are one of my favorites."

Savannah placed it on a shelf that Jonah had made across the top of the kitchen for storing dishes and such.

For hours, Savannah worked, putting away tin plates and cups and wooden spoons, and remembered them all. It was as if her mother had not gotten anything new in all these years.

Going through the crates made her feel young again, as if she were still living in the town of Dahlonega.

With each thing she pulled out, there was a memory and story she replayed in her head. How often had she washed these same dishes, dried them, and put them away?

The beautiful cabin, that was once lifeless and empty, was slowly coming alive and looking like her mother's home, housing all the things Savannah held dear.

*****

"Savannah," Jonah spoke softly as he knocked on the front door of the cabin.

She had been closed up for several hours and darkness was fast approaching.

"You can come in."

Jonah opened the door to find her sitting at the kitchen table holding a doll, with tears in her eyes.

"Are you okay?" he sat down beside her.

She nodded and half laughed through the tears. "This was *my* doll. The only doll I ever had besides the yarn dolls Mother made me. The morning I left with you, I left her to Mary. I felt you would think it was silly if I brought her, and I wanted you to think of me as a grown woman and not a child that still played with dolls."

He pulled her close to him as she cried and held on to the now faded old doll. "I am so sorry, Savannah. You must have hurt so, about so many things, and yet you kept all those emotions bottled up and to yourself. Can you ever forgive me?"

"Jonah, I have forgiven you many years ago. The truth was, I never held a grudge against you at all. I loved you from the very beginning and wanted to be your wife. It wasn't the doll I cared about."

"Then why, my sweet wife, are you crying so?"

"This doll, this faded old doll, represents my past. Those years of long ago when I felt like such a lucky little girl, with the best mother in the world and thought that a father was someone that only barked orders at you and never told you they loved you, that love only came from a mother. I know now, by watching you with our children, that is not the case at all."

"Thank you, there are times I feel as if I could do so much more for the children and take some of the load off you. You do so much for them all, and I know we all would be lost without you."

"Oh Jonah, you are the best Pa. Our children adore you. You not only tell them you love them each night before they go to bed and give them sweet hugs and kisses, but you show them every single day."

"Thank you, that means so much to me to hear you say that." Jonah looked around the kitchen of the cabin. "You have everything looking good."

"Thank you, I know Mother will love it."

"What are you going to do with your doll?"

Savannah stood up and took his hand and led him to what would become Mary's room. She had already placed one of her mother's quilts on the bed Jonah had made for her, and the room looked beautiful.

"This is where she belongs now," Savannah lay her up against the feather pillow.

Jonah put his arm around her. "You have this place looking like a home. Your family will be shocked and amazed to find their things already in place waiting on them."

"It wasn't just me, Jonah, you are the one who built this. You are the one that worked so hard to make this beautiful for people you don't even know."

"Not true, Savannah, I know them through you. For over ten years, I have listened to your stories and your heart, and I feel that I know them well. They are *my* family, too."

"Oh, Jonah, I am so glad you feel that way. They are all going to love you."

"And I am sure I shall them, also."

"I still have half the crates to unpack. I am sorry I have only made it halfway, but this has been very emotional for me."

"You have plenty of time, no need to rush. I only came because it is now dark, and we have eaten a long time ago. I left

160

you a plate in the warmer. Why don't you call it a night and start again in the morning?"

"Oh, Jonah, I am so sorry, I lost track of time and forgot to stop and make dinner. What did you eat?"

"Rose made chicken and dumplings the way you taught her, and she is quite proud of herself. I must say they are surprisingly good. I ate two bowls."

"That is wonderful, I am so immensely proud of her, and I shall tell her so. Thank you for giving me this time alone."

"I will do anything for you, Savannah. You are my love. I knew this would be emotional for you, and I told the children under no circumstances were they to knock on this door."

Savannah laughed. "It's hard for me to believe that curiosity didn't get the best of Catherine and she come wandering up."

"Let's just say I kept her busy in the barn."

"In the barn? What did you have her doing?"

"Shoveling out the stables."

Savannah chuckled. "And tell me how that went. I cannot imagine that being something she asked to do."

"Well, Matthew, of course, usually helps me, and for a six-year-old boy he does quite well. Catherine wandered in and asked if she could come tell you something important, and I made it a point to brag on Matthew in front of her. Pretty smart on my part if I do say so myself."

"Oh, Jonah, I can only imagine what happened next."

"Yes, she forgot all about the importance of having something to tell you and insisted that she could clean the stable better than Matthew, so I sent Matthew to play with Ricky Ayers and put her to work doing his job."

Savannah laughed a gut-wrenching laugh. "And tell me, Jonah, did she clean the stables better than Matthew?"

161

"Let's just say I had Rose draw her a washtub full of hot water. The bath could not wait until Saturday. She had more of the manure on her than she did on her shovel, and the smell wasn't that pleasant."

"Jonah, you are killing me! That is so funny! I bet she will never want to be better than Matthew again when it comes to cleaning the stable."

"I think it is safe to say that our sweet Catherine will never compete with him again when it comes to anything in the barn."

"I am surprised she lasted as long as she did."

"Well, I had already sent Matthew to play, and so she had no other choice. I did not let her off easy. And she has also decided that hunting just might not be something she wishes to do."

"Oh, really? Whatever made her come to that conclusion?"

"She said that cleaning stables and hunting and stuff for boys was stupid, and that girls are not supposed to do stuff like that."

"Wow, I am surprised she said that."

"Well, she made that statement with blisters on her hands and horse manure on her face."

"Poor Catherine," Savannah giggled, "I guess she got what she deserved. I better go in and love on her a bit."

"Oh, there will be no loving tonight, I am afraid. She has been fast asleep the past hour, worn completely out from working so hard."

"I can imagine."

"Come on, my sweet wife, let us go get you some of those dumplings. And since I am still awake, you can love on *me* all you wish."

Chapter Fourteen

Savannah walked around the quietness of the cabin that was to become her mother's new home.

She had worked hard for a couple of weeks, unpacking, and adding special touches here and there.

She made a beautiful tablecloth for the table Jonah had built and lace curtains for the windows. She even decorated each bedroom and personalized it to fit who it belonged to, knowing what they liked from the letters over the past ten years.

Savannah knew she had spent way too much time on the project, yet Jonah never once complained.

He and the children had stayed away and given her space for as long as she needed, and Savannah knew that it must be hard to find things to keep Catherine busy.

Jonah had done nothing but show her the kind of love any woman would desire, always loving, caring and gentle. They rarely had a harsh word for the other, and Savannah knew how blessed she was to be married to such a man.

It wasn't so long ago, when they first married, that Jonah had let her know more than once that she would never be more to him than a caregiver to Rose, and no matter how hard she prayed that he would fall in love with her, nothing she tried seem to work. In fact, it seemed that it just pushed him further away, until the point she gave up, and came to terms that she would have to live with him as nothing more than a friend.

Savannah sat down in the rocker that would become her mother's and thought back to the day Jonah first pledged his love for her.

They were married two years at that time with no physical contact, and she had just gotten back from nursing John Barge back to health, where she had been alone with John for a week.

They managed to bring him back with them from his rundown home, knowing that he was no longer able to live alone. It was the same day he moved into this very cabin to live out the rest of his life.

Jonah had told her earlier that he wished to talk to her about something. She guessed he wanted to talk about John or Rose, or the many things they had spoken of the past two years. It was never about them or their relationship because every time she tried, he would run off. It was never something he desired to speak of.

She was working on a crocheted blanket when Rose finally went to sleep that night.

Jonah covered up Rose in Clara's quilt and sat down beside her.

She was tired from the week past and so happy to be back home in the cabin she loved. The cabin Jonah had built, and she had hung curtains to make it a home.

"You are very talented, Savannah."

"Crocheting isn't that hard, Jonah."

"It's not just crocheting; it's everything. You are just magic."

"Magic," she laughed. "What do you mean?"

"Everything you touch turns to gold. Look at how Rose has turned out. She adores you, her momma. Do you know she cried for you two days after we left you?"

"Oh, Jonah, that is terrible."

"And look at how you made this house a home. It was a miserable place here without you."

"With Rose crying for two days, I can imagine it was," she winked.

"It wasn't just that, Savannah. I missed you. I missed you like I never thought I would."

"It isn't easy doing all my chores and yours, too, Jonah. I am sorry I had to send you back like that, but we could not take any chances that Rose might get sick; she is just too young to fight it off."

"I don't mean that. Sure, it was not easy doing all you do in a day, which I never realized until I had to do it. What I meant was I *missed* you."

"But you knew I was coming back. You had not lost me like you lost Clara."

"I did not think of Clara at all, Savannah. I could not stop thinking about *you*."

Savannah looked toward him and never missed a stitch. "I wonder why?" She needed to hear him say it.

Jonah took both hands and ran them through his thick dark hair. "There are days when I cannot remember what she looked like, Savannah."

"I am so sorry, Jonah. You say Rose looks just like her. You can remember her through your daughter."

"And that is what I do each time I forget. I look at her and that helps me remember."

"I'm sorry that Clara is not here with you now. I am sorry that you have had to go through so much pain. I am sorry that you had to marry me to take care of your daughter."

"Don't be sorry, Savannah," Jonah swallowed, knowing what he was about to say could change their relationship forever. "I am not sorry at all that I married you."

"You aren't?"

He slid the chair closer to her and took her hand in his. "I'm sorry that I have pushed you away so many times. I am sorry that I have taken you for granted. I am sorry if I have treated you as anything less than my wife. Please forgive me."

"It's okay, Jonah, I know why you married me. If it had not been for Rose, you still would not be married. I know you, Jonah, and I know how faithful you are to your love, to Clara. You do not have to explain to me."

"Yes, I do have to explain." I have been doing a lot of soul-searching the past week. I have searched my heart and realize that Clara no longer owns it."

"What do you mean?" She could feel herself starting to tremble.

"I am not sure exactly when it happened, Savannah, but slowly you started owning my heart, and I did not realize how deeply it went until I left you at John's, with him sick, and I feared that you might also get sick and that I could possibly lose you."

"What are you saying, Jonah?"

"I have fallen in love with you, Savannah. So deeply in love with you, it hurts."

She gasped. "Oh Jonah, please don't say it if you don't mean it."

He smiled. "I mean it, Savannah. I love you. I love you every bit as much as I love Clara."

"But I never wanted to take her place. I just wanted you to love me, too."

"And I do, Savannah, I love you. Will you please do me the honor of being my wife?"

Savannah giggled through tears. "I am already your wife."

"But I never asked you, not the way a lady should be asked.

"Yes Jonah, I will be your wife."

166

Jonah stood and pulled Savannah to her feet. "Do you think you might ever love me half as much as I love you?" He smiled that sexy smile that made her melt inside.

"I already love you more," she whispered.

Jonah pulled her close and pressed his lips to hers. The very taste of her was intoxicating, and he wanted her to melt in his arms.

Savannah moaned from the pleasure of his kiss, but unlike last time, he did not pull away.

"I love you too, Jonah. I think I have always loved you."

"Make love to me, Savannah. I want to be your husband, and for you to be my wife."

Jonah picked her up and carried her to their bed. "I will be gentle, I promise."

"I have never been with a man, Jonah. I hope I do not disappoint you."

"How could you ever disappoint me, Savannah? You are my wife, and I love you so."

He kissed her again and she welcomed it. This was the way marriage was supposed to be. She prayed this day was real, and she would not wake up to the sun, realizing it was only a dream.

Savannah opened her eyes as the memory left her. It was a day she would never forget as long as she lived.

She thought about that day a lot. The day she and Jonah became man and wife, like a husband and wife should be, sharing everything together, even intimacy.

And now, almost eight years later and having given birth to two children, it just kept getting better with each passing season. She loved the way he desired her, and told her so daily, but it wasn't just about her body, or what she could do for him as a woman, but he valued and respected her as a wife.

It was time to get back to the cabin. Her work here was finished.

*****

"Hurry and eat, children; we must be leaving soon." Savannah had not slept a wink the night before from excitement.

Today was the day they would all ride into the village and meet the stagecoach carrying her mother and siblings.

"Can I wear my new dress that Mrs. Ingalls made me?" Catherine came out of her room carrying the dress.

"Yes, you can, hurry up now, we don't want to be late." Savannah set the jelly on the table to go with the biscuits. "Jonah, hurry up and come eat," she called out, thinking he was still in the house.

"Pa went to the barn to get the wagon ready," Matthew answered. "He is putting in a few chairs for the ride back."

"Then you come and eat, Matthew. You shall be hungry before we get back."

"Okay, Momma. Shall I not wait on the others?"

"It's okay this time; we are all in a hurry."

"Do I look okay, Momma?" Rose asked, coming out of her room.

"You are beautiful, I love your new dress, and you and Catherine will match. Come sit and make a jelly biscuit and glass of milk. What is keeping your sister?"

"She is putting a bow in her hair. She says she wants to look nice for Momma Alice."

"I will make her biscuit then, and your Pa's too, and they can eat it on the way." Savannah never felt so rushed in all her life. The last thing she wanted was for the stagecoach to come in before they got to the stagecoach station to greet them.

"I'm finished, Momma," Catherine glided into the room, turning around so her mother could see her from every angle, proud of the way she looked.

"You look very beautiful, Catherine. Momma Alice will think so, too."

"Are you all ready to go?" Jonah stuck his head in the door.

"Yes, we are. Come along, children, let us go."

"But I haven't eaten yet, Momma," Catherine whined. "I am hungry."

"You can eat on the way; I made you a jelly biscuit. I have you one also, Jonah."

"You seem a bit flushed," he joked.

"That's putting it mildly. I am afraid we shall not get there on time."

"Joseph told you noon, and if that is the case, we have plenty of time."

"But what if the stagecoach arrives ahead of schedule, what then, Jonah?" Savannah was beside herself with worry.

Jonah chuckled. "Come on, everyone," he took his biscuit from her hand and motioned the children out the door. "Let's get started before your momma has a fit."

The ride on the way into the village was taking longer than it should, or so Savannah thought. "Why is it taking so long?" she asked. "I don't ever remember it taking this long when we rode into the village before."

Jonah laughed. "Savannah, we are only halfway there. Please calm down; I promise you that we shall make it on time. We started in plenty of time; I am not sure why you are so worried."

"And what if they arrive before us? What will we do then, Jonah?"

"Then I can assure you that they shall wait on us; what else are they going to do?"

"But I want to meet then at the stagecoach station when it pulls in. I have thought about this for weeks." Savannah rubbed her hands together anxiously.

Jonah reached over and took her hand to give it a light squeeze, "Savannah, my sweet wife, please take a very deep breath, and let it out slow."

Rose laughed, "You are funny, Pa."

"Do you think they will like us?" Matthew asked.

"They will like me more than you because I am a girl and you are a boy, and boys stink and play in manure," Catherine stated.

"We will have none of that today, young lady," Savannah scolded. "They are going to love all of you the same. I know your Momma Alice and Uncle Joseph and Aunt Mary, and they will love all of you."

"I am sure they are just as nervous as we are," said Rose.

Savannah smiled. Rose was much too smart for her age; that was something she had not thought about.

They had been from stagecoach to stagecoach for almost a month now, staying in different hotels, and were probably worn out and just as nervous, wondering if they were even going to like it in Arkansas.

They had no idea they had a beautiful new home that awaited them, and their things were already unpacked.

Jonah had even taken the wooden crates apart and made small furniture to go in their home for them to enjoy.

Everything was more than ready.

*****

"It's been a long time since we all came to the village together," Rose commented as they came close enough to see the buildings on the horizon.

"Looks like the village keeps growing, Jonah. Do you think the stagecoach is here yet?" Savannah strained to see.

Jonah looked toward the stagecoach station platform and was relieved when he saw it empty. Savannah would have never forgiven him had her family arrived before them.

Jonah pulled the wagon as close as he could get and put on the brake. "Told you we would make it before them," he smiled, looking her way. "Looks like we are an hour ahead of schedule."

"I am sorry I made such a fuss, Jonah, please forgive me. I guess I just wanted everything to be perfect."

He leaned over and kissed her. "There is nothing to forgive; I love you."

"Can we go to the mercantile and get some candy?" Catherine asked. "I have not had candy since Santa brought me some in my stocking."

"Yes, can we, Pa?" Matthew screamed. "I want a chocolate drop."

Jonah looked toward Savannah to see what her comment would be, not sure if she wanted them to sit and wait.

"Oh, go on. Would you take them all without me, Jonah? I don't want to leave this site until they arrive."

He chuckled and climbed down from the wagon. "Come on, children, let's go to the mercantile and hurry back before your Momma Alice arrives."

Jonah took Catherine and Matthew's hand and led them across the street, with Rose close behind.

Savannah sat down on a bench on the platform in front of where the stagecoaches stopped and watched her family as they went into the mercantile.

Jonah was such a wonderful Pa, and she had no doubt that they would each come back with a few pieces of candy.

Today was the day she had been praying and hoping for ever since her father passed away, and it was finally here. God truly was a good God and answered prayers.

She'd always been afraid that when her mother grew older and needed more help with things, she would not be there to do so, and now it seemed everything was falling into place, just the way it should be. She would be able to take care of her mother for as long as she lived.

Savannah pinched her cheeks to give them some color and hoped her mother would think she looked healthy, and not tired and as worn out as she felt. She hoped, as rushed as she felt this morning, it did not show, and that her hair was still up in the bun she had become accustomed to wearing.

"Hello!" Dottie called out, running across the street toward her. "I saw your family in the mercantile, and Jonah told me you were out here waiting on your family to arrive."

"Hello, Dottie," Savannah got up and embraced her. "Yes, today is the big day. I am just so excited."

"Well, I won't stay; I wouldn't want your mother to see you talking to me, not a good Christian woman like yourself; whatever will she think?"

Savannah smiled. "I truly hope you do not mean that Dottie. First, Jesus loves all of us, and second, my mother is nothing like that. My brother Joseph might be blown away by your dress," she laughed, "but they will think nothing of us knowing each other."

"My dress?" Dottie looked down at her tight-fitting red dress and laughed. "Perhaps you are right, and for that matter alone, I will not stay, but I did want to come and tell you hello."

"Well, I am glad you did, Dottie. By the way, I love the new dress you helped Jonah pick out. Don't you think it looks good on me?"

"It truly is beautiful. I was not sure if he would tell you that I helped him. I saw him trying to pick out a dress, and he asked me if I knew about what size you would wear. You know men know nothing about things such as that."

"Yes, I imagine so. And it fits me perfectly."

"But, of course," Dottie laughed. "I am really enjoying the dress shop, and they have other things besides just clothes there; I was on my way over there now."

"I will have to take a look the next time we are here."

"Yes, I think you will enjoy it. Your mother will, also."

"We are both so used to sewing our own clothes and not used to shopping for anything other than material."

"Well, it's time you pampered yourself."

"Not sure what that is, but I like the idea."

"You are worth it. If you would excuse me, I am going to run along and let you greet your family," Dottie gave her another quick hug and kiss on the cheek. "Until next time."

"See you later, Dottie."

Savannah watched her family walk back across the street and just as she predicted, each child carried a small brown bag that Savannah knew held chocolate drops, peppermints and gum balls.

Never could she remember ever going to the mercantile in Dahlonega with her father and him buying her anything. But then, that was a lifetime ago and nothing that mattered now.

"Do you want a piece of candy, Momma?" Rose offered.

"You are extremely sweet to offer, Rose, but no, thank you. You save it for yourself."

"Pa got me two chocolate drops and peppermint. I like chocolate drops. Do you, Momma?" Catherine asked.

"Savannah, Catherine asked you a question," Jonah nudged her.

"I am sorry, what did you say, Catherine?"

"I asked you if you liked chocolate drops."

"Yes, but I don't want any, thank you."

"You are certainly deep in thought." Jonah sat down beside her. "If it is on schedule, it shouldn't be much longer now."

"I feel as if I might lose my breakfast," Savannah moaned.

"Are you serious? Do you feel ill?"

"Oh Jonah, I have butterflies in the pit of my stomach. I don't think I have ever been this nervous in all my life."

"Savannah, you look beautiful. The children look beautiful. Their new home awaiting them is beautiful. Everything is going to be okay."

"I am aware of that, so why do I feel this way, Jonah?"

"Because you are excited to see your family again after all these years. You are filled with many emotions. It's been ten long years, and you cannot imagine what they will look like and wondering what they will think of you."

"You know me so well, Jonah. I just never thought I would see them again, you know."

"But you are. They shall be here at any moment."

Savannah fidgeted back and forth with nervousness. She knew this would prove to be the longest wait of her life.

Chapter Fifteen

"We are almost there, Mother," Joseph said, looking out the window of the stagecoach, "I can see the buildings a few miles ahead.

"Are you sure this isn't just another stop before we get there?" Mary asked. She was tired of traveling.

"No, Mary, this is the village Savannah spoke of. We are in Arkansas. Savannah, Jonah and the children should be there to greet us," he assured her.

Alice wiped the tears from her eyes and focused on the buildings growing larger in the distance.

"Are you okay, Mother?" Joseph took her hand. "Why are you trembling?"

"I just can't believe in a few moments we will all get to see her again. It has been much too long, Joseph, much too long. I never thought this day would come."

"Mary, let's let Mother get out first; is that okay with you?" He wanted to give them each time to greet her separately.

Mary nodded in agreement and took a deep breath. This was it. She was about to meet her sister for the first time.

"Thank you, I know you are tired as we all are; I just want Mother and Savannah to have a moment alone.

"That's okay, I am a bit nervous anyway."

"No reason to be. You are going to love your big sister; she's even better in person."

*****

"Here it comes, Momma, here comes the stagecoach!" Matthew screamed out, jumping up and down on the platform.

"Children, let your momma greet them first, okay?" Jonah pulled Matthew and Catherine back a bit to give Savannah the space she needed. "Why don't you three sit back down on the bench, and you can greet them in a moment?"

Savannah stood, made one last look back at Jonah with tears in her eyes, and waited for the stagecoach to come to a stop.

"Whoa," the driver called out to the team of horses, bringing the stagecoach to a stop in front of the platform. "We are here, folks," he said as he jumped off and headed for the door.

Alice stuck her head out and smiled as the driver took her hand and helped her down.

"Oh, Mother!" Savannah ran to her awaiting arms and cried. "Oh, Mother, how I have missed you!"

"I have missed you, too, Savannah, more than you could ever imagine. Here, let me look at you!" Alice pulled back with tears in her eyes and looked her daughter over from head to toe.

"You are just as beautiful as the morning you left, only now you are a beautiful grown woman."

Mary stepped off the stagecoach and smiled at the sister she could not remember. "Hello, Savannah, it is nice to finally get to see you in person."

Savannah hugged Mary tightly. "The last time I seen you, you were just a baby. My, you have grown into such a beautiful young woman."

"Thank you--Mother says I look like you."

"Savannah!" Joseph called out, jumping from the stagecoach, and almost knocking her over with his embrace. "We are here, Savannah, we are finally here!"

"Joseph, I have missed you so much! I am so glad you never gave up begging Mother to come."

"Never! I knew she would give in sooner or later. And you must be Jonah," Joseph held out his hand in greeting and Jonah grabbed on tightly.

"Please forgive me; I got so caught up. Yes, this is my husband, Jonah, and this is Rose, Matthew and Catherine. And children, this is your Momma Alice, Uncle Joseph and Aunt Mary."

"So nice to meet you all," Jonah nodded. Savannah has been praying for this for years."

"We both have," Joseph smiled. "I can't believe we are here!" Joseph threw his arms in the air and screamed out. "We are here! The Bowens are finally here!"

Alice laughed, "Everyone is going to think you lost your mind, Joseph."

"I don't care, Mother, I don't care. I am just so happy that we are finally here, after all the years of begging you to come."

"Hey, Momma Alice, it is nice to meet you," Catherine took Alice's hand.

"Well, hello there, sweet girl," she bent down to her level. "It is very nice to meet you also, and you too, Matthew and Rose. I have heard so much about you all."

"Nice to meet you, too, Ma'am," Rose nodded.

"Oh, do call me Momma Alice. I am thrilled to be a grandma, and what a shame I have had to go through the last almost eleven years of being one and not once hear myself called that."

Rose smiled, knowing that she thought of her, too, as her granddaughter, not just Matthew and Catherine.

Jonah looked up at the crate on top of the stagecoach. "I assume that is yours?"

"Yes," Joseph answered, "it contains a few things we needed on the ride here, everything else we already sent; I trust you received it already?"

"We did, all ten crates of it."

Alice chuckled, "Please forgive me, Jonah, there was just so much I could not part with, and I knew that when we find a home of our own, I will need most of it. The truth is, though, that it all contains memories that I just could not leave behind."

"No apology needed--we understand. Joseph, can you help me get this onto our wagon, and we will be on our way?"

"Yes sir," Joseph said, helping Jonah get the heavy crate onto the wagon.

"Mother, do you need anything here in the village before we head home? We live about ten miles from here, so we normally only venture here once or twice a month."

"Do you want to go to the mercantile and let me buy some flour, meal and sugar and anything else you might need? We did not come to be a burden on you, and I know it will take extra food to feed us. I do want to help out."

"Jonah purchased supplies not long ago and we have plenty, so that is not necessary. But thank you."

They had already stocked her mother's kitchen with the things she would need and could not wait for her mother to realize it all.

"Then I insist, the next time we come to the village for supplies, that I am buying them; it's only fair."

Savannah laughed. "Whatever you say, Mother."

Alice Bowen had not changed at all, always wanting to do her fair share.

*****

Savannah loved the ride home, listening to several conversations going on at once.

Rose was telling Mary all about Grace and Elisa, her two best friends, the boys at school and about her momma being the teacher.

Alice was holding Catherine and telling her and Matthew about all they had seen on the stagecoach on their ride from Dahlonega to Arkansas, and Catherine and Matthew were mesmerized, taking in every word.

Joseph was asking Jonah all about the harvest and what needed to be gathered, and about his barn and how many animals he had. He also told him about the farm they sold and the horses he hated to part with.

Savannah closed her eyes and listened to the many conversations taking place.

This was the day she had waited for, and she realized how silly it was that she had been so nervous. Did she expect her family to be disappointed in her, or was it just that so many years had passed with nothing besides a few letters, and there was a part of her that felt like she was greeting strangers?

*****

Jonah stopped the wagon on the hill, just as he had almost eleven years before, so they could see the farm below.

"This is our home, Mother," Savannah said. "It is easier to see it from up here. We call this the valley."

"Oh, it is just beautiful!' Alice exclaimed. "Jonah you have both done such a fine job."

"Your letters didn't do it justice." Joseph could not believe it was such a nice place.

"Which house do you live in, Savannah? Did someone move in next to you?" Alice could not figure out why there were two cabins so close together.

"Remember, Mother, I told you about Papa John and the cabin Jonah built for him right after he got so sick and almost died?"

"Yes, I remember, but that was many years ago, and I thought you told me it was a very small cabin. Those look like two fairly size cabins down below."

Savannah giggled, as Jonah put the horses back in motion and started down the hill to her family's new cabin. "Yes, it was small, Mother. Our home is there, to the right. To the left was Papa John's cabin, but Jonah added on to it, and now it is going to be your home, for the three of you."

"What?!" Joseph choked back tears. "No way; you are joking, right, Savannah? That isn't our home."

"Jonah, you built us a home?" Alice cried. "Oh, my goodness, how will we ever repay you?"

"Family doesn't repay family," Jonah said. "You all just being here with Savannah and your grandchildren is payment enough."

"It's very pretty," Mary stated. "It's prettier than our place back home, Mother."

"Well, of course it is," Alice said. "That old house had been there for years. I just don't know what to say."

Jonah stopped the wagon in front of their new home and jumped off. "Come see if you like it before you say anything," he laughed, taking Savannah's hand, and helping her down.

Savannah went to the door and opened it. "Come see, Mother."

Joseph helped Alice from the wagon, and both walked slowly to the door, looking around at their new home.

"Oh, my goodness," she cried. It's our things, Joseph and Mary, they have our things already in place." Alice broke down and shook with sobs.

"I love you, Mother. I have always loved you and missed you since the morning I left you. Jonah and I wanted to do this for you. You deserve it. You have always worked hard for everything and done so much for so many. You truly deserve it."

Joseph and Mary also stood in tears, looking around their new home.

"Come," Savannah smiled. "Come and see your bedrooms."

"We each have a bedroom?" Mary was surprised.

"Yes, yours is there," Savannah pointed. "They aren't huge rooms but will serve their purpose and give you all your privacy."

Mary walked into the room and smiled at her. "It's our doll."

"No, Mary, it's *your* doll."

Mary gave Savannah a genuine hug. "I love you Mary, and I am glad you are here."

"Thank you, I love you, too."

"Oh Savannah," Alice called from her bedroom. "You made me a sewing and quilting area; everything is so organized and neat. I just love it."

"I wanted you to feel at home, and I remembered how nice you always kept your things."

"No way," Joseph yelled. "A rifle, you are giving me a rifle!"

Jonah walked into his room and took the rifle off the wall and handed it to him. "Savannah got me a new one for Christmas, and I noticed you didn't send one in the crates, so I am giving you my old one. It's old, but it's still a dandy."

"Thank you, Jonah, I shall take care of it. I never actually had one of my own. We sold Pa's before we moved."

The next hour was spent visiting and looking around their new home while Matthew and Catherine ran around the cabin and played.

It was an emotional time for all.

A time to be reunited.

A time to laugh and to cry.

A time to remember.

A time to let go.

A time to heal.

181

A time to forgive.

Savannah once again had a complete family. No more broken pieces, or a long distance between them, and she knew that for the rest of her life, no matter what should come her way, God was truly in charge. He had proven that today, by bringing her family to Arkansas.

*****

Savannah lightly tapped on the front door of her mother's cabin around eight o'clock the next morning.

In all the years she had lived with her mother she never knew her to sleep past six, always up and always working at something.

Joseph opened the door with a cup of coffee in his hand and smiled. "Good morning, Sis, sorry we slept late. Come on in."

"Good morning," Alice called out, rolling out a pan of biscuits. "I never intended to sleep so late."

"It's only eight, Mother, you didn't sleep late at all."

"Joseph laughed. "You know Mother, always up at the crack of dawn. Honestly, I am too, but I guess the trip just wore us all out. Seems a bit odd not to have to milk the cow and gather the eggs and tend to horses."

"I was going to invite you to the house for breakfast, but I see you are already making yours."

"Well, you did leave us all this food, so it would be a shame to let it go to waste," Alice laughed. "And besides, I have not made biscuits in over a month; it feels nice to be cooking again with my old mixing bowl and my cooking ware. Would you like a cup of coffee?"

Savannah helped herself to a tin cup from the cupboard and poured herself a cup. "Well, this is nice, just go next door and get a cup of coffee. I do believe I could get used to this."

Mary came dragging her feet into the room. "I feel like I have been run over by a stagecoach."

Savannah laughed. "I am sure it will take several days to get settled in and get over the long ride west. If you want, Mary, after you eat breakfast, come on out to the house and visit with Rose. The children all plan to play in the creek today. It is their favorite thing in the summer. I can hardly keep them out of it."

Joseph washed out his cup in the basin of hot water and placed it back in the cupboard. "Please tell Jonah I will come out shortly and help him; I don't intend to be lazy and sleep late every morning."

"Oh, Joseph, please don't think you have to work like a work horse. This is your home; please enjoy yourself for at least a few days. Borrow one of Jonah's horses and get to know the area. Ride out and meet the neighbors and introduce yourself."

"Maybe I shall do that. I would love to see the area and what all you have spoken of the past ten years."

"And Mother, you and Mary can meet the neighbors at church next Sunday."

"Oh goodness," said Alice, "this is Sunday, isn't it? Are we keeping you from church? I lost track of what day it is with the long journey west."

"Jonah and I decided that since we were all up so late and this was your first full day here, we aren't going this morning. There is always next Sunday, and everyone knew my family was coming yesterday, so they won't worry about us."

Savannah drank the last of her coffee and washed her cup. "I shall see you later; please feel free to come to the house anytime. Let's do dinner together this evening and let me cook for you."

"Only if you let me cook for you tomorrow," Alice grinned, loving being close to her daughter once again.

"Mother, you just have no idea how I am looking forward to eating *your* cooking again. That sounds like a great deal to me!"

*****

"Sorry I slept so late," Joseph said to Jonah upon entering the barn. "Savannah said I would find you out here."

Jonah greeted Joseph with a hug. "Think nothing of it. When we start gathering the harvest, then you can get up extra early; as for now, just relax."

"That is what Savannah said, but relaxing is not something I am used to, Jonah. But I have to admit it was nice sleeping until seven and not having anything I was responsible for."

Savannah told me you have been the man of the house since you were eleven. I think you deserve to take a break; you have clearly earned it."

"You know, Jonah, this was the first year I didn't plow the field or plant the seed, because I knew we would be leaving before it come in. It felt strange. I thought I heard my father at least one hundred times scream at me and say, '*get off your butt, boy, and go to work; you have to earn your keep around this house!*'"

"Savannah told me how hard he was on all of you. I am sorry you had to go through that."

"Can I talk to you about something; I mean just you and I, man to man?"

Jonah put down the brush he was brushing Midnight with and looked at Joseph to give him all his attention. "Sure, what's on your mind?"

"I didn't fully understand why Savannah left us when it all happened. I mean I was just seven years old at the time. It wasn't until years later that I learned the truth, and that you traded your land and cabin for my sister's hand in marriage."

"I did. I guess you were pretty angry with me."

"I was. I was angry with Father as well. Always thought you two never had a right to do what you did to her without even asking, and with just two days' notice. She did not even have time to tell me goodbye. Savannah was like a second mom to me, and me waking up to find her gone crushed me."

"You are right, Joseph; I had no right to do that. In fact, it was plain selfish of me. I was only thinking about heading west and getting away from Dahlonega and the memories of my late wife, the wife I loved with all my heart. I didn't think once about Savannah, or what it might do to her, or what she might want, or even think about it for that matter."

"But meeting you yesterday and seeing you now, seeing how you and Savanah interact with one another, you don't seem like the type of man that would do that at all, and honestly, I am still puzzled by it all."

"Thank you for saying that. I have felt guilty over my actions for years and apologized to Savannah countless times. She has such a forgiving heart. I love your sister, Joseph. She and those children are my life, and I don't intend to ever hurt her again."

Joseph nodded. "Thank you for talking to me about this. It has really bothered me all these years. When I was a little boy I wanted to get on my horse and ride here and kill you and bring my sister back home. In my mind, you were keeping her hostage."

Jonah nodded sadly.

"But when I got a bit older, and Savannah started explaining it all to me through her letters, I knew how much she loved you, and then how much you loved her."

"So, you are no longer angry at me, then?"

"No. Now when I think back, I am glad you took her away from that, away from Father, but at the time I was just being selfish and wanted her home because she was the peacemaker between Father and me. When she was not there anymore, it was hard on me; he was hard on me."

Jonah placed his hand on Joseph's shoulder. "I'm truly sorry, Joseph, please forgive me."

Joseph nodded. "I am good now. Especially now that I met you and can see how much you love her, and what kind of man you are. Just know, Jonah, I am not used to that, so I may be a little rough around the edges."

"I am glad you are here, Joseph."

"Can I ask you something else, Jonah?"

What's that?"

"When I came into the barn you hugged me. Why did you do that?"

"Because we are family. I am glad you are finally here. I know how much you missed your sister and how much you wanted to come here, and I love you. I think, in the years to come, you and I will become close, or at least I hope so."

Joseph fought back tears. "My father never once hugged me in my eleven years with him, never even once. It was a great feeling."

Jonah smiled. "So, are you ready to saddle this horse up and go exploring?"

"Yes sir, I would love to do that."

Chapter Sixteen

The valley was as beautiful as Savannah always described in her letters. Trails wide enough for wagons ran everywhere through the woods that Savannah told him made a huge circle to everyone's home in the valley and to the church. Just stay on the trail, she told him, and you will be able to say hello to everyone.

Joseph left a bit after lunch and had already met the Ingalls'. He liked Tom and Nancy and even met their daughter, Grace. He could tell they were good people and invited him in for coffee.

He knew Nancy Ingalls was Savannah's best friend here in the valley and had delivered both her children. They were a lot alike with their fiery spirits.

His mother was the total opposite, though, always allowing his father to tell her what to do and order her around, never appreciating anything she ever did.

To him, she did nothing right. He was glad his mother was finally free of him and now had a beautiful new home and was near her oldest daughter; he was so happy for her.

Joseph could see the church in the distance and made the horse go a bit faster.

The church was beautiful, with a steeple, just as Savannah had said.

He noticed a cross buried in front of a pile of rocks and knew this must be John Barge's grave. Savannah spoke of him often in her letters, and he knew how bad it hurt them when he died.

He could hear someone talking loudly inside and went closer to the door. Finding it ajar, he decided to investigate.

"Hello," he called out, pushing the door open a bit further to look inside."

"Well, hello there." A sandy-haired man was standing behind the pulpit. "How can I help you?"

Joseph walked toward him and extended his hand. "I am Joseph Bowen, Savannah Bell's brother; we just arrived yesterday."

"Yes, yes," he smiled and shook his hand in greeting. "I am Pastor Corbin Anderson. The Bells told us you were on your way, so nice to meet you. I guess that is why I didn't see any of you in church this morning?"

"Yes sir, but we will all be here next Sunday. My mother does not believe in missing church. We were just all exhausted from the long journey and lost track of what day it was."

"Completely understand. So how was your journey west?"

"Very long, but it was nice seeing the countryside. Neither of us had ever been out of Dahlonega."

"Then I am glad you were able to come. I look forward to meeting the rest of your family."

"My mother is glad there is a church close enough for us to attend and a school for my sister, Mary."

"Savannah hoped since we built the church and school you would all come. It was quite remote here for a while. Still isn't as populated as most communities but we expect more to arrive in the years ahead."

Joseph looked around the church. "You did a nice job on this place. It's also very peaceful here."

"It is. I stayed after church today to practice my sermon for next Sunday. It's always peaceful here."

"No harm in that. I guess this is where Savannah teaches school?"

188

"It is. The children all love her, too. She has done a lot for my boys. They were struggling in their reading and writing until she started helping them."

"She's always been the smartest in the family."

"No doubt about that. Do you read and write well, Joseph?"

"Well enough, I guess. Mother's been teaching us since I can remember, and I attended school until my father died, and then mother finished teaching me at home while my sister went, so I could help out around the farm."

"I see. Savannah told me how hard you worked. How do you like the valley so far, Joseph?"

"I like it a lot. I've just come from the Ingalls' and was on my way north to meet the Ayers family."

"There are some incredibly good, godly people that live in this valley. Make sure you meet my boys as well, Nathaniel and Josiah; they are not that much younger than you, maybe you will have a lot in common."

"I'll do that, sir. It's so nice to meet you; I will go and let you get back to what you were doing."

"Have a good day, Joseph, it was nice to meet you, too."

Joseph closed the door as he exited and climbed back on Midnight, never feeling so much freedom in all his life.

It felt good to ride through the valley and not have to rush, not to have a million things to be responsible for and get finished before dark. It almost made him feel guilty.

He had been working and doing things around the farm since he was old enough to walk. He could not ever remember having a childhood, or friends to play with except his sister, Savannah. Mary was always too young and to herself and had her head in her books as she got older.

His name had been *boy* as far as his father was concerned.

Boy, get off your butt.

Boy, go get the cow milked.

Boy, go gather the vegetables.

Joseph wished he could forgive his father and let it go, but he was almost certain it would be a thorn in his side that he would carry to his grave.

He could see the Ayers' home in the distance and their barn to the right. It was a two-story home with big porches and a swing on the front.

There was a huge stack of firewood by the house, neatly stacked and covered to stay dry, and in the distance, fields of vegetables.

Joseph climbed off the horse, tied it to the hitching post, and stepped up on the porch. There seemed to be no sign of life anywhere, and he thought that perhaps they were not home.

He quietly knocked on the door and waited.

A small girl with light brown hair answered. "Hello, who are you?"

"I am Joseph Bowen," he smiled, "And who are you?"

"My name is Janice Ayers."

"Hello, Janice, is your parents' home?"

"Janice, you do not supposed to open the door to strangers," another girl said, coming up to the door.

"Hello, I am Joseph, Savannah Bell's brother."

"You mean Mrs. Bell, our teacher?"

"That's right, and who might you be?"

"I am Glenda Ayers."

"Is your parents' home, Glenda?"

"No, but my sister is. Peggy!" she called out.

An older girl come to the door and stepped in front of Janice and Glenda. "Go play, you two, I will take care of this." She looked at Joseph and smiled shyly. "How can I help you?"

For a moment, Joseph could do nothing but stare. She was the most beautiful girl he had ever laid eyes on, with her dark hair and beautiful smile. Why had Savannah not told him of her beauty?

"Excuse me," she said again. "How can I help you?"

"I am sorry, forgive me. I am Joseph Bowen, and you are?"

"My name is Peggy Ayers; can I help you with something?"

"Ah, no. I mean, yes. I mean, I am your teacher's brother. I am Savannah's brother--Mrs. Bell."

Peggy grinned. Joseph was cute, and she could tell she made him nervous but was not sure why.

"It's nice to meet you, Joseph. Mrs. Bell told the class that you and your family was moving here from Georgia."

"It is nice to meet you, too. Are your brothers and parents' home?"

"No, they rode into the village to get my brothers each a haircut and I am watching after my sisters while they are gone."

"I was just stopping by to meet everyone and say hello."

"Would you want some water? I know that is quite a ride."

"I would like that, thank you very much."

"Hang on, I will be right back." Peggy shut the door and left Joseph standing there waiting.

Within a few minutes she came back with a tin cup filled with cold water.

"I am sorry I cannot invite you inside, but I am not supposed to let someone I don't know in without my parents being here. We can sit on the front porch if you like and talk."

Joseph looked toward the wooden porch swing. "I would like that. Do you want to sit over there?"

"Okay." Peggy shut the door and walked with him to the swing.

"This is a nice swing; your father must be quite a craftsman."

"Yes, he built most of our furniture. He sells things to the mercantile also."

"Jonah is also great at building; I am looking forward to learning a lot from him. What about your sisters?"

"They are playing with the dollhouse Daddy made them for Christmas; they are okay."

"So, how long have you lived in the valley?"

"Almost seven years now."

"Do you like living here?"

"Yes, especially since Mrs. Bell became our teacher; she is wonderful."

"I agree with you; my sister truly is wonderful. Where did you live before you come to the valley?"

"We moved here from Cleveland, Georgia. My daddy wanted to settle out west."

"We just moved from Dahlonega, Georgia. We did not live too far from one another. That is really amazing."

"Are you and your family going to stay here or go back to Georgia?"

"We are going to stay here. We have a cabin right by Savannah and Jonah's. Jonah was so kind to build on to John's cabin and allow us to live there."

"That is good. He seems very nice."

"What are your brother's names, Peggy?"

"Daniel, Jerry, Powell and Ricky."

"Are you the oldest?"

"No, Daniel is the oldest, then me. I am almost fifteen. How old are you?"

"Almost eighteen."

"Do you still go to school?"

"No, not for a couple of years now."

"I will go another year or two. Momma is glad Mrs. Bell is teaching us; I think everyone in the valley is."

"She is smart; you could learn a lot from her."

"I have; she is fun to learn from. I am sorry I cannot ask you to come in. I guess my parents would not mind, knowing you are Mrs. Bell's brother."

"No, it's okay. That is a good rule to follow, not letting in anyone you don't know."

"We never have visitors anyway, unless it's the neighbors."

"Yes, you are farthest away from the village."

"My daddy goes once a month and carries the furniture he makes. And picks up supplies. Next month the girls will get to go."

"You take turns? I guess that is a good plan. So, do you have a boyfriend at school, Peggy?"

Peggy giggled. "No, I thought Josiah was cute, but Grace likes him, and she is prettier than me."

"You mean Grace Ingalls?"

"Yes, do you know her?"

"I met her earlier, yes. But Peggy, I do not think she is prettier than you."

"You don't?"

"No, I don't. In fact, I have not seen anyone yet as pretty as you."

Peggy blushed. "Thank you."

"Do you walk to and from school?"

"Yes, we all do. There is no other way to get there unless Daddy takes us with the wagon, and he says he is too busy to do that twice a day, that it doesn't hurt us to walk."

"Makes sense, I used to walk to school myself. When school starts back, would you mind if I come and walk you home from school sometime?"

"Okay, if you want to," she smiled.

"Do you ever come over and visit with Rose Bell?"

"No, we are not really close friends, although I do know her and think she is sweet. I sit in the back of the class; Mrs. Bell has us sitting by age."

"You can meet my sister in church Sunday. She is almost thirteen; she will be going to school with you also."

"Okay, I will like that. I don't have a lot of friends here in the valley, except my sisters and brothers."

"Would you care to sit with me at church on Sunday?"

"Yes, and I can introduce you to my parents."

"Okay, great, since I don't have any friends here, either."

"So, we can be friends, then. That way we cannot say that anymore," Peggy laughed.

"Yes," he chuckled. "Well, I guess I better get back home; Jonah might need my help with something. Please tell your parents I came by to meet them, and I will meet them Sunday in church."

"I will, thank you for stopping by. I enjoyed your visit." Peggy walked Joseph back to his horse.

"Likewise. Have a good day," Joseph tipped his hat.

He felt giddy as he rode back toward the Bell's farm. He knew without a doubt that he had just met the woman who would become his wife someday. He always knew she would be in Arkansas.

*****

"The roast was wonderful," Alice wiped her mouth. "I do believe it is much better than mine."

Savannah laughed. "No way, Mother."

"It really was good, Savannah, but then everything you make is good," Jonah leaned over and kissed her on her cheek.

"Mary, do you want to come in my room and talk, after I help with the dishes?" Rose started stacking the plates.

"Yes, we can do that." Mary answered.

Alice shooed them both away with her hands. "Go on, girls, I will help with the dishes. I trust that is okay, Savannah, and you are not going to run me out of your kitchen?"

"I guess not this time, but we won't make this a habit. Go on and have fun, girls." Savannah wanted her sister to become good friends with Rose, knowing it would make her like living in the valley and not miss Dahlonega as much.

"Do you want me to help you with the dishes, Momma Alice?" Catherine asked.

Savannah giggled. "Catherine, you have never done the dishes; you can't even reach the water basin."

"But I can stand on a chair, can't I, Momma Alice?"

"I tell you what," Savannah suggested, "Why don't all of you go and listen to Momma Alice read the Bible? I would love it if she does the honors tonight."

"Are you sure?" Alice hated leaving her with all the dishes.

"Yes, I am sure. You can even read from *your* old Bible; it's on the hearth."

Alice went to pick up her Bible. "Savannah, you kept it after all these years?"

"Of course, I did. You did not expect me to get rid of it, did you? It is the only thing I had that made me feel close to you."

"She reads from it every night and always has," Jonah told her. "Even when I had given up on God, she never gave up that one day I might see the light again."

Matthew took Alice's hand and led her to the rocking chair. "Come on, Momma Alice, and read it to us. I want to hear how you read it to Momma when she was a little girl."

Alice sat in the rocker and smiled. There had been way too many tears the last couple of days. She opened her Bible, ran her fingers across its pages, and began to read in Thessalonians.

"Rejoice evermore. Pray without ceasing. In everything give thanks: for this is the will of God in Christ Jesus concerning you."

Savannah sat down beside Jonah and lay her head on his shoulder. Hearing her mother read from her old Bible brought everything together. The dishes could wait.

When she was younger, and her father had been yelling and talking down to her mother all day, she would get the Bible each night and read it aloud and tell her how much she and her father loved her.

Her mother told her that her father loved her, even though he never said it himself. Never did her mother ever say an ill word against her father. She was a woman of honor and respect.

Alice Bowen was the most amazing woman that ever lived, and she was proud to call her Mother.

*****

Harvest time came to the valley. Everyone was up early and in the fields.

Savannah missed John and the way he helped. It always brought back memories during harvest time.

Mary had never been used to hard work outdoors but did not complain, and Savannah was proud of her for trying, for she wasn't about to let a six- and seven-year-old work harder than she did.

Catherine and Matthew were another year older and worked almost as hard as anyone.

"Looks like God has blessed us again this year," Savannah told her mother, bending over to pick the green beans that hung thick on the vine.

"Do you string them up and put them in the underground cellar to dry?"

"You know I do, just like you taught me."

"I'm so glad you paid attention to me while you were growing up. I am afraid I have been too easy on Mary." They both looked

196

her way and chuckled at the faces she made as she picked a bean, one at a time, very slowly.

"She may want to go back to Georgia after this, Mother."

"Nah, it's about time she learns how to live life on a farm-- won't hurt her none."

For a week they all worked and gathered vegetables during the day, and in the evenings, they would gather around and eat dinner and read the Bible. It was a hard week, but the food was plentiful, and Savannah was grateful.

*****

School was starting back, and a part of Savannah hated leaving her mother each day. She so enjoyed spending time with her and catching up.

Summer was over, and the children depended on her.

She felt bad for neglecting Jonah. Since her mother came, she hardly spent any one-on-one time with him at all.

"Do you hate me?" Savannah asked, lying in bed beside him.

"Why would I hate you? Is there a reason I should?"

"Since my mother came, I have not spent much time with you."

"I see you every day."

"Jonah, you *know* what I mean," she smiled and laid her head on his chest.

"Oh, that," he laughed. "I have tried to be patient, because I know you need this with your mother and family. I know things will get back to normal soon."

"Please forgive me. School is starting back, and I promise I will get back in a routine of being a better wife and mother."

"You could never be a better wife and mother, when you are already the best."

197

"Mother and I talked about this today. She is the one who brought it to my attention."

"I am confused."

"That if she is not over here, then I am over there, and you and the children need me to be like it was before they came. That *you* especially need me to be your wife."

"I see. Does your mother think I am not happy with the situation?"

"No, she said you were wonderful and a very patient man. But she has a plan."

"And what plan is that?"

"That we will only have dinner together on Fridays and take turns cooking. It's her turn this week."

"Savannah, I truly don't mind for you to spend time with your mother; I know how much you both have to catch up on."

"Shhhh," Savannah put her finger over his lips to quiet him and kissed him deeply. "I am missing my husband. Does he miss me as much as I miss him?"

"Oh, he misses you all right."

"Just how much does he miss me?" she smiled.

"He misses you a whole lot; in fact, he's willing to show you just how much!" Jonah pulled her closer and kissed her again.

She could hardly wait.

Chapter Seventeen

The first day back at school was going better than Savannah could have imagined.

Mary seemed to like it at the Valley School. Even though she had met the other girls already at church, Savannah knew school would be the place they would be able to grow even closer.

Savannah looked at the class, who was working quietly on their lessons and wondered what Jonah, Joseph and her mother were up to at home.

Her mother was probably about to bake something for their dinner or cookies to offer the children after school.

She might also be hard at work cutting out the new dress she promised Catherine the night before. She always lived up to her promises and would not rest until she had seen them through.

Jonah and Joseph were probably busy doing something in the barn, perhaps brushing the horses or cleaning the stables, or maybe even making another piece of furniture with the last crate.

Joseph was never far away from Jonah, always willing to help wherever needed. She wasn't sure if it was because he feared that Jonah would yell at him if he wasn't constantly working, the way their father had, or if it was that he enjoyed having an older man as a father figure who actually seem to care.

Savannah was grateful they had bonded quickly, and knowing Jonah, he would do all he could to make Joseph feel special and appreciated.

Just a few days ago Joseph had walked to the school with her alone to help her carry a few things. She remembered the talk very well.

"Are you looking forward to starting back?" he asked.

"Yes, I suppose. I have mixed emotions."

"Do you not like being a teacher?"

"Oh, sure, I love it. It is just that I am afraid Mary may not like it here as much as she did in Dahlonega, and I truly wish for her to be happy. I also hate leaving Mother there alone all day. I do not wish for her to be bored. The valley isn't as populated as Dahlonega, with neighbors coming in and out, ordering her baked goods or having her alter their clothing."

Joseph laughed. "Savannah, you worry way more than you should. Mother has never been bored a day in her life. Trust me, she will always be able to find something to do to keep her occupied. And if you let her, you would never have to cook another day; she loves it so."

Savannah nodded in agreement. "Yes, but you see, my dear brother, I am my mother's daughter, and I love it as well. What about Mary? Do you think she will like it here as much as back home?"

"I wouldn't worry about Mary; she is adjusting. I heard her tell Mother last night that she really liked Rose and couldn't wait to get to know the other girls better."

"I am so glad to hear that. I was afraid after the harvest she would change her mind about the valley."

"Did me good to see her work so hard. She was beginning to be too prim and proper," he laughed. "And that is no way to be on a farm."

"What about you, Joseph? Be honest. Is the valley all you hoped it would be?"

"All that and more. I was shocked to find you and Jonah already had a cabin for us, waiting. I was expecting to find a piece of land and help the men erect us a home. It is beautiful. And I know Mother loves it, she has never had such a nice place to call home before."

"But do *you* really like it here?"

"Of course. And remember me telling you in a letter that I would find the woman I am to marry here? And I did that in the first few days."

Savannah looked quickly at him in amazement, "Are you speaking of Peggy Ayers? I have seen you sitting by her at church."

"I do."

"Do tell me all, little brother."

"The day after we arrived, I used Jonah's horse as you suggested and went to meet everyone; do you remember that?"

"I do."

"Well, Noel and Marylou Ayers had gone to the village with the boys to get haircuts, and Peggy was there watching her little sisters."

Savannah smiled. "Peggy Ayers?"

"Of course, the one and *only* Peggy Ayers, soon to become Peggy Bowen in the next couple of years; she just doesn't know it yet."

"You are serious, aren't you, Joseph?"

"Have you ever known me not to be serious? She is beautiful, isn't she?"

"Yes, all the Ayers children are, but beauty only goes so far, Jonah; you hardly know her at all. How can you make this prediction by looking at someone?"

Jonah clucked his tongue. "I hardly believe you of all people could say this. Was it not you that told me once in a letter that you had a crush on Jonah years before he ever asked Father for your hand in marriage? Besides, I have spent the last couple of months sitting by her at church."

"Okay, you have me on that one, and yes, you are right. Just to let you know, Peggy is an amazing young lady, and I think she will make you a great wife someday, but there is only one problem."

"And what is that?"

"She has to feel the same about you in order to say yes."

"This is true; I don't have a hundred acres to offer in trade for her hand, so I will have to do this with my charm and good looks only."

Savannah laughed. "You are too funny, Joseph. So, what are your plans to win her over?"

"Oh, that's easy. I will continue to sit with her at church, and I plan to be at school at the end of each day to walk her home. That is, of course, if I am not needed on the farm for those couple of hours."

"I see. So, what do you think her parents will think about your courtship?"

"They seem to like me well enough at church, and I will win them over completely in no time. When I ask for their blessing for her hand in marriage, they will be thrilled to give it to me."

"I love your confidence, little brother, and I love you, too."

"Not as much as I love you, Sis."

Savannah smiled, thinking back, and looked toward the back of the room at Peggy, who was hard at work.

She had no doubt that, one day, Peggy Ayers would in fact become her sister-in-law.

*****

"What a wonderful idea, Savannah," Katie Anderson commented. "To have a women's committee one Saturday a month, so all of us could get together and do crafts, quilt and sew. I just absolutely love this!"

"I was so hoping you would. I am glad you all came," Savannah poured each of the women a cup of coffee and sat down at the table to pick up her crocheting.

"It amazes me that you, of all people, think of all these wonderful ideas," Marylou smiled, sewing the sleeves on a new dress for Janice. "Not that you are not smart enough to think of things, by any means, but you don't have enough hours in the day as it is, spending so much time with all our children."

Nancy laughed, "Savannah is just smart like that. So, what are you making?" She looked toward Savannah.

"I am making all of my students a new hat for Christmas. If Pastor Anderson doesn't object, I would like to place a Christmas tree in the school this year."

"Why would you think he would object?" Katie asked.

"Well, with it being a church and all."

"I don't see any harm in decorating the church," Alice jumped in, "Do you, Katie?"

"Of course not, but if it would make you feel better, I will ask him tonight and see what he thinks."

"Thank you, and that brings me to another idea I wanted to talk to each of you about, because I need your help."

"Count me in, whatever it is," said Alice. "I feel I don't help enough."

"Of course, you do, Mother."

"We are just glad to have you here with us." Nancy patted her arm, lovingly.

"I was thinking that we could have a Christmas Dance, and let the children decorate. We talked about having an annual dance before we built the church and school, and yet it's been a year now, and we have yet to do it."

"I don't think the church is big enough to have a dance in," Marylou said.

"No, I agree, but what if we have it in one of our barns? Ours has a wood heater, and it's plenty big enough, and I know Jonah wouldn't mind; in fact, if I know my husband, he will be helping us decorate."

"Savannah," Nancy screamed, "That is a wonderful idea." Do you know how long it's been since I went to a dance? Why, that would be never," she laughed. "I think the children would love it, and I know us adults would, wouldn't we?

"Count me in," Katie nodded her head. "I am sure Corbin would be thrilled also, anything to bring the community together, he is all for it."

Marylou chuckled. "Me too, and I am sure Noel would love it; he's been known to dance a jig or two every now and then."

"Who will play the music?" Nancy asked. "I don't think anyone here in the valley can play an instrument. I know Tom and I can't."

Savannah smiled, "Well, you see, ladies, I have already thought this through; I just need to get Jonah to take me into the village, so I can ask the band that plays there what they will charge to come play for us."

"Do you think they would, Savannah?" Alice could not imagine them riding so far just to play for a few people in a barn.

"They would if the money were right. I was thinking maybe we can have a fundraiser to raise the money."

"I'll pay for it," Alice quickly volunteered.

"Mother, it could be quite expensive, I am sure."

"I said I will pay for it; just find out how much they charge."

"Are you sure, Mother?"

"Of course. I had money, expecting to build a house, and found it already built. Please let me do this; I would love to."

"You are so kind to offer. What do the rest of you think?"

"That truly is kind of you," Nancy agreed. "Tell me what you want us to do, Savannah."

"Let me talk to Jonah first about the barn and then ask about the music, and I will let each of you know. We can have the dance the Saturday after school is out for Christmas break, right before Christmas. But I really do want to get the children involved as much as possible. We can start decorating a week before the dance."

"Thank you, Savannah," Katie smiled. "We are blessed to have such a creative lady who has the best ideas. It is time we did something fun. This valley would not be the same without you."

*****

Savannah was thrilled to be on her way into the village with Jonah alone. It was not very often they were able to venture off, just the two of them.

"It was nice of your mother to volunteer to take care of things until we return."

"I am just so happy Mother is there. I never dreamed she'd be close enough to babysit."

"Lucky for us," he laughed.

"I am excited to be going off for the day with you. It has been so long."

"The last time you rode into town with me, John was still alive."

"Oh, my, then it really has been a long time. Do you think we could eat at Annie's?"

Jonah smiled. "Yes, my sweet wife, you must be craving ice cream?"

"You know me well," she giggled. "Do you think the band will come play for us?"

"I guess we will just have to find out. Would you like for me to ask?"

"No, I can ask. I just hope they are playing today, as they usually are when we go into town. I am sure the mayor pays them something to play as they do."

"I am certain of it."

"Are you positive you don't mind us using the barn for the annual Christmas dance?"

"The annual?" laughed Joseph.

"Of course; this will be the very first year."

"I see."

"And just wait until I tell you the plans I have."

Joseph laughed aloud. "Do tell me all."

"I am going to have everyone bring several covered dishes and desserts. My mother will be thrilled to get involved in this."

"Yes, I can see as she would."

"And I have several games in mind to play. Oh Jonah, the barn will come to life with paper flowers and colored chains, mistletoe, and a Christmas tree."

"Sounds like you have the visual, now to just bring it to life."

"Thank you for letting us use the barn," Savannah looked at him for a moment before whispering, "You truly don't mind, right?"

"No, my sweet wife, I do not mind. What do you need me to do?"

"I was so hoping that you would ask. Could you build a stage?"

"A stage?"

"Nothing huge, just a platform that the band can stand on."

"Is that necessary?"

"But of course. Well, I mean if you do not mind. Just think of the beauty of it all," Savannah spread out her arms as if she were seeing it all right before her very eyes.

"I guess, in that case, I will do the best I can."

"Oh, thank you, Jonah," she clapped her hands together. I am just giddy with excitement."

"I guess we need to hope that the band will agree to this. Won't be much of a party without music."

"I have another plan if they decline, but I trust that it won't be needed."

"I like that. A woman with not only plan A, but plan B as well."

"Look Jonah, we are almost here," she squealed and pointed to the buildings up ahead.

"You seem like a child coming to town for the very first time. You were not this excited when we all rode in to get your family."

"Oh, I was too nervous to be excited," she laughed.

"And you are not at all nervous that you are about to walk up to those four men and ask them if they will come play for your dance?" Jonah could see the band playing in the gazebo.

Savannah clapped excitedly. "They are here! I was worried they wouldn't be."

Jonah chuckled at her and stopped the wagon close to the mercantile. "Would you like for me to go with you, at least?"

"No, thank you. You can go get your hair cut and I will go talk to them and meet you in a little bit at the mercantile. We need to get a few supplies, and I need a bit more yarn for the children's Christmas hats."

Jonah kissed her as he was lifting her off the wagon. "Sounds like a plan, pretty lady. I will see you soon."

Savannah took a deep breath and let it out slowly as she began walking toward the gazebo where the band played. Surely, they would stop long enough to speak to her if she walked close enough. Everyone took a break sometime.

Several people were standing around the gazebo, listening to the beautiful music the four men played.

The melody was amazing as the harp, the cello, the ukulele, and the violin played in perfect harmony.

Surely, these men would charge a lot to travel ten miles to play in a barn for a small crowd on the Saturday before Christmas. Savannah was determined to ask anyway.

After all, if they said no, there was always plan B.

After playing a couple more tunes, the men bowed and everyone clapped, including Savannah.

"Might I speak to you a moment?" she asked the man playing the violin, who seemed to be the one in charge.

"Yes ma'am," he nodded. "How might I help you?"

"First of all, might I say, your music is beautiful."

"Thank you, we appreciate it. We do enjoy playing."

"My name is Savannah Bell," she extended her hand.

He took her hand and smiled. "Nice to meet you, Savannah. I am Larry Tomlin, and this is my brother Bob, and our friends, Darryl Jameson and Leroy Banks."

All the men smiled and nodded at her as they placed their instruments back in their cases.

"Do you men ever play anywhere else?"

"We do. Let me guess, a wedding?"

"No, sir. I live in the valley about ten miles from here, and the community there was hoping to have a Christmas dance the Saturday before Christmas. That is, of course, if we can find someone to play the music."

Larry smiled and looked back at the other three men. "What do you say, men, would you be interested in playing for a Christmas dance?"

"Will there be any single women there as pretty as you?" Darryl grinned.

Savannah could tell he was joking, by the way he said it.

"Only my mother; I am afraid the rest are married. There is only twenty-five of us that live in the valley and most of those are children. I am the teacher there, and we were hoping to have a Christmas dance, play some games, and have a good time celebrating the birth of Jesus."

"I suppose there will be good food, also?" Bob asked.

"Yes sir, and lots of desserts. You men will be welcome to eat as much as you like. We will gladly pay you whatever you charge for your time."

Leroy closed the case on his ukulele and picked it up. "I don't know about you boys, but I am all about that dessert; what do you say?"

Larry nodded. "You say it's the Saturday before Christmas? What time were you thinking? It's a bit far to travel by night back to the village."

"You are more than welcome to stay in our barn, where the party will be. It's very warm, and we have cots to sleep you, if you want to start back the next morning. You are also more than welcome to attend church with us on Sunday before you journey home."

"Sounds like a nice offer. What do you boys think?" Larry asked.

The three men nodded their approval.

"As I said, we will pay you whatever you charge."

"I tell you what, little lady," Larry smiled. "You feed us and put us up for the night, and we will call it even. It is not every day we get asked by such a beautiful lady and get invited to church, too. These old boys need church."

All three men chuckled. "About as much as you do, Larry," his brother Bob piped in.

"Are you serious; you will come and play for nothing? You mean it's no charge?"

"Oh, there is a fee. We are trusting the food and desserts will be amazing. Since we will be staying the night, let us start around four, and it can last as long as you want it to. We will be there about three to set up and get ready to play."

Savannah shook Larry's hand again. "Thank you, sir, thank you so much. The others will be excited."

Larry nodded and smiled. "It was nice to meet you, Mrs. Bell. We look forward to it."

Savannah could not wait to get back and tell the other women they agreed to play, and for no charge. She never expected that.

There was so much planning to do--how would she get it all finished with everything else she was responsible for? But then, as Jonah said, most of it she brought on herself.

Chapter Eighteen

"Just how much do you like that boy?" Marylou asked Peggy, as they were preparing dinner.

"Are you talking about Joseph, Ma?" she asked, knowing very well who her mother was speaking of. For the last several months, they had sat together at church each Sunday, and he had walked her home from school every day since it started.

"Who else would I be speaking of, Peggy?"

"What do *you* think of him, Ma?"

Marylou laughed. "I like the way you turned the question back at me, but I asked you first."

"I like him a lot, Ma."

Marylou smiled. "I thought as much. He does seem like a very well-behaved young man. I am just concerned about his age."

"We are only three years apart. You and Pa are four years apart."

"But you have two more years of school, at least."

"They will pass by quickly. I think he really likes me, Ma. He says I am even prettier than Grace Ingalls."

"Well, there is one thing I can say about that young man; it doesn't look like he is going to give up. You are right, he really likes you."

"What does Pa say about him?"

"Your Pa doesn't care what man you choose, Peggy, as long as he is good to you and makes you happy."

"Does Pa think I am too young to have a boyfriend?"

Marylou placed the biscuits in the oven and chuckled. "I married your Pa at sixteen, so I guess he won't say much. Just be careful, Peggy; I don't want to see you get your heart broke if someone more his age comes along."

"Joseph isn't like that, Ma."

"I hope you are right."

When Peggy was finished and the table set, she left the kitchen feeling deflated. That was something she had yet to think of.

Did Joseph only like her because she was his only choice? After all, she was the oldest girl that was single in the valley. What if an older girl moved into the valley? Would he stop sitting beside her in church and walking her home from school?

Maybe that was something she would have to speak to him about tomorrow after school.

Over the past five months, they had gotten close enough that she felt she could freely talk to him and share her heart.

She knew that more settlers would be coming into the valley soon enough. Maybe it was time to find out just what his intentions were.

*****

"Bundle up, children; it's cold outside. Remember, I want you all to go home and make a list of ideas for the dance. We will start decorating in exactly two weeks. I will go over them all and consider the best ideas. Class dismissed."

Savannah glanced out the window and smiled when she saw Joseph standing there like always, waiting on Peggy, no doubt. Even the cold did not stop him.

"I didn't think you would come today." Peggy shivered, buttoning her coat all the way up.

"Why not? I haven't missed a day since I met you."

"It's just so cold today, I thought you might stay home."

Joseph shook his head. "It's the only way I get to see you. I can handle the cold."

"Thanks for coming, I enjoy you walking me home."

"Here, let me carry that for you." He took her book and her lunch pail out of her hand. "I enjoy walking you home, also."

"Thank you."

"Peggy has a boyfriend," Powell snickered, running past them both.

"Is he right, Peggy?"

"Right about what?"

"Do you consider me your boyfriend?"

"Well, you are my friend and a boy, so…"

Joseph stepped in front of her, so she would be forced to look at him. "But am I your boyfriend?"

Peggy smiled. "I like to think of you as that, yes."

"Good, I was hoping you would say that." He started walking beside her again, going as slow as possible. Joseph wanted to stretch the three miles out as much as he could. Just being near her was his favorite time of the day.

"Do you think of me as your girlfriend?"

"I do. May I hold your hand?" He took her gloved hand in his and saw her blush.

"Can I ask you something, Joseph?" She had been pondering the question since last night at dinner and just how she would ask him.

"Sure, you can ask me anything."

"I know there is not a lot of girls in the valley, and I am the oldest. What if Grace was older than me, or maybe Elisa? Would that make a difference?"

"You think I only like you because you are the oldest?"

Peggy shrugged.

"I knew from the moment I laid eyes on you that you were the most beautiful girl in the valley. In fact, you are the most beautiful girl I have ever laid eyes on. Your age had nothing to do with it. If you were only twelve, I would still wait on you as long as it took for you to get old enough to marry me."

"Marry you?" Peggy was taken aback.

"Yes. I am going to marry you someday, Peggy, for I cannot imagine my life with anyone else."

"But you have only known me a few months."

"I didn't need a few months to know that," he squeezed her hand tighter.

"But you haven't even kissed me yet." Peggy stopped in her tracks. What did she just say? Oh, how she wished she could take it back.

Joseph smiled and took her face in his hands. "You are only fifteen, and I don't desire for your Pa to come after me with his rifle."

"I shouldn't have said that," she blushed again.

Joseph kissed her lightly on the lips and pulled away with a smile. "One day, Peggy, I will take you in my arms and kiss you the way I want to, but for now, I will respect your age and hold your hand."

Peggy walked the rest of the way home, not remembering much after that. There was one thing she knew for sure--when the day came and he asked her to be his wife, her answer would be yes.

*****

"I thought I would find you out here," Joseph entered the barn, finding Jonah hard at work. "What are you building?"

"Your sweet sister asked me to build a stage for the dance."

"A stage? Can they not just stand on the ground and perform?"

"Now, that is a question you need to ask your sister. She is as beautiful as the sunrise in the mornings and loves me more than I deserve, but I still can't figure her out sometimes."

Joseph laughed. "Do you need some help?"

"Nah, I got two more weeks; it gives me something to do while it's cold outside."

"What if it snows and the dance has to be cancelled?"

"I don't think your sister has thought about that, but if she has, I am sure she has another plan B."

"Jonah, when did you know you loved your first wife?"

"Clara? Why do you ask?"

"Is it possible to know you are in love at first glance? I mean, to know just by meeting someone that it is the person you want to spend your life with?"

"Peggy Ayers, am I right?"

"Yes, I just wish she were old enough now to marry me."

"Whoa, slow down Joseph; you have plenty of time."

"Two years seems like an eternity."

Jonah nodded his head. "I understand, and yes, I knew the moment I laid eyes on Clara that she would be my wife; there was not a doubt in my mind."

"Yet, it took you a while to know you loved my sister?"

"That was only because my heart still belonged to Clara. If I had met your sister first, there is no doubt, I would have loved her the same way--instantly."

"I kissed her today."

"And how did she respond?"

"Well, it wasn't a real kiss--just a peck on the lips, really. I wanted to kiss her for real, but I know it's too soon, and if I can't pull her in my arms right now, it's better just to wait, right?"

215

Jonah put down his hammer and sat down on the edge of the platform he was building, motioning for Joseph to take a seat.

"Son, I understand how you feel. Hormones can be the devil at times, and yes, it is better to wait a bit. You shall know when the time is right to ask her to be your wife, and everything will fall into place."

"I've never felt this way over anyone before."

"And you are sure she is the one?"

"Without a doubt. I have been looking at the land from the school to her home, and I would like to build a cabin there someday. There's not much farming land around it, but I was thinking if you would let me continue to help you, then maybe we can plant the other field to the left of Mother's cabin and there would be enough for all of us and plenty also for you still to sell at the market. I am a good hunter, too, and I could sell the skins for extra money, or trade for supplies."

"I'd say that is a good idea, and yes, there is plenty enough room here for you to plant and to help me. I could use the help; I am not growing any younger."

"Thank you, Jonah. I wasn't sure how you would feel about that."

"When the time comes to build your cabin, I'd also be happy to help you. You could start off with something small, the way Savannah and I did, and build on as your family grows."

"Thank you. You are an exceptionally good builder, and I will appreciate the help. I know I could learn a lot from you."

"Noel Ayers is also a great carpenter, and I am sure when the time comes and you ask for his daughter's hand in marriage, he will be glad to lend a hand. I am sure he will be happy you want to build so close to them."

"Two years is a long time, but she is worth the wait."

*****

"I cannot believe the band wanted no pay for their time and travel." Nancy took the coffee from Savannah's hand and sat down at the table to continue her sewing.

"It was truly God, I tell you. He is smiling down upon us with His favor. Would any of you other ladies like a cup of coffee?"

"I will take one, Savannah," Marylou smiled.

Katie raised her cup, "Might as well give me a refill."

Alice put down her sewing and took the paper and pen beside her and started to make a list. "Let's talk about who is going to do what, so we don't all end up bringing the same thing."

Savannah laughed. "I see who I took after, Mother; I am also a list maker. That is a very good idea. I will be terribly busy with the children doing the decorating, but I will furnish the milk, coffee and lemonade, if that is okay with everyone?"

Alice wrote it down on the list. "And I will bake three cakes, a couple of cobblers and cookies. Oh, and I will also make fried pies; everyone seems to like that."

"Sounds good," Nancy commented. "I shall make lots of fried chicken; we need to thin our chickens out a bit, so I should have plenty. I will also do mashed potatoes and leather britches with cornbread."

"How does cornbread dressing sound with gravy?" Marylou asked. "And also, biscuits. We must have biscuits, and I will bring plenty of homemade jelly and apple butter.

"Sounds good," answered Katie. "So, what should I bring?"

Savannah thought back to when they built the church. "Bring several of those wonderful sweet potato pies that you are famous for, and your barbeque pork chops were wonderful."

"Corbin just butchered three of our hogs, so there will be plenty of that."

"Remember, ladies, we will be feeding twenty-nine people, so be sure to make enough. I am sure the band will eat enough to pay their wages."

"Do you need any help decorating?" Alice offered.

"Not from any of you. You will each have enough cooking to do to keep you busy. The children, Joseph, and Jonah will help me with the decorating."

"And what if it snows?" asked Nancy.

"Oh, do not even voice that," giggled Savannah. "It is not going to snow; we must pray that God holds off until *after* the party. I am so excited about this, and believe it or not, your children have turned in some really good ideas. Tomorrow we will discuss them in class and make plans on what comes next to our first annual Christmas party."

Katie shook her head and chuckled. "First annual--I like the sound of that. We could not have picked a better teacher for the Valley School. You amaze me, Mrs. Bell."

"Now, now, call me Savannah when the children are not around. I happen to be younger than all of you."

"Yes, younger and smarter," added Alice. "It runs in the family."

All the women laughed.

It pleased Savannah to see her mother joking and happy once again.

She knew the rest of her life would be the best of her life.

*****

"I have spent the weekend going over all the ideas you submitted for our first annual Christmas dance, and I must say that I am overly impressed with your ideas. Keep in mind, though, that we cannot use them all, but I did pick the ones that I thought would be a good fit and work well together."

Catherine raised her hand.

"Yes, Catherine?"

"I don't know how to dance."

Savannah smiled. Leave it to her daughter to totally change the subject.

"Catherine, it doesn't matter whether you know how to dance or not. It is a Christmas party to celebrate the birth of Christ. We will have fun and play games and eat lots of great food. Whether you decide to dance or not makes no difference."

"Okay," Catherine pouted.

"Now, back to what I was saying. Nathaniel, Daniel, and Josiah, I am going to leave it up to you three to pick us out a Christmas tree and bring it to our barn. The tree was a great idea, Josiah, and you will need Daniel and Nathaniel to help you with that."

"When do you need it there?" he asked.

"We will all meet in the barn tomorrow and spend the rest of the week getting ready for the dance. You can bring it to the barn whenever you all have picked one out and cut it down."

"Yes, ma'am."

"Mary and Rose, you girls oversee bringing the greenery into the barn. There is still greenery all throughout the valley with holly bushes and such. Gather and bring as much as possible. You can discuss where you will meet in the morning, as well as you boys for the tree, and Rose, the greenery was a great idea."

Rose smiled and nodded her head.

"Glenda, your mother told me she has been making extra candles and has many to share. Please do not forget to bring them to the barn with you in the morning. It was a great idea, Glenda, and I think the candles lit everywhere is going to be so beautiful and make the barn look like Christmas time."

"What time should I be there, Mrs. Bell?"

"Nine o'clock, just as if you were coming to school."

"Yes, ma'am."

"Elisa and Grace, your mothers both told me they have many quilts that are stored away that have Christmas colors. Please gather all you can find and bring them to the barn in the morning. We will take very good care of them. Grace, what an excellent idea about the quilts; that will be a nice added touch."

"Jerry and Powell, please fix as much popcorn tonight as possible. I am sending extra popcorn with you so you should have plenty, and try not to eat it," she giggled, "for I know it will be tempting, but we shall need as much of it as we can get. We shall be stringing it this week to decorate with. You can carry it in an empty flour sack; Mrs. Ayers told me she has plenty."

"Do you want us to string it at home?" Jerry asked.

"No, we shall all work on that in the barn."

"Yes, ma'am."

"Powell, that was a great idea, by the way."

Powell smiled and sat up straight, proud his idea was chosen.

"If I did not call your name, please do not think you shall have nothing to do, as we are making ornaments and paper chains and flowers for the tree, and everyone will stay very busy and have a job to do. I expect the ones that do not have to gather something from the woods tomorrow to be here by nine, and the ones that do, to do it as quickly as possible, then come as soon as you can.

"It's going to be a fun, remarkably busy week. We must be finished by the time we leave Thursday, because there is no school Friday, and the dance is Saturday. That gives us just three full days to finish."

"I didn't get anything to do," Catherine pouted, crossing her arms.

"Catherine, did you not pay attention to what I just said? You shall *all* have plenty to do, including you. Now stop pouting, or I shall leave you in the house tomorrow working on paper chains alone."

"Yes ma'am."

"As always, children, bundle up and I shall see you all in the morning. Class dismissed."

"Mary and Rose, I want you both to walk on with Matthew. Catherine and I shall be right behind you; I would like to speak to her a moment alone."

"Okay," Rose nodded. "Matthew, get on your coat and let's go."

"Am I in trouble?" Catherine asked, the moment everyone left the school.

"I am very disappointed in you, Catherine."

"But why, Momma? What did I do?"

"You speak without raising your hand and pout for no reason. You also do the same thing at home."

"Am I supposed to raise my hand at home?" She was confused.

"No, I mean you pout and complain and always try to be better than your brother. Do you have any idea how much your Pa and I love you?"

Catherine started to cry, and Savannah sat down beside her and pulled her close.

"I don't want to disappoint you; I can't help it if I forget to raise my hand."

"Catherine, your Pa and I think you are such a special, beautiful girl, and we love you very much. We love you just the way you are. You do not have to compete or be better than anyone to earn our love. But when you are at school, you must follow the rules as everyone else does."

"I am sorry; I just wanted something special to do. You didn't like my idea, did you, Momma?"

Savannah chuckled. "It was a wonderful idea having everyone in the village a present under the tree, but the truth is, I already have every student a gift that will be under the tree."

"Really? So, you did like my idea?"

"I did. Maybe you can help me place each gift in a bag and decorate it for me."

"I would like that. Why didn't you tell the class you liked my idea?"

"As I said, there is no competition. Do you know that Jesus loves it when we do something for others, and we never tell a soul that we did it?"

"Really? Then how will anyone know we did it?"

"We know, the person we help knows, and Jesus knows. No one else must know, Catherine. It's called boasting and boasting isn't a good thing."

"I guess I boast a lot, huh, Momma?"

Savannah smiled and hugged her again. "Yes, little missy, you do boast an awful lot, but today is a new day, and you can always start out fresh from today on."

"Okay, Momma, I will try my best not to boast, but I know that it won't be easy."

Savannah ruffled her hair. "Just take one day at a time. Now let us get home and cook dinner."

Chapter Nineteen

The next three days were bustling with activity. Savannah kept the barn doors closed and the heater going so the children would stay warm.

Jonah and Joseph were the only adults Savannah allowed in the barn to help. She wanted it to be a surprise to the rest of the community. Besides, she knew the women were busy baking and cooking.

"It's beautiful, Mrs. Bell," Mary said, standing beside her, admiring the barn and all the hard work from everyone.

Savannah put her arm around her sister and gave her a side hug. "Remember, it's okay to call me Savannah when all the other children have gone home."

"Just habit, I guess. Mother is going to be so surprised."

"As well as all the other adults. So, do you see anything we have missed?"

"What about the top of the tree, Momma? It needs something," Rose stated.

"Do you remember the paper angel Mother had on top of the tree back in Dahlonega?" Savannah asked Mary.

Mary smiled, "I do. Do you think we can make another one?"

"I am sure of it. Let us girls get together tomorrow and make one. I think I have some white cloth left over from the tablecloths we made."

"I am tired, Momma. Can I go to the house?" Catherine whined.

The other children had been gone a couple of hours, and Savannah was still trying to do the finishing touches.

"Yes, you may, and Matthew, you can go with her. Tell Momma Alice that we will all be in shortly; she is making us all stew tonight."

Matthew and Catherine took off out of the barn to find Momma Alice.

"I guess I worked them too hard," Savannah laughed.

"So how does it look?" Jonah called out at the other end of the barn, referring to the stage he and Jonah had been working on.

"It is wonderful, Jonah. You and Joseph have done a fantastic job with it."

"It was mostly Jonah, "Joseph commented. "I've only helped today."

"I would have been finished days ago, had my sweet wife not had me doing other things also." Jonah winked, making Savannah laugh.

"Yes, but the tables you constructed look wonderful, you have to admit. Everything looks wonderful; there is no way we could have done this without you and Joseph. And just think, next year at the second annual Christmas party, you will not have to work so hard, because everything is already built."

Jonah rubbed his head, "And just what am I supposed to do with a stage and two long tables until then?"

"You can put your feed and hay on the stage and tools on the tables, silly man. Have no fear, I know you can use them, and next year we will just clean them off again."

"You seem to have this all figured out." Jonah loved the way anything Savannah touched was beautiful, as if she were magic.

"Well, one of us has to," she joked. "Let's call it a day and go have some of Mother's stew and cornbread."

"Sounds delicious."

*****

"Oh, Savannah, it's beautiful," Mary gasped, after Savannah sewed the finishing touch on the angel they would use for their tree topper.

"It really is, Momma." I am glad I noticed that something was missing from the tree."

"Me too, Rose, I would have never noticed until it was too late to do something about it. You are a very smart young lady."

"You are the one that is smart, sending Catherine to Momma Alice's house to keep her occupied so we could make the angel."

"I have been known to be smart from time to time," winked Savannah. "What ever happened to the angel Mother made?" she asked Mary.

"She fell apart after all the years of using her, and Mother threw it away a couple Christmases ago, saying she was going to make a new one, but she never got around to it."

"I remember that angel well, it was one of my favorite things about Christmas. I am glad you are with us in Arkansas this year, Mary."

"Me too."

Savannah looked at her and smiled. "Do you really mean that? I was afraid you wouldn't like it here."

"At first, I did not know what to expect, and I knew I would miss Chrissy so much, but after meeting Rose and the other girls, I love it here. And our home is beautiful, and I love my room."

"I am so glad, Mary. I knew you would love Rose, but I was afraid you would miss home and your friends there too much."

225

"I only had one good friend, and we are writing. I have many good friends here. And most of all, I love having you as a teacher."

Savannah chuckled. "Now, that is a great compliment. I love being your teacher, to all of you." She pulled both girls close in a group hug.

"What do you say we go to the barn and have Joseph place our angel on top of the tree?"

*****

"I suspected you'd be like this," Jonah laughed, watching Savannah rush around the kitchen trying to finish the things she needed to do, so she could clean up and concentrate on the night ahead.

"Like what?"

"You know, like what. You have been going like a crazy woman again since daylight. The same way you acted the day we rode into town and picked up your family."

"Oh Jonah, what if the band doesn't show up? It has been a couple of weeks since I spoke to them. What if they changed their mind, or just forgot?"

"You worry way more than you should for things you have no need to worry about."

"You didn't answer my question--what if they don't show up?"

Jonah took her by the shoulders and forced her to sit down. "Take a breath and let it out slow."

"Jonah, this is not funny at all."

"I wasn't being funny, my sweet wife. You and so many others have worked very hard, and tonight is going to be amazing. What is the worst thing that can happen?"

"We have to shift to plan B."

"And *what* exactly was plan B?"

"That we have the party with *no* music."

Jonah laughed. "See, then everything is going to be okay. We are going to have a Christmas party with or without music."

Savannah stood and kissed him. "Yes, we certainly are. Thank you for making me breathe."

*****

"They are here!" Matthew called out, running into the barn where Savannah was placing the lemonade on one of the long tables.

"Who is here, Matthew?"

"The four men from town that play music."

Savannah ran out the door to greet them. "Hello," she called out. "Over here!"

"Told you they would show up," Jonah commented, coming up behind her.

"You are right once again; whatever would I do without you? They are right on time, too. It's three o'clock."

"Hello, ma'am, we made it," Larry jumped off the wagon and shook Jonah's hand. "Larry Tomlin here, and this is my brother Bob and our friends, Leroy Banks and Darryl Jameson."

"Nice to meet you all," Jonah nodded. "Do you men need some help unloading?"

"No thank you, we can manage. Where would you like for us to set up?"

Jonah and Savannah led the men in the barn and Larry whistled, "Man oh, man, this is the place right here. Mrs. Bell, you have outdone yourself."

"It wasn't just me; I had a whole classroom of children and a couple of adults that helped also. My husband Jonah built a stage. You can set up over there."

"A stage?" Bob seemed shocked. "How many people did you say would be here?"

"Twenty-nine counting you four, and many are children who are very excited about hearing music and dancing," Savannah answered.

"Then we will do the best we can, Mrs. Bell. We thank you for inviting us to come. Come on, boys, and let us get set up."

Savannah looked at Jonah and smiled, watching the men set up their instruments.

It was all coming together, her dream of having a Christmas dance complete with a band, and everyone had worked so hard to see it come to life.

Just one more hour and she would light the candles. Right now, it was time to go get ready.

*****

"May I have this dance?" Jonah asked, holding out his hand to Savannah, who had been busy running around making sure everyone else was waited on and happy.

"I have never danced before, actually," she smiled.

"Nothing to it, just follow my lead. If we do not start this thing, no one is going to dance."

"Maybe you are right." Savannah followed him to the middle of the barn as the music played and he took her in his arms.

"Have I told you lately how beautiful you are, my sweet wife?"

"Not today," she giggled.

"Then you are more beautiful today than you were yesterday. I am so proud of you. This place looks amazing, and it was all *your* imagination come to life."

"Thank you, and thank you for building the stage. I know you have other things you could have been doing besides helping me set up for a dance."

"It was no bother. I would do anything for you; you should know that by now."

"All this hard work, and come Monday, we will have to tear it all down."

"Yes, and next year make it beautiful all over again, but that is life."

Savannah smiled, "Yes, that is life."

"See, I told you that we had to start this thing. Looks like the others have followed our lead."

Tom and Nancy were now slow dancing, along with Corbin and Katie, and a few of the younger children were laughing and starting to join in.

"Can I have this dance?" Joseph smiled at Peggy, who was standing beside her mother, Marylou. Peggy looked at her mother for a moment, knowing she had never danced in her life.

"Well, go on, Peggy, don't keep the boy waiting," Marylou pushed her toward him, and reached back to take Noel's hand. "Well, don't just stand there, let's dance."

Peggy followed Joseph to the edge of the dance floor.

He pulled her closer and started to sway back and forth. "I am afraid I have never done this before, but I don't think anyone is paying much attention to us. It looks like they are each in a world of their own."

"Me, either. Thank you for asking me."

"There's no one else I'd want to dance with. I want you to know that I think you are beautiful tonight, Peggy."

"I made me a new dress. I wasn't sure what was appropriate for a Christmas dance."

"You are an exceptionally good seamstress. It's incredibly beautiful, just like you."

"Thank you. You look good yourself."

"Mother made me a new shirt. She said I wasn't about to wear any of my old ones to the dance," he laughed.

"Your mother is sweet. She reminds me a lot of Mrs. Bell."

"Thank you, they are quite the pair when they get together. I am so glad they were able to reunite."

"It was nice getting to work with you the past few days, decorating the barn."

Joseph nodded, "It was. I think my sister had something to do with that; I mean, me being allowed to stay and help and all. She knows we don't get a lot of time together."

"Mrs. Bell is awesome; I am so glad she is our teacher."

"So, tell me, do you like me as much as you do Josiah?"

"Josiah?" Peggy was confused.

"The first day I met you, I asked you if you had a boyfriend and you said you thought Josiah was cute, but your friend Grace liked him."

Peggy giggled. "You remembered that?"

"Never forgot it, not for a second." He looked Josiah's way, who was in the corner talking to Grace.

"Yes, I like you a lot more than I do Josiah. In fact, I forgot all about Josiah the moment you stepped off my porch."

"I like hearing that. In fact, that just made my day."

"It's true. These past few months have been wonderful, getting to know you."

"For me too, Peggy."

"May I have your attention please?" Pastor Anderson called out when the music stopped. "We are about to eat, along with the band. They deserve a break," he laughed. "Let us pray over the food.

"Father, we come here tonight to celebrate Your birth. And what could be more appropriate than to celebrate it in a barn, as you were born in a stable. Father, bless everyone here, for they have worked so hard to make this beautiful that we all might enjoy. Bless this band for the distance they have come to entertain us. Bless this food and let it nourish our bodies and bless the hands that prepared it. In Jesus' name we pray, Amen"

For the next hour, everyone ate and swapped stories around the table. After they had their fill, the band picked up the pace and played a few faster tunes. Savannah loved hearing the instruments together, especially the violin; she was sure it was her favorite.

The children loved laughing and dancing and bobbing for apples. Even Catherine was dressed and at her best tonight.

"Looks like my daughter is smitten over your brother," Marylou whispered in Savannah's ear, watching them dance. They had been inseparable since it started.

"Trust me, Marylou, he has it just as bad for her."

"Yes, I can see that. He is a good boy, your brother."

"Yes, ma'am, he certainly is."

"She looks at him as I used to look at Noel. If my calculations are right, it won't be too long, and we shall be planning a wedding instead of a Christmas dance."

Savannah shook her head and agreed. "Looks like you might be right."

"You did a fine job, Mrs. Bell," Pastor Corbin walked up. "Don't recall ever seeing a barn dressed up this nice in all my life."

"I agree," said Katie, who was standing behind him. "I know the children helped, but it was under your guidance. Simply beautiful."

"Thank you both, and thank you for all the cooking you have done. Your sweet potato pies are amazing."

231

"Katie and I wanted to say goodnight; it's getting late and church comes early. We thank you again for all your hard work. Will I see you all at church in the morning?" He looked at Marylou as well as Savannah.

"We will be there," Marylou answered.

"Yes, and guess who else is coming? The band plans to spend the night and come to church with us in the morning, before they head back to the village."

"Savannah, that is wonderful news, thank you for inviting them. Well, goodnight," he nodded.

"Are the Andersons leaving?" Nancy asked. "I had no idea it had gotten so late; the band must be exhausted."

"Yes, I can imagine they are. It has been such a wonderful night," exclaimed Savannah. "I guess all good things must end, and Pastor Anderson is right; church comes early."

*****

Jonah entered the barn, where the band was sleeping on cots. "Savannah sent me to bring you all to the house for breakfast."

"After all I ate last night, I am not sure I could eat another bite," Larry rubbed his belly.

"She got up early and made fresh biscuits, eggs and tenderloin, and of course, there's a fresh pot of coffee and flap jacks with molasses."

"You don't have to convince me; I can always hold food like that," Leroy laughed and headed out of the barn toward the house.

"Might as well come with us," Jonah encouraged the other men. "If you know my wife, she will not be satisfied until you have had a bite of something."

Bob laughed, "Yes, I imagine so. You are a lucky man, Mr. Bell."

"I couldn't agree with you more."

*****

"It is a pleasure seeing the church so full this morning, especially after the wonderful time we all had last night," Pastor Anderson said. "I was afraid some of you might still be in bed."

Everyone chuckled around the room.

"Since this is the last Sunday before Christmas, I wanted to share with you all the Christmas story of Jesus' birth. I will be reading from Luke, Chapter 2:1-7, if you want to follow along in your Bibles.

"And it came to pass in those days, that there went out a decree from Caesar Augustus, that all the world should be taxed.

(And this taxing was first made when Cyrenius was governor of Syria.)

And all went to be taxed, everyone into his own city.

And Joseph also went up from Galilee, out of the city of Nazareth, into Judaea, unto the city of David, which is called Beth-lehem; (because he was of the house and lineage of David:)

To be taxed with Mary his espoused wife, being great with child.

And so it was, that, while they were there, the days were accomplished that she should be delivered.

And she brought forth her firstborn son, and wrapped him in swaddling clothes, and laid him in a manger; because there was no room for them in the inn.

Pastor Anderson closed his Bible and walked in front of the altar.

"Now, some believe that it wasn't actually a stable that He was born in, but a room on the lower level of a home where they

233

placed their animals to sleep. You see, back in that time, a home had two levels. The top level was where everyone slept and they had their guest room, but because of the census taking place, all the guest rooms were full.

"The lower level was where they housed their animals, and a manger was a trough or long open box that they fed the animals from.

"Some believe he was born in the spring or in autumn, and not in the winter at all.

"But whether He was born in a relative's home on the lower level, or in a stable, whether he was born in the spring, autumn or winter, He was born of a virgin.

"He was God, sent down in the flesh, to live and die for each of us. The Messiah, who lived and walked among us, and lived a perfect life. He bore our stripes and took on our sin, so that we might be forgiven and have eternal life.

"He rose again in just three days, and now lives inside each of us that believe, with His Holy Spirit.

"And even though Christmas is a time of gift-giving and celebrations and candy canes and presents, it is a time to look back at our Savior and thank Him for coming to this earth to die, so we could live."

Alice Bowen looked around the church and smiled. It did her heart good to see how happy her Joseph was sitting beside Peggy, and Mary beside Rose.

Being in the presence of her family gave her joy, especially being with them in the Lord's house.

Thank you, Lord, that you placed it on Joseph's heart to keep on at me until I obeyed and brought us all out west. I know this is the happiest I have felt in many years.

She opened the hymnal and started singing along to Amazing Grace.

Chapter Twenty

"It's coming down pretty hard out there," Jonah announced, coming in the front door, and shaking the snow from his coat.

Savannah rushed to the window to look out. "I was so hoping it wouldn't start; I had a great lesson planned today that the children would love."

"I'm sorry, but you said if it was snowing hard, to stay inside, and you must take your own advice. Who knows how long this will last? And with the blizzard-like conditions, a person could get turned around easy out there."

"But Pa, I left my slingshot at school yesterday," Matthew pulled over a chair to stand in so he could look out the window better.

"Sorry, son, you can get it when you go back to school in a few days. I have a feeling it's going to take a while for this to stop."

"But it's not that bad yet, Pa."

"It's bad enough, now get down and run and play in your room. I don't want anyone leaving the house until the snow and hard winds have stopped."

"Can we go play in it, Pa? I want to build a snowman," Catherine begged, jumping up and down.

"Do as your Pa says," Savannah pointed, "Go to your room and play with your dollhouse; no one is going anywhere today."

Jonah pulled her close and hugged her. "I know you are as disappointed as the children that you can't go to school today."

She laughed and pursed her lips, pretending to be Catherine. "Yes, you know me well."

"Well, I am not disappointed," piped in Rose. "I am going to bake cookies and a pie for dinner tonight. Do you think Mary can come over and spend time with us?"

"I am going out now to string a rope from our cabin to theirs and tell her there is no school this morning. I will ask her if she wants to come back with me."

"Why don't you just ask them all to come over and we can be snowed in together? Tell Mother to bring her sewing, and we will make the most of our time." Savannah kissed Jonah on the lips and winked. "And don't get lost out there; I would hate to have to come and find you."

*****

"I know you are disappointed about school being out today, Savannah, but I am loving this time together--you and I sewing by the fire and Mary and Rose baking pies in the kitchen, the children playing in their rooms, and Jonah and Joseph doing whatever it is they do in the barn," Alice laughed.

"Yes, you are right, Mother, this really is wonderful. I am glad you all decided to come wait out the snow with us."

"We will find our way back to the cabin before bedtime. The rope Jonah hung will guide us home."

"You are all welcome to camp out with us, Mother. It will be fun. We can make popcorn and you can read to us from your old Bible."

"Let's do, Mother, I would love to spend the night," Mary called from the kitchen.

"In that case, how can I refuse? So, what is on the menu for dinner? Would you like for me to cook for everyone tonight?"

Savannah smiled, remembering back when she was a little girl and it snowed in Dahlonega, Georgia. "Do you remember what you always cooked us when it snowed?"

"Mush, I called it, and you all loved it."

"Yes, mush, made from corn meal and it tasted so wonderful with cold milk poured on top."

"I can do that; it will be good on this cold day."

"What are you making now, Mother?"

Alice pulled the thread through and broke it off using her teeth before tying it in a knot. "I promised Catherine another dress, and I am also making a matching one for her doll."

"Oh Mother, between you and Nancy, that child has more dresses than all of us put together."

"And what is the harm in that?" Alice grinned. "Do you remember the blue dress I made you just before you left with Jonah to come out west?"

"Of course, I do. How could I ever forget it? It was the dress I wore when I married him."

"I wish I had of had more time to make you a few more things before you left, but there just wasn't enough time."

"I understand, Mother, and thankfully you taught me to sew, so I was able to make my own dresses. I wore that dress until I wore it out and used the good parts of the material in a quilt I made for our bed; that way I could always keep the memories."

"Now that the girls have gone to Rose's room, I can speak freely. There is something I have been wanting to speak to you about since we arrived and never had the chance until now."

"Then talk to me, Mother."

"Did you ever resent me for not standing up to your father?"

"About what? I am not sure which time you are speaking of."

Alice chuckled. "Just as I thought. Joseph always told me how he felt about him, but you have never said a word."

"It wasn't my place to disrespect Father."

"He was hard on you, wasn't he?"

Savannah looked up from her sewing and smiled. How would she speak freely and not disrespect him? How could she tell her mother how she never once felt loved from him?

"I am sure Father was raised in a time when things were even harder than it was for us, and he was just trying to prepare us for when we were grown and had to do it on our own."

"Savannah, you know what I am talking about. I wasn't deaf and blind. I knew he was hard on you and your brother."

"Yes, Mother, Father was hard on us. Perhaps that is the way his father also treated him, and he knew of nothing else."

"I met your father back in 1810. There wasn't much in Dahlonega back then, certainly no single men, and the boys at school were very immature."

"You never told me how you met him, please go on."

"Your father lived a few farms over and worked extremely hard. I cannot ever remember him attending school. He was a few years older than me, so maybe he did."

"Did your family know his family?"

"I suppose; I cannot remember that. I was just sixteen when I met him at a church social. I remember he was so handsome and older than the other boys, and I was smitten."

"But you didn't get married right away?"

"It was two years later. Oh, he wanted me to marry him sooner, but my Ma and Pa didn't like him, and I wanted to respect their wishes."

"So, what made you marry him?"

"I was eighteen, and he talked me into running off and getting married. I will never forget the look on my Pa and Ma's face when they found out. I always hated I hurt them so."

"But you were eighteen; it looks like they would have wanted you to get married and have a family of your own."

"They did, just not to your father. They didn't like the way he treated me, and my ma said I would live in a life of misery if I married him, but I was in love and I thought that perhaps he would change after we got married."

"And did you live in misery?"

Alice looked toward the fire in deep thought, so many memories flooding her mind. How could she explain it to her daughter?

"Savannah, you need to understand that I was raised to respect your father, just as my Ma respected mine."

"But Grandpa was good to Grandma, right?"

Alice smiled. "He was. I do believe I had the absolute best father a girl could possibly have. Jonah is so much like him; in the way he treats the children and you. It reminds me so much of my father."

"Did you live in misery?"

Alice closed her eyes to fight back the tears. "You have no idea during that first four years how many times I wished I had listened to my pa and ma. He never once laid a hand on me, and for that I was grateful, but his cruel words cut me to the bone."

"So only the first four years?"

"You were born four years after we were married, and you were my heart. I loved you so much that I tried not to dwell on Mitchell. I cooked for him and cleaned and pleased him as a wife, but it was never as you and Jonah are. I am glad you are happy, and you don't have to go through what I did."

Savannah smiled and reached over and placed her hand on her mother's arm. "It's good to talk about it, Mother. It is good to get it out. Father can no longer hurt you."

"But did you ever resent me for not standing up to him?"

"You were the absolute best mother; you still are. I never once resented you; I only felt bad for you, and I always thought that was the way a marriage was supposed to be. I found out, though, that it is not. There is a lot of good men in this world, and Jonah is one of them."

"Yes, he is. One of the best, and for that I thank God. I was so afraid, the morning you left, that he would mistreat you after he got you away from us. I prayed to God to go with you and protect you, and for you not to hate me for what I allowed Mitchell to do."

"I've had an incredibly good life, Mother. I never once hated you. I always knew you had nothing to do with it, that it was all Father's doing, and because it was Jonah, I did not hate him either. I hated leaving you and Joseph and Mary behind, but I was thrilled to be Rose's mother and Jonah's wife."

"I am so glad. So many years we have had to be apart."

"Yes, much too many, but we must not look back and think about the past. You are only forty-nine years old, Mother. You are still a very beautiful young woman, and I pray someday a man comes to the valley that sweeps you off your feet. A man that will cherish you and love you the way you deserve."

Alice laughed. "I am not beautiful and hardly a young woman."

"I beg your pardon. Of course, you are."

She rocked back in her rocking chair and chuckled. "I cannot imagine it, and I am not sure I would want to start over. I honestly love the way things are now. I love being here with you and the grandchildren. As much as I thought I did not want to leave Dahlonega and the memories, I realize they were mostly not good ones."

"I am so sorry, Mother. I'm sorry you lost Grandpa and Grandma at an early age, but because of that, you really have no other family in Dahlonega."

"You are right; my family was out here in Arkansas."

Savannah chuckled, "And Joseph was not about to give up."

"No, he never did. He told me every day since you left that one day he would get on his horse and ride to Arkansas. Then when your father passed, he started begging Mary and I to come, too. I guess I should have come sooner; I hope you don't feel that I loved you less because I didn't."

"Of course not. I knew you had your own business of baking and sewing, and you wanted Mary in school. I understood, and still do."

"Mary loves it here, and I was afraid she wouldn't. She did not want to come."

"I know, but I knew that once she met Rose and the other girls in the valley that she would be okay. You have done good by her, Mother; she is a very respectful young lady."

"Thank you. I am afraid I was a bit too easy on her. Lucky for her that she was only six when your father died, so she does not remember that much about him. He never paid her much attention; it was Joseph he was always after."

"Yes, Joseph and I have spoken. I hate that he endured that, but he seems incredibly happy now."

"Oh, yes, he is. I am glad he has Jonah to be a father figure in his life, and a very good one at that."

"And he has fallen hard for Peggy Ayers. Did you see how they acted at the dance? Marylou seems to think we will be decorating for a wedding one day."

Alice grinned, "Oh yes, he has it for her badly. And she is right, he swears that one day he will marry her."

"So, he told you that as well?"

"Not long after he met her. If there is one thing I know about your brother, when he truly wants something, he doesn't give up."

Savannah nodded and laughed, "You are right about that. He has grown into such a fine-looking young man. I think he and Peggy make an adorable couple."

"He looks just like your father. Your father might not have been the best father or husband, but he was a nice-looking man, or at least I always thought so."

"Yes, he was. I am glad, though, that he acts like you. Joseph has your kind ways. I am also glad you are opening up about Father. I've never heard you say one cross word about him."

"I never once talked back to him when he was alive. So many times I wanted to, especially when he traded your hand in marriage for land, of all things. But when I told you that you were leaving and you seemed more concerned about taking care of Rose than becoming Jonah's wife, I knew that a part of you was excited about the journey."

"I had a crush on him for so long, Mother."

"Why did you not ever tell me? We used to talk about everything, or so I thought."

"He was a married man; I could only imagine what you would have said."

"I guess you are right; it would have been different if he were single."

"Mother, he was fourteen years older than me," Savannah laughed. "I hardly think being single would have made a difference."

"Perhaps you are right," she smiled, "but in any case, it all worked out, and he is amazing."

"That he is. I wonder what he and Joseph are up to in the barn?"

"Perhaps they are building you something. Do you think Jonah ever gets upset that Joseph is right underfoot?"

"Of course not; he loves Joseph. Matthew has followed him around ever since he's been able to walk, and Jonah loves it."

"I am glad there is a wood heater in the barn, or else they would not be able to stand this cold. Do you think it will ever stop snowing?"

"I hope so. Looks like we are in for a terrible storm. Could be out of school a few days." Savannah stood and walked toward the kitchen. "Would you like a cup of coffee, Mother?"

"Yes, I would love one, thank you. I am so enjoying this day with you."

"You and I both. We needed some down time after the Christmas party--that about wore us all out."

"You, more so than me. All I had to do was bake a few desserts, which I love."

"Rose is just like you. That child could stay in the kitchen." Savannah handed Alice a cup of coffee and sat back down.

"Momma, can I go out and play now?" Catherine asked, dragging her feet into the room.

"No, little missy, you may not. You know what your pa told you, and it's not going to change."

"But I am bored inside. It's not fair that Rose has Mary to play with, and I have no one."

"You have your brother. You two need to start getting along and find something to do together."

"Matthew isn't here, and besides, I don't like playing with him; he always tries to be the boss of me."

"What do you mean, he isn't here?" Savannah asked, concerned.

"He put on his coat and hat and left to go to the barn with Pa."

"When did he leave? I didn't see him leave!" Savannah jumped up from the chair and ran to the window.

243

"He left out of the back door right after Pa and Uncle Joseph went to the barn and told me he was going, too. I told him Pa would be upset, but he wouldn't listen."

"Oh, Catherine, why didn't you come and tell me when he left?" Savannah scolded, grabbing her coat off the rack.

"Do you not think he went to the barn?" Alice asked.

"I can't be certain, Mother; the wind and snow are terrible out there. Please stay here with the children, and I am going to follow the rope to the barn to make sure he is out there."

"Okay, please be careful."

Savannah buttoned her coat all the way and pulled her hat down over her ears, dreading going out in the cold.

She felt around the edge of the house, with the wind and snow feeling like razor blades cutting into her face and found the rope, just as Jonah said.

Slowly she made her way toward the barn, holding tight to the rope, with the wind so strong it was pushing her back.

Dear Father, please let Matthew be in that barn.
Please do not let him have taken off to get his sling shot.
He would never make it out here in this weather.

Savannah made it to the barn door, and with all her strength, pushed it open against the roaring wind.

"Goodness, Savannah, you shouldn't be out in this weather," Jonah came rushing to her and shut the door back.

"Matthew!" Savannah called out, running around the barn frantically, looking in all the stables. "Matthew, where are you? Oh, God, Jonah, please tell me Matthew is in here with you?"

"No, he's in the house with you!" Jonah caught her before she fell to the ground in sobs.

"Jonah, Catherine just told me he went out the back door this morning, saying he was coming to the barn with you! I just found out; he is not in the house!"

244

Jonah ran to the stable to saddle Midnight, "I bet he went to the school in search of that sling shot."

"Oh Jonah, the weather is too bad; he will get lost out there!" she cried.

"Joseph, take your sister back to the house and stay there until I get back with Matthew."

"You need me, Jonah; two of us will be better than one looking for him." Joseph wanted to help in any way he could.

"No, I need you to stay with the women and see that your sister gets back to the house and doesn't try to come looking for us, should I not make it back soon."

"Jonah, you will never find him in this!" Savannah was frantic.

"I have no choice. Go back to the house and pray. Pray harder than you've ever prayed in your life." Jonah took off out of the barn on Midnight, and within seconds, vanished from their sight.

Chapter Twenty-One

Jonah rode as hard as Midnight could possibly go through the blinding snow, praying he did not accidently step on his boy who could have possibly fallen and be freezing to death at this very moment.

"Matthew, where are you!" he yelled.

Oh, how could you possibly hear me in this howling wind?

Why son, why did you have to go after that sling shot?

Why could you not have listened to me?

You never disobey me, so why now?

Jonah slowed a bit and tried to look more closely at where he thought the trail was that carried his son to school each day.

Oh, dear Lord, please let me be in the right place.

Please wrap my son in Your arms and keep him warm.

Guide me to him, Father, please guide me to him.

Jonah rode through the biting wind and snow for what seemed to him like hours, and he prayed. He could barely see beyond four to six feet, and the snow that had already fallen was at least a foot already.

"Matthew, son, where are you?" he screamed again.

Yelling so much his throat felt sore and raw, he was afraid if he did not find him soon, the snow would completely cover him, and there would be no way to find his lifeless body.

There were so many memories. His son had been his sidekick for the past seven years and had followed him everywhere. How would he ever make it if he could not find him in time? What would this do to them, to their marriage? He was not as strong as Savannah; he knew that.

Jonah never wanted Savannah to get pregnant. He was afraid that he would lose her during childbirth, just as he lost Clara, but when she got with child, she assured him that everything was going to be all right, and his only choice was to trust in God and pray that she was right.

He thought back to the night Matthew was born and how afraid he was that something would happen, but with Nancy Ingalls' help, everything went smoothly, and Matthew was born healthy and screaming.

Matthew, his only son.

I want to have the faith Savannah has, Lord.

Forgive me for turning away from you when Clara died.

I know I am not a perfect man, but please do not take my only son.

Jonah thought about Jesus dying on the cross so many years ago. God's *only* begotten Son.

I am not strong like You, Father.

You saw what happened to me after Clara died; You saw how I fell apart.

Please do not test me again. I am not strong like Savannah.

I know I will fail miserably.

He deserves a life, Father, to grow up and have a family of his own.

Jonah made it to the school and tied Midnight to the railing.

"Matthew!" he screamed, bursting through the door. "Are you in here?"

There was nothing but silence and darkness, with little light coming in through the outside windows.

Jonah knew where Matthew sat and looked frantically for the slingshot to see if he had made it to the school. There was nothing.

Quickly he looked around the other desks and, on the floor, to see if perhaps it had been somewhere other than his desk. Still nothing.

Jonah knew he had made it to the school and somehow got turned around on his way back. Grabbing one of the children's scarves that was left behind, he wrapped it tightly around his face and nose, leaving just enough room for him to see, and headed back out the door into the blinding snow.

*****

Savannah paced the floor and prayed.

Father, please keep my baby warm. Wrap him in your arms, like only You can.

You are the almighty God, and I know you can keep his little body from freezing to death.

Send an angel, dear Father, to keep him warm.

"I should go try to find him." Joseph looked out the window. "He's been gone much too long."

"No, Joseph, I know you are a man now, but we don't need you lost out there, too. You don't know this territory like Jonah does, and you can't see your hand in front of your face with this storm," Alice tried to calm him down. He had been rubbing his hands together, staring out the window for over an hour.

"I lied to you, Momma," Catherine came running into the room crying.

"What do you mean?" Savannah screamed. "Did you know Matthew wasn't going to the barn?"

"Yes, he told me not to tell you, and that he would be right back."

"Oh, Catherine! What you have done is an awfully bad thing! You should have come and told me right away!"

"You told me not to tell on him all the time. I didn't want to be a tattletale," she cried.

"Now, now," Alice jumped in. "What's done is done. Catherine, why don't you go to your room and play with your dollhouse?"

Catherine took off in sobs.

"Joseph, go latch the back door tight, so Catherine can't go looking for her brother; I can just see her doing something like that," Savannah said. "I am so upset with her right now."

"Savannah, she is just a child, and you have been telling her to stop telling on her brother. I have heard you," Alice reminded.

"But this was important, and she should have known it was dangerous out there."

"She is only six years old; how could she have known?"

"Oh Mother, what are we going to do if Jonah can't find him? What if Jonah gets turned around out there himself?"

"Savannah, we have all prayed, and we have to trust that God shall help Jonah find him and keep him warm until he does."

Savannah buried her face in her hands and cried. "Oh, Mother, I don't want to lose my baby!"

Alice put her arms around her and held her close. "Dear Jesus, help us."

"Open the door!" Jonah pounded with his foot.

Joseph hurried to the door and found Jonah covered in snow, carrying Matthew in his arms. "Quick, get some water boiling, and blankets."

"Thank You, Jesus!" Savannah cried. "Oh Jonah, you found him!"

Jonah lay him on their bed and started rubbing his cold arms. "He's still alive, but so cold. I am so thankful I found him when I did."

Savannah brought blankets to wrap him in, and Alice started the pot of water to boil.

"Is he going to be okay, Pa?" Rose had never seen anyone so blue.

"Yes, he is, we just have to get his temperature back up," Savannah answered. "Where did you find him, Jonah?"

"I will tell you everything soon; right now, we just have to keep rubbing his arms and legs. Can you hear me, Matthew?"

"Son, it's Momma, please talk to us."

Matthew moaned, and Savannah cried out. "Thank You, Jesus, thank You for keeping my boy alive."

"Here, see if he will drink some hot broth; that will help bring his temperature up." Alice handed a cup of broth to Savannah.

"Come on son, take a sip of this." Savannah tried to give him a sip, but it just seeped out of the corners of his mouth.

"Jonah, are you sure he is okay? Should we go for a doctor?"

"Savannah, the doctor is ten miles away, and there is a blizzard out there. No one would make it that far. He will warm up in a little bit."

"Here's the hot water," Alice said. "I already had some on the stove about to do dinner, and I have just put more on."

"Get some rags wet from the hot water, and let's wrap his body in them," Jonah urged.

Alice and Savannah went to work wrapping his body and rubbing his arms and legs.

"I am so sorry, Momma," Catherine cried, standing at the foot of the bed.

"What are you sorry for?" Jonah asked.

"It's a long story, Jonah," Savannah answered. "Joseph, would you take Catherine to the other room and try to find her something for dinner? Rose and Mary, you can go eat something as well. We will call you when he wakes up."

"But Momma," Catherine hung on to the bedpost, afraid Savannah was angry with her.

"It's okay, Catherine, go with the others, and we will talk later."

Joseph took her by her hand and led her out of the room.

"What was that about?" Jonah asked.

"As I said, it's a long story. I cannot think about that right now. Do you think he is warming up any?"

"Look at his eyes," Alice pointed.

Matthew's eyes were closed but fluttering.

Savannah got down at his ear. "Son, please wake up and talk to me. Can you hear me?"

"So cold," Matthew's teeth chattered.

Savannah smiled at Jonah; happy he was coming around. "Yes, son, it's cold, but we are going to warm you up."

Savannah could not stop the tears; she had never felt so grateful in all her life.

Jonah placed his hand on her shoulder and nodded, with tears in his eyes. God had been so good to them. He had heard his prayer and answered.

"Come on, son, let's sit you up some and try to drink a little of this broth," Jonah lifted Matthew a bit and gave him more of the broth. Matthew drank, slowly.

Savannah fell into her mother's arms and shook with sobs. "Oh, Mother, that was so close. He's going to be all right."

"Our Father is a good God. It was not Matthew's time to go. He is going to have a long life ahead of him," Alice rubbed her daughter's back as she did when she was a child.

251

"Momma," Matthew coughed out the word.

Savannah got close to him once again. "Yes, son?"

"I went to..." his voice trailed off.

"You went to the school to get your sling shot?" she finished what she thought he wanted to say.

He nodded yes.

"Did you find it?" Savannah knew it was not the time to scold him now; that would come later.

"Pocket," he coughed.

Jonah got up and motioned for Savannah to follow him.

"Mother, would you stay and keep trying to give him broth? I will be right back."

"Certainly."

Savannah followed Jonah to Matthew's room, since he was in theirs, and he shut the door.

"He's going to make it," he broke down and cried. She hugged him close and let him cry. It was not often in their marriage she had seen her strong husband cry.

"It's going to be okay, Jonah, you found him. I am so proud of you."

"Savannah, I need to talk to you. I need to tell you what happened."

"Let's sit down on the bed, and you can tell me everything."

"I couldn't find him, Savannah. I searched everywhere I thought he could be. I knew I could not give up, or our boy would die, but I couldn't find him, and I was so afraid I was going to freeze to death myself before I did. I just kept thinking what you would do if we never made it back."

"I'm not going to lie; I was worried, too. I do not know what I would have done if it wasn't for Mother. She kept me calmer than I would have been. We both just continued to pray and asked God to show you where he was and keep him warm."

"Savannah, you may not believe what I am about to tell you. I mean, it's hard enough for me to believe it myself. Maybe I was just so cold that I was becoming delusional."

"What is it, Jonah?"

"You will never believe how I found him."

"Where was he, Jonah?"

"I knew he made it to the school because I couldn't find his sling shot. When I started back, I moved a little further out, the way the wind was blowing, thinking maybe the wind had taken him off where I thought the trail was. The snow had already covered my tracks, so it was hard to tell where I had been, and I couldn't see well enough anyway."

Savannah took his hand. "Go on."

"I prayed, Savannah. I prayed as I prayed when you were with John, and I thought I might lose you to sickness. I begged God to show me where he was and keep me alive long enough to find him and bring him back here."

"And He did. He heard your prayer."

"I heard a voice, Savannah."

"You mean Matthew? You heard Matthew calling for help?"

"No, it wasn't Matthew. As you could see, Matthew almost did not make it. If it had been much longer, we would have lost our boy today."

"Then who, Jonah? Who did you hear?"

"It was John."

"Papa John?" Savannah asked, confused.

"Yes, I am sure of it. I heard him yell through the wind that he was under the tree, and then I saw him."

"You saw Matthew?"

"No, Savannah, I saw Papa John. He was standing right next to me and pointing at the tree."

"Oh, my, you saw Papa John?" Savannah cried.

"Yes, he was wearing the new shirt that you buried him in. I swear, Savannah, if it weren't for him showing me, I would have never found him. Matthew was completely covered in snow. I found him by digging where John showed me to look."

"Oh Jonah, don't you see? John told us that we had saved his life twice, and he would one day find a way to pay us back. Our sweet Papa John saved Matthew's life."

"But Savannah, listen to what you are saying. How is that even possible? Papa John died; we both know that."

"I guess some things just aren't meant to understand."

"I never believed in ghosts, and I am still not sure if I do."

"Maybe it wasn't a ghost. Maybe it was an angel that God allowed you to see, that looked like someone you recognized, so you wouldn't be afraid."

Jonah nodded. "Perhaps you are right."

"I prayed for God to send an angel to keep Matthew warm and show you where he was."

"And He did just that. Our boy is alive and going to make it because God is so good."

*****

"Catherine, can we come in?" Savannah had told Jonah what happened and wanted to speak to her daughter before she fell asleep.

"Yes, Momma."

"We want to talk to you about what happened today," Savannah closed the door behind her.

"Is Matthew going to die?" she cried.

Jonah sat down on her bed and picked her up and sat her in his lap. "No, Catherine, Matthew is not going to die, but he came very close."

"I am sorry, Pa. I should have told you when he left, but he asked me not to tell, and I am always getting into trouble for telling on him."

"You are right," Savannah said softly. "And I am sorry I yelled at you earlier."

"It's okay, Momma, I am sorry I didn't tell you. It's all my fault that Matthew almost died."

"No, Catherine," Jonah said. "If it is anyone's fault, it is Matthew's for not obeying me."

"I am just so confused. Do you want me to tell on Matthew or not?"

Savannah chuckled. "Use your judgment. If you are telling on him to get him in trouble for doing nothing and make yourself look better, then no. But if you are telling us that he is about to do something dangerous, then yes. Do you understand what I mean?"

"I think so. Today was dangerous, and I should have told you."

"Yes, today would have been a great day to tell on your brother."

"Am I in trouble?"

Jonah hugged her tight and kissed her on the cheek. "No, you are not in trouble."

"Is Matthew in trouble?"

"Would you want him to be?" Jonah asked.

"No, Pa. I think him almost dying is enough punishment."

"That's my girl. I am so immensely proud of you for saying that. That just proves you are growing up, and as much as you act like you do not care about Matthew, I know that you love your brother very much."

"I do, Pa. I do love Matthew, and I am glad that he is going to be okay."

"Can I ask you something, Catherine?" Savannah asked.

"Yes, Momma."

"Why did you tell me you lied? Why didn't you keep me thinking that he told you he was going to the barn?"

"Because Papa John told me to tell you the truth."

"You saw Papa John?" Savannah and Jonah swapped glances.

"Yes, I dreamed about him. I fell asleep and I dreamed he woke me up and told me to come and tell you the truth. He told me not to ever lie again, that it wasn't nice to lie to my momma."

So much had happened in a day.

So many things that could never be explained.

Thank you, Papa John, thank you.

Thank you, Father, for loving us the way you do.

Chapter Twenty-Two

"It is so good to see your color is back and your appetite," Savannah kissed Matthew, as he sat eating biscuits at the table.

"It looks like maybe us three could venture back to our own house," Alice said, looking out the window. They had been held up for three days since the storm started.

Jonah laughed, "Do you not like our company?"

"Well, I for one have loved it," Mary smiled. "It's been fun staying with Rose."

"Well, Rose is more than welcome to come over to our house and stay with you anytime." Alice carried the dishes to the wash basin.

"Oh, no you don't," Savannah gently pushed her mother aside. I will do these. You are free to go back to your house. I know you, and I know you are wanting to get back to your things."

"It's a good thing I already started a fire for us," smiled Joseph, putting on his coat and hat.

"Son, you are wonderful to think of that, but how did you know we were going back today?"

"Mother, I was going back with you or without you. I love Jonah, but I can only take so much," he joked, making everyone laugh, including Jonah.

"Well, okay then," Alice put her coat on as well. "Rose, would you like to come over a bit and visit with Mary? I am sure you two girls can find something to do in her room or talk about whatever it is you two talk about."

"May I, Momma? May I spend the night with Mary?"

"If your Momma Alice doesn't mind. Might as well enjoy the day. Looks like we will be out of school a few more days with the depth of this snow."

"Can I go too, Pa?" Catherine asked.

"Well, maybe you should ask Momma Alice if she minds you going?"

"Not at all, let's get your coat and hat on," Alice took her hand and led her to the rack beside the door.

Within minutes the house emptied out.

Jonah looked at his son who seemed to be in slow motion, eating, picking at his biscuit. He knew it would take him several days to be back to his usual self physically and emotionally. He had not acted like himself since it happened.

"Is something on your mind, son?" Jonah asked.

Savannah left the dishes in the basin and came to sit back down; she knew this was the time that she and Jonah needed to talk to him about what happened.

"I guess you are angry with me, aren't you, Pa?"

Jonah looked at Savannah and she nodded at him to go ahead. After all, it was Jonah who had risked his own life to find him.

"I am not angry with you, son, but I am *very* disappointed in you."

"I thought I could hurry to the school and back, and you would never even know I left."

"Don't you think I would have seen the sling shot and know you had to have gone to retrieve it?"

Matthew hung his head. "I guess I didn't think of that."

"Son, I told you not to go outside. I told you how dangerous it was out there. You have never once ever disobeyed me, and I can't for the life of me figure out why you did this time."

Matthew's eyes filled with tears. "I am sorry, Pa. I promise never to disobey you again."

Savannah reached over and lovingly took his hand. "Matthew, we almost lost you out there. Do you realize that disobeying your father almost cost you and your father your lives?"

"I tried to find my way home, but I couldn't see the trail, and it was so cold. If it were not for Papa John telling me to lay down and curl up at the tree and him keeping me warm, I would have frozen."

Savannah gasped and looked at Jonah. "You saw Papa John?"

Matthew nodded. "Yes, he told me that he loved me and that I needed to stay still, so Pa could find me. He lay there with me and kept me warm."

Jonah smiled at Savannah and reached to wipe a tear from her face.

"Do you believe me?" Matthew asked. "I was afraid you would not believe me."

"Yes, son, yes, we believe you," Savannah wiped another tear.

"I was afraid no one would find me, but he told me that Pa was on his way, and if I didn't say still that I would get lost."

"I am glad you obeyed Papa John," Jonah ruffled his hair as he always did, and Matthew smiled.

"Is Papa John a ghost?"

"Savannah shrugged. "I have no idea, Matthew, but I do know one thing; Papa John loved you very much, and maybe he found a way to come back and help you. It was not your time to go to Heaven yet."

"I know; that is what he told me. But I never got to thank him for helping me."

"It's okay, son; I think he knew."

"I hope so. I was so scared until I saw him, and he stayed with me. I asked him if he was going to come back with me, and he said he couldn't, but that he loved me and for me never to disobey you again."

"That is incredibly good advice, son. I am glad he was there to keep you safe."

"I'm so sorry, Pa. I really am."

"I know you are, and I forgive you."

*****

Springtime came to the valley, and Jonah welcomed it.

Even though there was much work to be done with the plowing and planting seed, he was tired of the cold and snow, and he wished to never have to go through another winter like the one that had just passed.

"Do you mind if I take off?" Joseph asked.

Jonah drank a ladle full of cold water and wiped the sweat from his brow. "Off to see Peggy?"

"Yes, sir, to walk her home from school."

"Don't mind at all. You have been helping me since sunup; you deserve a break. I think I will walk with you and walk my sweet wife home."

"Now you're talking. I know she will love that."

"Guess I need to learn from you younger guys about romance these days."

Joseph laughed. "I don't think you have any trouble in the romance department. My sister adores you."

"And I adore her. Well, let us get started; our women are waiting."

*****

"Thank you all for turning in your assignments on time. I shall go over them this weekend and hand them back come Monday. Be careful on your way home and have a great weekend. I shall see you all at church on Sunday."

The children quickly gathered their books and exited the school.

"What are you doing, Pa?" Rose asked, walking out of the school, with Mary right beside her.

Jonah placed his finger on his lips, indicating for her not to let his presence be known. "I come to walk your mother home from school. Please go on ahead and take Matthew and Catherine with you; we will be along shortly."

"Okay, we will see you back at the house."

Peggy smiled at Joseph, who was always there waiting for her like clockwork and had yet to miss a day. "It is good to see you."

"And it is always a pleasure to see you; it is the highlight of my day." He took her book and lunch pail and started walking.

Peggy giggled. "It is also mine."

"Isn't the weather beautiful? No more waiting days to get to see you because of the snow."

"Yes, it was a hard winter. Would you like to stay for dinner after you walk me home?"

"Really? Is that okay with your parents? I have been in the valley almost a year and never once stepped foot inside your home."

"Yes, my Pa told me to ask you. He said they might as well invite you in and really get to know you, because it doesn't look like you are going anywhere," she laughed.

"Uh oh, does that mean he *wishes* I'd go somewhere?"

"Not at all; my parents like you very much."

Joseph reached down and took her hand. "Can I show you something?"

"Sure, what is it?"

Joseph turned and started through the woods.

"Where are we going?"

"You will see; just trust me."

He pulled her along, until he got to the place he dreamed of building a cabin someday.

"Do you know if anyone claims this land?"

"No, it is still unsettled."

"How do you like it here?"

"It's beautiful. I love the creek that runs close. Why do you ask?"

Joseph took both her hands in his and admired her beauty. She had the most amazing eyes.

Shaking, he took a ring out of his pocket and held it up for her to see.

"I have been saving for months to buy you this. It will be a symbol of my love for you and show the world that you belong to me, as my girl. Marry me, Peggy. Marry me, and let's build our cabin right here. Let's claim this for our own. You would be close to your parents, and I would be close enough to still help Jonah on the farm, so we can also plant enough harvest for us."

Peggy's eyes grew wide. "But I still have another year of school after this one. Ma wanted me to go until I was seventeen."

"I've waited a year; what's one more? At least we shall wait and be engaged."

"But you still have not *really* kissed me yet," she smiled.

Joseph took her face in his hands and pulled her close. "You have no idea how long I have wanted to do this." He kissed her passionately and left her breathless.

Peggy gasped. "So that is what it is like to *really* be kissed."

Joseph chuckled. "Will you marry me next summer, Peggy?"

"I will. I will marry you, Joseph, I cannot wait to be your wife. I will wait to wear this *after* you speak to my parents."

"You make me so happy, Peggy. I am so glad I moved to the valley. I always knew you'd be here.

I will ask for your parents' blessing tonight after dinner. I love you, Peggy Ayers. Now, before we leave these woods, may I have one more kiss?"

*****

Jonah stood for the longest and watched Savannah make notes.

Since Mary moved to the valley, she walked home with Rose, and Savannah was normally the last to arrive, always holding back to do the planning for the next school day.

Never once had Jonah walked her home from school. Maybe it truly did take a younger man, like Joseph, to teach him a thing or two about romance.

"Have I told you lately that I love you?" Jonah walked toward the front of the classroom.

Savannah looked up and smiled. "Not today you haven't."

"I love you more today than I did yesterday, but not as much as I will love you tomorrow."

Savannah stood and wrapped her arms around him. "To what do I owe this pleasure? You coming to walk me home from school? And what is this?"

"It is wildflowers I picked along the way."

"How romantic; I don't get flowers often."

"And that is a shame. I will have to do much better than that from now on."

"I love you, Jonah Bell," she kissed him deeply.

"Not as much as I love you, Savannah, my beautiful wife. Are you ready to walk home?"

"I am," she giggled. "Thank you for coming for me."

"And thank you for just being you. I could not imagine my life with anyone else."

"You know, I sometimes wonder what would have happened if you had not have had one hundred acres and a cabin to trade my father for my hand in marriage."

"I try not to think of that. Where my life would be now, had I never married you."

Savannah smiled. "Does this mean you might be walking me home every once in a while?"

"Maybe," he winked. "You sure deserve more than I ever give you."

*****

"Dinner was delicious," Joseph stated, wiping his mouth.

"Thank you, Joseph, I am glad you could stay for dinner," smiled Marylou, getting up from the table to stack the dishes.

"Here, let me help you," Joseph stood.

"Why don't you go out with me to slop the pigs, Joseph," Noel placed his hat on top of his head, "and let Peggy and Glenda help with the dishes? By the time we return, they shall be finished, and we can have dessert."

"Don't you want Jerry and I to slop them?" Daniel asked, confused. It had been their job for the past couple of years.

"No thanks, Daniel, I thought Joseph might want to see the back side of the farm, don't you, Joseph?"

"Yes, sir, I would like that." Joseph knew that Noel intended to speak to him alone. For almost a year, he had been courting his daughter, and it was time he got to the bottom of his intentions. Joseph thought it would have come way before now.

Joseph followed Noel to the back yard. He could hear and smell the pigs before they were even close enough to see them.

"Been raising hogs ever since I can remember," Noel said, pouring the slop into the trough.

"Looks like you have quite a few."

"Yes sir-ee, I have a lot of mouths to feed."

"Yes sir. Is there anything you need me to do?"

Noel put down the bucket and looked toward Jonah. "No, son, I just wanted to have a moment alone with you."

"Yes sir, I understand."

"Do you? Do you know why?"

"I am guessing it is about your daughter. You want to know my intentions?"

"Yes," he nodded. "Now the truth is, Joseph, I have liked you from the very start. You seem like a nice young man, and I can tell you treat my daughter with respect."

"Yes sir, I wouldn't do anything in the world to hurt her."

"Wouldn't you? I mean, what if another girl comes along that you like more?"

"That will not happen, sir. I want to marry your daughter next summer, after she finishes school. The truth is, I asked her today and was going to ask for your and Mrs. Ayers' blessing tonight after dinner."

Noel smiled and rubbed the hair underneath his hat. "And what did she say? Did she say yes?"

"Yes sir. I also gave her a ring, which she has not put on until I ask you."

"And what if I didn't give you my blessing; what then?"

"Then I would keep coming around daily and pray you get to know me, and know that I am an honorable man, and I plan to treasure your daughter and build a life with her. I will treat her with kindness and cherish her."

265

"And what if I still said no?" he grinned again.

Joseph looked toward the ground and thought a moment before looking back at Noel. "Then I would wait another year until she was eighteen and ask her to run off with me and marry me, because frankly, Mr. Ayers, I cannot imagine my life without her."

Noel pursed his lips and nodded. "Do you know that Marylou and I ran off and got married? Her parents thought she was too young, so we took off and didn't tell anyone."

"No, sir, I didn't know that."

"Not sure Peggy knows that, either."

"I love your daughter, Mr. Ayers. I would like to claim some of the land between the school and here, deeper in the woods and build a small cabin there before next summer, so we will have a place to live."

"I see. So, you will not be taking her far from home, then?"

"No sir, I know how that feels from when my sister moved far away."

"You have no plans of going back to Georgia?"

"No sir, Arkansas will be my home until I take my last breath."

"I like you, Joseph, just as I said, and after our talk, I do believe that I like you even better than I did."

"Thank you, sir. Does this mean you will give me your blessing?"

Noel smiled. "I will give you my blessing, son. In fact, we will look at this land you want to build a cabin on, and I will help you build it."

"Thank you so much, sir."

Noel put his arm around Joseph and started back toward the house. "Now let's go get Marylou's blessing and see that ring of hers."

*****

"Can I talk to you, Mother?" Joseph entered the house to find Alice washing dinner dishes.

"Well, there you are, I was beginning to get worried about you; you are usually always back before dinner."

"I am sorry, if I had known Peggy's family were going to ask me to stay for dinner, I would have let you know."

"They asked you to stay, did they? I am glad. It's been almost a year since you have been courting their daughter."

"Come sit, Mother, I want to talk to you about something."

Alice dried her hands and came to the table. "I hope something isn't wrong."

"Not at all, Mother," he smiled. "In fact, everything is perfect."

Alice placed her hands on his and smiled. "You asked Peggy to marry you, didn't you?"

"I did, and I asked for her parents' blessing. How did you know that?"

"I knew you would before long. I am happy for you, son. I know how much you love Peggy; any fool can see that."

"Are you upset that I didn't talk to you about it first?"

She chuckled. "Of course not. I think if she were older, you would have asked her the first month we were here. Sometimes it takes love a while to grow, and then there are times when you just know."

"That's how I felt about Peggy, from the first moment I laid eyes on her, I knew, Mother. I just knew that she was the woman that would be my wife someday."

"I like Peggy, and I am happy for you both. When do you plan to be married? Isn't she still in school?"

"Yes, she wants to go one more year. We will be married next summer."

"Next summer. Gives us plenty of time to plan a wedding. I am sure your sister will be thrilled to decorate and plan something nice. Do you both want to live here with us? I don't mind, and we have plenty of room, thanks to Jonah."

"That is what I want to talk to you about."

"You're not moving back to Georgia, are you?"

Joseph laughed. "Now, Mother, why would you even ask such a thing as that? You know me better than that, especially as long as it took me to get you to move out here."

"What then? Where shall you live?"

"I have found land I would like to stake my claim on, between the church and the Ayers farm. I want Peggy to be able to stay close to her family."

"So, you shall build your own cabin then?"

"Yes, and Noel Ayers told me he would help me build it. I want to be finished before next summer."

"You amaze me, son. You had the move out west all planned out, and now you have your wedding and future planned, but then you had to grow up way before you should have, and I shouldn't be surprised."

"I won't go far, Mother. I will still be close enough to help you do whatever you need of me."

Alice patted Joseph's hand. "Son, I knew the time would come that you would have your own life and your own wife, and when you are married, your wife comes right after God. Don't worry, I have not gotten so old that I still can't take care of myself."

"And I shall never get so far from any of my family again that we can't see each other and help each other out. I love you, Mother. Thank you for being you."

"Let me give you the money to build the cabin for you and Peggy."

"That's not necessary, Mother; I planned to take out a loan at the bank in the village."

"Son, you know I have the money. I planned to build a cabin for all of us when we arrived, but Jonah had already built one. I spoke to Jonah and I have tried to give him money to pay him back, but he would not hear of it. I would love to, Joseph. Let me do this for you. We will call it your wedding gift."

"Mother, I don't know what to say. That is a lot of money."

"After selling the land we got from Jonah and our land back home, I have more than enough. I insist."

Joseph laughed. "Thank you so much Mother, I am so grateful."

"Don't thank me, thank God; after all He is the one that provided it."

"I just can't wait to get started, and since I have a little more than a year, it will give me plenty of time and I won't have to rush."

"You've never built a cabin before, Joseph," Alice reminded.

"No, I haven't, but Noel and Jonah has, and they have both offered to help. And for that, I am grateful. Besides, I am a fast learner, and I don't intend to let them do all the work."

"I believe that, Joseph. I know you. Now that we are having this talk, and Mary is out at Savannah's with Rose, I want to tell you something."

"What's that, Mother?"

"I am sorry for the way your father treated you all those years, especially after Savannah left. I should have stood up to him, and I did not, and for that I am sorry. Can you ever forgive me?"

Joseph did not know what to say for a moment. His mother had never spoken ill of his father, nor allowed him to. "Why bring this up now?"

"Because it must be said. I watched and made sure he never laid a hand on you, but now I realize his words were sometimes worse than a beating."

"Thank you."

"For what? You have nothing to thank me for."

"For saying that you wished you had stood up to him. For saying you are sorry. That means a lot."

"I guess, deep down I didn't know what to do, and I walked on pins and needles, not wanting him to lash out."

"I understand, Mother. It is okay. I forgive you," he leaned over and kissed her on the cheek. "I have never been upset with you, and I never blamed you. I am simply happy you can live out the rest of your life in peace."

"Thank you for begging me to come to the valley. I am happy here."

"We all are, even Mary, just I like I knew we would be."

"I'm really happy for you and Peggy, son."

"Just pray that this next year goes fast and then slows down from there on out," he laughed. "I can't wait to marry her, Mother, and build a life and have children of my own."

"You are a fine young man, son. I am so proud of you."

Chapter Twenty-Three

"I appreciate you picking me up this morning for the trip into town, Mr. Ayers." Joseph climbed up on the wagon, excited to be going into the village to buy some of the materials to get started on the cabin he and Peggy would call their home someday.

Noel set the wagon in motion, "Don't mention it, son. I was hoping for a chance to get to talk to you more. It seems like each time you have eaten with us lately we never seem to get a moment alone. Also, since you are going to become my son-in-law, maybe it's time you start to call me Noel."

"Yes, sir."

Noel chuckled. "I like you, Joseph. I think I liked you from the first moment I met you. I have to be honest, though, and tell you that I was a bit concerned at first, because Peggy was about to be fifteen at the time, and I wasn't sure what your intentions were."

"Yes, sir, I can understand that. I was willing to wait as long as it took."

Noel nodded. "I can see that. Been a year now and she is about to turn sixteen, and I know you will wait on her another year and be as respectful to her as you have been so far."

"Yes sir, indeed. Will prove to be the longest year of my life, I am sure."

Noel laughed. "I remember so well when Marylou and I were younger, so I know what you are going through, son. At least with us starting to build the cabin, it will keep your mind occupied and go by much faster."

"I genuinely want to thank you for helping me build the cabin. I know a lot about farming, but as I said before, I don't know a lot about building."

"I didn't know that much either when I was just eighteen. You learn by watching and doing, son, and I know you will learn a lot in the next several months. I am glad we do not have to rush. Do you plan to move in after we are finished? I am sure we will be finished with the cabin before you and Peggy get married next summer."

"I had not thought a lot about that. I guess I could. At least I would be much closer to come visit her with me living next door. How do you feel about that?"

Noel looked his way and grinned. "Well, Joseph, you are there most the time anyway, so I reckon it won't be much different than it is right now."

Joseph chuckled. "I guess you are right about that. I do hope that does not bother you. I can come less if it does."

"Not at all. I enjoy getting to know you, and I like seeing my Peggy happy."

"Thank you, because even though I would cut down my visits if you wanted me to, it would not be easy at all."

"I understand. Don't think I'd want to go a day without seeing Marylou either."

"Do you think you could teach me how to make furniture? I was thinking that we would need a table and chairs and a bed, as well as a cupboard and maybe a chest of drawers."

"I think I could manage teaching you that, if you are willing to pay attention and learn."

"Yes, sir, that I can do."

"So, tell me about your pa, son. Peggy said he died a few years back?"

"Not much to tell, really. He was a farmer in Dahlonega but made most of his money through gambling. He passed when I was eleven, and I took over the farming."

"That's a mighty big job for an eleven-year-old."

"He'd been teaching me since I was seven. Wasn't nobody else there to do it. I am sure I didn't do as good as a grown man could have done, but with Mother directing me and helping all she could, we managed."

"I'm proud of you, son. Not many boys would have done that. Yes, sir, I knew from the moment I met you that I liked you, and now I understand why. Not a lazy bone in your body, and I do believe that you are going to learn all there is to know about building in no time at all."

"Thank you, sir. I appreciate that."

Joseph liked Noel. It seemed that all the men of the valley were good men and treated their wives with respect and were great fathers to their children. It was not something he had ever been used to.

It would be a different world from here on out, and he hoped that he could be half the husband and father the other men seem to be.

"As soon as we drop off this furniture to sell at the mercantile, we will go to the hardware store and sawmill and load up. Are you excited about starting the cabin tomorrow?"

"Excited and a bit nervous, if that makes much sense."

"Makes a lot of sense, son. Building a cabin and getting married is a big step for anyone. You are absolutely positive this is what you want though, right, son?"

"I've never been more positive of anything in my life."

273

Noel smiled. "That's what I thought. Well, let us get this show on the road then." Noel urged the team to go faster and headed into the village.

*****

"Would you like some help with the fried chicken, Momma?" Rose asked.

"No, I think I have this, but if you want to whip up some dessert, that would be great. I bet the men would love some of your fried pies."

"Mine aren't as good as yours, but I shall do my best." Rose went right to work gathering the things needed to make the pies.

"Your pies are delicious and never think otherwise. Jonah, Joseph and Matthew left early, and I am sure they will be ready to eat when we arrive."

"What can I do, Momma?" Catherine asked.

"You can gather the plates and fold the napkins to put in the picnic basket, and thank you for asking, Catherine."

"You are welcome, Momma. I am so excited to be having a picnic where they are building Uncle Joseph's cabin."

"It will be Peggy's cabin too, Catherine," Rose commented.

"Does that mean she will become my aunt Peggy?"

"Yes, it does," Savannah smiled. "As soon as they are married, she will become your aunt Peggy."

"That is good, because I like her a lot. Do you think they will let me go spend the night sometime when Janice does? We are best friends."

"Catherine, let's worry about all that when the time comes. I am sure Peggy and Joseph will like their time alone for a while."

Savannah loved her daughter's excitement. Truth was, she was just as excited for the future and what it held for her brother and the valley, as more cabins were built, and more families moved in.

Twelve years ago, she would have never dreamed that any of this would be possible, and she was sure she had never been as happy as she was at this moment.

"Can I come in?" Alice yelled, sticking her head inside the door.

"You know you can," Savannah laughed. "I see you beat us with your cooking."

Alice brought in a loaded picnic basket and set it down on the kitchen table. "That is only because I don't have as much to do as you do each morning. The chicken smells wonderful."

"Thank you, and Rose is making fried pies."

"Oh, good, I love your fried pies, Rose."

"Thank you, Momma Alice. Where is Mary?"

"She is primping and will be here shortly. I am afraid she has a crush on one of the Anderson boys."

"Is that so?" Savannah looked at Rose.

Rose giggled. "She thinks Nathaniel is cute."

"Well, well, I guess I learn something new every day," Savannah joked.

"Joseph has been giddy with excitement these past couple of months. All he talks about is the cabin and getting married next summer," Alice sat down in the rocking chair.

"I'm just glad school is out for the summer, so Peggy won't have to concentrate on schoolwork. Poor thing, the last few weeks of school was hard on her, hearing the hammering and building going on so close. I supposed I'd be the same way, though, if it were Jonah and I."

"Just wait until school starts back, if you think she has it bad now," Alice laughed. "I predict with all the men helping, the cabin will be finished before winter."

"Is Joseph going to go ahead and move in, Mother?"

"He says he is. It will put him closer to Peggy. I don't think we will see too much of him after that. At least not after his work is finished here with Jonah."

"I am sure of it, but I am just glad he is happy." Savannah loved seeing her brother happy, knowing how unhappy he had been so much of his life.

"There she is," Alice stated as Mary walked through the door.

"You look nice, little sister," Savannah smiled.

"Thank you. Do you like the new dress I made?"

"It's beautiful. You are going to be a great seamstress, just like Mother."

"Well, you aren't too bad yourself," said Alice. "I guess it runs in the blood."

"You taught us well, Mother."

"You both are smart women. You can do anything you set out to do."

"Well, the chicken is finished. How about the pies, Rose?"

"Give me another half an hour and it will be."

"Great, are you girls ready for a little walk?" Savannah placed the chicken inside the basket.

"Can I take my dolly?" Catherine asked. "Janice is going to bring hers, too, and we are going to play."

"Sure, that sounds like a good idea. I am eager to see what the other ladies bring. We are going to have quite a feast."

*****

Savannah snuggled close to Jonah after the children had gone to bed. "What a day we have had."

"The cabin is looking good. I never expected anyone but Noel and I to help. I was surprised when the other men and boys come running to pitch in."

"Jonah, you know that's how they are here in the valley. That is the best part. We are like one big family, each helping the other."

"Yes, they are all good people, that is for sure. And the best part is when all you ladies come bringing food."

Savannah laughed. "I think the other women enjoy it as much as I do."

"None of them cook as good as you do, except for maybe your mother."

"Oh, Jonah, you are terrible."

"No, I am honest. I have the best cook and the most beautiful wife in the valley." He kissed her, and she giggled.

"Flattery will get you everywhere."

"That's what I am hoping."

Savannah reached over and turned down the wick on the oil lamp, knowing it was she that was the luckiest woman in the valley.

*****

"What do you think?" Noel asked, driving the last nail in the steps to the front porch.

Joseph stood in awe and smiled. "I am not sure what to say. You have all been wonderful to help me this way, especially since I had no idea what I was doing."

"You can't say that any longer," Jonah added. "You have worked as hard as anyone."

"I don't know about the rest of you, but I enjoy doing something different every once in a while, besides plowing, planting and harvesting," Tom laughed.

Pastor Anderson put his arm around Joseph. "When is the big day? Have you set a date yet?"

"Peggy and I were hoping the weekend after school is out for the summer. We've waited a long time as it is."

All the men laughed, understanding what he was talking about.

"And we have not spoken to you about it yet, Pastor Anderson, but we hope you will be okay with performing the wedding?"

"I would love to. I normally suggest counseling to make sure it's what you both really want, but seeing you two together this past year, I have no doubt you are both very much in love and ready to get married."

"Yes, sir, that we are. I can't wait until school gets out today to show Peggy. I never dreamed we would be finished before winter."

"A lot can be accomplished when five men get together," Noel stated, putting his tools back into his wagon. "So, I guess you will be moving in soon, to be closer to Peggy?"

"Yes, sir, plan to do just that this weekend. Mother and Savannah said they are making curtains and a tablecloth and all that stuff that women do."

Jonah laughed. "Leave it up to your mother and sister to add the finishing touches and love every minute of it."

*****

Joseph's heart skipped a beat when he saw Peggy emerge from the school and head in his direction. Never had he seen a woman so beautiful in all his life, and just think, in a few months she would become his wife.

"Is it finished?" she asked with excitement.

Joseph pulled her close and hugged her tight as if he had not seen her in weeks. "It is, and everyone is gone. I have been waiting two hours to take you to the cabin and show you everything."

Peggy laughed. "It's not like I haven't seen it every day for the past few months."

"True, but you haven't seen it completely finished, with no one there but me."

"This is true. So, are you ready to take our walk?" She placed her hand in his. Her favorite time of the day.

"Been ready," he chuckled. "I asked Pastor Anderson today if he would marry us. I guess he already assumed he was going to."

"Did you tell him the weekend after school is out?"

"I did. Seems like a lifetime away."

"It does, but at least now you shall be closer to me and can have dinner with us each night."

"Not like I am not already doing that now," he chuckled.

"But now you shall not have far to go home and can stay a bit later."

"I would like that. I was talking to your Pa and he and I agreed that we would build a barn for us so we can get a couple horses of our own. We will need them going into the village once a month for supplies."

"And maybe we can get a cow for milking and a few chickens. The eggs would be good."

"Hard to believe we are going to have our own place together." Joseph turned down the road the wagons had made toward the cabin.

Peggy stopped walking when the cabin came into sight. "Just look at it, Joseph; it is beautiful."

"Your father is a wonderful carpenter; he is the one that came up with the design--me and the others just followed along."

"Come on, I'll race you." Peggy turned loose of his hand and started running.

"Oh, you think you are faster than me, do you?" Joseph yelled and took off after her, getting to the porch just a few feet ahead of her and lifting her into his arms.

Peggy laughed, out of breath, "I guess you are faster, after all."

Joseph opened the door, still holding her in his arms and carried her inside before setting her down. "Welcome home, Peggy."

"It's beautiful, Joseph, and Mrs. Bell told me today that she and your ma is making curtains."

"They are."

"My mother is making a quilt for our bed as our wedding gift. It is going to be beautiful."

Joseph pulled her close and kissed her passionately. "The hardest part from here on out is waiting to take you in my arms as my wife and knowing we never again have to be apart, even for one night."

"I am looking forward to that, also. I cannot wait to become Mrs. Peggy Bowen."

*****

Alice spread the tablecloth over the long table as Savannah finished hanging the matching curtains. Together they had worked hard the past couple of days, making Joseph and Peggy's cabin look like a home.

"So, what do you think, Mother?"

"I think it is beautiful. I am so happy for them both, especially for your brother; he deserves all this and more. He has been such a wonderful young man and son and was forced to grow up way too fast."

"I don't think he would have had it any other way, Mother."

"Maybe," Alice sat down at the table to rest a bit. "yet still. He never really had a childhood. He became a man at eleven years old."

Savannah sat down beside her and placed her hand on top of her mother's. "Mother, you must stop beating yourself up over the past. You are and have always been a wonderful mother; we could not have asked for anyone better. What Father did and how he acted was not your fault."

Alice wiped a tear. "Maybe, maybe not. It's still good to see him so happy now, and you, too. Now the only one I have to worry about is Mary."

"You don't need to worry over Mary; she loves it here in the valley and has a good head on her shoulders. I have seen her change a lot since you moved here. She is truly growing up before our very eyes."

"Yes, she really has, and some of that is because she has a very good teacher."

Savannah smiled, "And a very *good* mother."

*****

Springtime had to be Savannah's favorite time of the year, and she especially loved the long trips into the village with Jonah, when her mother volunteered to watch the children, so she and Jonah could have a little time alone.

It had been another long winter, yet successful as far as the second annual dance went. The band from the village had gladly come again and played music. It was almost as if they were becoming family, right along with the others in the valley.

"Just listen to those birds sing, Jonah, don't you just love it?"

"What I love is that winter is over and spring is here, and I get to spend the day with my beautiful wife and be selfish that

281

she is spending the day with me and not running around trying to do for everyone else."

"I am so sorry, Jonah; you must hate that I try to do so much."

"Not in the slightest, my sweet wife. I would not want you any other way."

"I know you have to get your hair cut and we are going to eat at Annie's, but do you think I might look at a few decorations for the wedding? It will be here in just a couple of months."

"Not at all. I am sure you have something in mind, just as you did the dances at Christmas."

"I do," she smiled. "You know me well."

"Then I will head to the barber first, and you can take your time shopping." Jonah pulled the wagon close to the mercantile and helped her down, before heading in the opposite direction.

"Look who's here!" Dottie screamed, running her way.

"Dottie, oh my goodness, just look at you!"

Dottie laughed. "I guess I look a bit different than the last time you saw me, but heavens, it has been a while since you have come to town."

"Yes, it certainly has. So, tell me what's going on with you?" Savannah could not believe that Dottie was dressed in a modest dress and had her hair down, without all the makeup.

"I no longer work at the saloon, Savannah. I decided that I am getting too old to chase after men to earn a living. Mrs. Palmer hired me at the dress shop, and I have been earning a decent living, living a decent life."

Savannah hugged her tight. "I am so proud of you, my friend, and you look beautiful with your hair down, and I love the dress."

"Thank you. It's about time I started looking like a decent person, don't you agree?"

"Oh, Dottie, you were born beautiful, and always have been, but I do love this new look on you."

"I have a confession to make," Dottie smiled.

"Oh, do tell."

"Mr. Garcia from the bank told me he always thought I was beautiful and asked me to dinner. He treated me so well, with no strings attached, and I thought maybe someone could possibly see me as someone other than a tramp."

"You were never a tramp, Dottie."

"Savannah, you are too kind, but the truth was, I was just that, and you know it. So, anyway, I asked Mrs. Palmer if she would hire me, and she said she would love to, if I quit the saloon and wore the dresses from the dress shop."

"That's wonderful, Dottie, and you seem so happy."

"I am. It feels good to know people aren't judging you when they look at you."

"Did you think I did that?"

"Not you, Savannah. You were the only one that was treating me with kindness. You are a godly woman, and it shows."

"You are sweet, and I thank you. So, what happened to Mr. Garcia?"

Dottie laughed. "He seems to be smitten, as well as I. We have been dating a couple of months now."

Savannah clapped her hands together in excitement. "That is the absolute best news, Dottie! I could not be happier for you! You deserve the best."

"Thank you, and I better get back to the dress shop; my break is over. It was so good seeing you again."

Savannah watched as Dottie took off toward the dress shop at the end of the street. People really could change, and she thanked God for helping Dottie see herself as He saw her, someone who deserved the very best.

Chapter Twenty-Four

"What do you think, Peggy?" Marylou asked her daughter as she stood in front of the mirror after trying on her dress for the first time.

"Momma, it is beautiful, thank you."

"It is the first wedding dress I have ever made, but I do think it turned out nice."

"It is gorgeous, yes. I love it, and I know Joseph will love it. I cannot believe we are getting married next week."

"Me either, it seems like just yesterday he asked you, and here you are about to become his wife. It is what you want, right, Peggy?"

Peggy smiled at her momma who now had tears in her eyes and hugged her. "Don't cry, Momma, I want you to be happy for me, and yes, I cannot wait to marry Joseph."

"Oh, I am, just seeing you in your wedding dress got to me. You are about to leave, and I will miss you."

"I won't be but a little way from you. We will be neighbors."

"I know all of this, yet still, it will be different. Just know I am happy for you and I genuinely love Joseph, and I know he will be very good to you."

"He already is, and I shall be good to him."

"Yes, you will make him a great wife, and you will be a great mother someday."

"It's because I had a great role model to take after. You are the best."

"Thank you, Peggy, I don't feel like the best at times, but I thank you for saying that."

*****

Savannah stood looking at the school from the back of the room after all the students had left. It had been a long year, but summer was here and now there was a wedding to get ready for.

"A penny for your thoughts," Jonah said from the doorway.

"Oh, Jonah, I am so glad you are here. How is it that every time I truly need you, you just show up?"

Jonah laughed. "I thought I might walk my beautiful bride home on her last day of school, since I have been so busy and have not done it often enough throughout the year."

"Well, I am very glad you came."

Jonah smiled. "Why do I get the feeling I am about to get myself some work to do?"

Savanah giggled. "You know me well, my handsome husband."

"So, what do you need of me?"

"You know the wedding is in just a couple of days, and I need to decorate the church for it."

"Yes, and just what does that mean?"

Savannah spread her arms as she spoke and walked toward the front of the church. "I was thinking you could build a small arch."

"An arch?"

"Yes, you know, an arch, so I can decorate it with flowers, and they can stand under it to get married. Just something simple."

Jonah belly laughed. "Savannah, I have learned that nothing is simple with you."

Savannah walked back to him and put her arms around him. "But you love me, right, Jonah?"

Jonah kissed her on the lips and nodded. "That I do, my sweet wife. I guess I could build you an arch."

"And that, my handsome husband, is why you are the best husband in this valley."

*****

"Why do I feel so jittery?" Joseph asked Jonah on their way into the village to pick up his suit.

"It isn't every day that one gets married."

"But I am the one that asked her, and I have waited on this for two years, ever since I laid eyes on her, and tomorrow is the big day, and I am sick to my stomach over it all. Is this normal?"

Jonah laughed. "Yes, it is perfectly normal. You aren't getting cold feet, are you?"

"Are you kidding? I can't wait."

"Then what exactly is it that you are nervous about?"

"Everything, just everything," he threw up his hands, causing Jonah to laugh harder.

"Well, don't be. Everyone in the valley is excited for you and Peggy, and we will all be there cheering you on, on your big day."

"Can I tell you something and you not laugh at me?"

"I'm sorry, please forgive me for laughing. I just remembered how nervous I was also."

"It's okay, I understand. It's just that it isn't really the wedding I am nervous about."

"Oh?"

"Jonah, I mean, Peggy and I…" his voice trailed off.

"You are nervous about being alone with her on your wedding night, for the first time?"

"Bingo, go ahead and laugh if you want."

Joseph, I am not going to laugh; I totally understand. You are excited yet nervous because you have never been with a woman like that before, and you want it to be perfect."

"Yes, yes, see? You do understand."

"I promise you that tomorrow night, everything is going to be perfect, and you are going to wake up the next morning and wonder why you were nervous at all."

"You are right, I know."

"And as the years go by and you two truly become more accustomed to each other, you will know what the other is thinking, and even be able to finish each other's sentences. You will be one flesh, and your favorite time of the day will be when the rest of the world sleeps, and it's just you and her and you lay in each other's arms and share thoughts and dreams."

"My sister is lucky to have you," Joseph smiled.

"I'm the lucky one, and you are lucky too, Joseph. Peggy is a beautiful woman who seems to adore you. You two are going to have a very happy life together."

"Thank you. And thanks for the talk. This was not something I could have talked to Mother or Savannah about."

"I guess not, and Joseph, I hope you know you can talk to me about anything. You are young enough to be my son, and I love you."

"Would you stand by me tomorrow as my best man? That would mean a lot to me."

Jonah smiled. "Thank you, and it would also mean a lot to me. I would love to."

*****

"Can I come in?" Noel knocked lightly on the door.

"Yes, Daddy, you can come in."

287

Noel came into Peggy's room and shut the door behind him. "It's about time to ride to the church and I wanted to take a moment to speak to you, if I might?"

"Sure, Daddy, I am glad you come in; I wanted to speak to you, also."

"Oh, really, is everything okay?" he asked.

Peggy smiled. "Everything is wonderful. I just wanted to thank you for agreeing to walk me down the aisle and being the best daddy, any girl could have hoped for all these years."

"Your momma told me how pretty the dress was on you, but goodness, it is more beautiful than I ever imagined. You, my beautiful daughter, are going to cause that young man to fall deeper in love just by looking at you."

"Oh, Daddy, you are silly."

"No, it is true. I remember when I married your momma and realized that she was about to become my wife and how beautiful she was, and that in just a few hours it would be just she and I, and I was overwhelmed with happiness."

"I am happy too, Daddy. I love Joseph and cannot wait to become his wife. Thank you for all you have done for both of us."

"You are my daughter, and he is about to become my son, and I will help you in any way that I can for as long as God lets me live."

Peggy kissed Noel on the cheek. "I love you, Daddy."

"I love you, my beautiful daughter. Are you ready to head to the church? Savannah is going to have Joseph inside waiting on us, and she has the band here playing some soft music."

Peggy giggled. "Mrs. Bell thinks of everything."

"That she does."

*****

Savannah was waiting outside when the Ayers family arrived. Everything had gone just as she had planned so far, and she thanked God for the beautiful weather.

"Right on time," she smiled.

"We had a great wedding planner," Marylou laughed.

"Children, go on in and take a seat. Marylou, Jonah is waiting just inside the door to escort you to your seat and then he will stand beside Joseph," Savannah directed.

"And what do we do?" Noel asked, climbing off the wagon to help Peggy down with her long dress.

"When the music starts, I will open the doors and I will walk in first to the front to stand beside Peggy, as she asked me to, and when you see me stop, you both will walk in slowly, Peggy holding on to your arm, taking a step then pause, a step then pause, got it?"

Noel chuckled, "I think so, the worst thing we can do is either walk too fast or too slow. I'm not real experienced in the wedding department."

Savannah smiled. "You will be fine. Are you ready, Peggy?"

"I am."

When the music started, Savannah walked slowly to the front of the church.

"Everyone rise," Pastor Anderson said, as everyone rose to their feet and faced the door.

Joseph gasped as Noel and Peggy stepped to the entrance of the church.

Peggy was even more beautiful than he remembered, with her hair pinned up on her head and a few curls cascading down. Her dress fit her body like a glove, with the white lace going all the way to the floor.

This was about to be his wife, and he could not hold back the tears.

Jonah placed his hand on top of Joseph's shoulder, letting him know he understood.

Noel escorted Peggy to the front of the church, under the beautiful arch that Jonah had built, and placed her hand in Jonah's.

Pastor Anderson smiled at the two young adults and began. "Dearly beloved, we are gathered here today in front of these witnesses of family and friends to join these two together, Joseph Mitchell Bowen and Peggy Ann Ayers, in holy matrimony. Who gives this woman to be wed?"

Noel stood. "Her mother and I do."

"If there is anyone here today that can show just cause why this man and this woman should not be wed, let them speak now or forever hold your peace."

There was a brief silence in the church.

"Marriage is not to be taken lightly. It is the bond between one man and one woman, as they join together with one flesh, to love each other and respect each other all the days of their life. Let us pray."

Joseph could do nothing but stare into Peggy's eyes, with his own filled with tears and mouth the words, I love you.

"Dear Father, standing before you are two young people who are very much in love. Father, we ask you to place your protection over their marriage and help them to grow deeper in love and closer to You, always knowing that with You, Father, anything is possible, and even on the cloudiest of days, there is always a brighter tomorrow. Amen

"Joseph and Peggy, I have watched you two young adults grow over the past two years, and I am proud of each of you. May I say that if you always place God at the head of your marriage, always praying together, and talking through anything that may come your way, you will have a long and happy life together.

"Joseph, do you take this woman, Peggy, to be your lawfully wedded wife, to have and to hold, in sickness and in health, for richer, or for poorer, loving and cherishing her all the days of her life, forsaking all others, as long as you both shall live?"

"I do," Joseph smiled at her.

"Peggy, do you take this man, Joseph, to be your lawfully wedded husband, to have and to hold, in sickness and in health, for richer, or for poorer, loving and respecting him all the days of his life, forsaking all others, as long as you both shall live?"

"I do," Peggy squeezed Joseph's hands tighter.

"Then, by the power vested in me and the state of Arkansas, I now pronounce you husband and wife. Joseph, you may kiss your bride."

Joseph pulled her close and kissed her for the first time in front of anyone else.

"Let me now introduce to you Mr. and Mrs. Joseph Bowen."

Everyone stood and cheered as they joined hands and walked back out of the church.

"Jonah and Savannah would also like for me to announce that everyone is invited back to their barn for the reception and some music."

*****

"Why didn't you ask me to help you?" Nancy asked Savannah at the reception.

"Because I knew you would, and Mother and I wanted this to be something that the community didn't have to help with, but something you all could come and enjoy."

291

"You have outdone yourself, Savannah, everything is beautiful."

"Thank you," she laughed. "We have been planning it a while, but really just threw it all together in a week."

"I had no idea," Marylou come up behind them. "I would have helped if you had asked."

Savannah laughed. "Please don't be offended. You had your hands full making the dress, which was absolutely beautiful, by the way. Mother and I wanted to do it, for them."

"My wife performs miracles," Jonah commented, hearing the conversation going on.

"Oh, Jonah, it wasn't all me; you and Mother and the children helped, too."

"Nah, I just swept the hay off the stage," he laughed.

The evening was beautiful, as everyone ate and danced, and Joseph and Peggy cut their cake.

As they were leaving to head back to their cabin in Jonah's wagon they had borrowed, everyone threw rice and waved goodbye.

Joseph and Peggy were finally man and wife, and Savannah couldn't be happier seeing the love on each of their faces as they said, "I do." It was a wedding to be remembered.

*****

Savannah could tell something was bothering Jonah as they put the children to bed. It had been a long day, from sunup until way past sundown, and Savannah guessed he was showing the signs of a man who was beyond tired.

"Are you okay, Jonah?" she asked, as he was getting into bed.

"Can I talk to you about something?"

"Sure, you know you can. I can tell something is bothering you."

"You were beautiful today, standing there beside Peggy. I am glad she asked you to be her maid of honor."

Savannah smiled. "Thank you, and you were handsome standing beside Joseph, but that isn't what this is about, is it?"

"Sort of, yes."

Savannah snuggled closer. "What's wrong, Jonah?"

"I am just so sorry, Savannah, that our wedding wasn't like that. When I saw you standing there today and saw Joseph crying watching Peggy walk down the aisle, I understood how he felt because I love you that much. And I felt bad that you were not able to experience what Peggy did."

"Jonah, I know that you love me, and I understand about all that and why it wasn't possible back then. You still loved Clara when we said I do."

"I did, and I hate myself for forcing you to marry me and forcing you to leave your parents, and forcing you to move out west, and forcing you to become an instant mother. You are right; I did not love you when I said I do, but today, some thirteen years later, I love you more than anyone I have ever loved in all my life."

"Shhhh, it's okay, Jonah. One day you will stop beating yourself up over all of this. I forgive you. And if I had had a choice in the matter, I still would be with you here today. I have told you all this before."

"You have, but today just made me realize that you have gotten so much less than you ever deserved. You deserved a beautiful wedding dress and a cake and flowers and a man that cried when you walked down the aisle."

"And yet, I have a man that loves me every bit as much as my brother loves Peggy--even more so, because we have had thirteen wonderful years together and have three beautiful children. I do have a man that has cried for me and makes love to me late at

293

night when the world is sleeping. I have a man that would lay down his life for me, and I know it."

"I would, in a heartbeat."

"So, you see, Jonah, all the wedding dresses and cakes or anything else, for that matter, doesn't change a thing. Please do not worry about our past. Let us just look ahead and concentrate on tomorrow and the week after that, knowing that our love will conquer anything that might come our way."

"I love you, Savannah."

"And I love you, Jonah. Thank you for making today special for my brother and being a Pa to him that he never had."

"And thank you for making it the most beautiful wedding and working so hard for so many. You are such a special lady."

"We are a team, Jonah, you and me. And with God, nothing is impossible."

*****

Savannah did not feel like she was about to be thirty years old in a few weeks, and yet at times she felt as if she had lived a lifetime with Jonah, here in the valley in Arkansas.

What a beautiful day it was to be sitting on the ridge overlooking the valley and their farm below with her journal in her lap.

It had been much too long since she had opened its pages and shared her life or poetry.

As I sit here with the sun shining on my face, I am reminded how blessed I truly am.

This is my favorite spot, the same spot where Jonah stopped the wagon almost fourteen years ago, and we decided that this would be where we made our home. And we have.

And even though that distant day seems like yesterday, so much has taken place.

Rose is now going on fourteen and such a beautiful young lady, who is so eager to help in any way she can; whether it be taking care of her younger siblings or helping cook or clean. I have so enjoyed being her momma, and I know that she would have made Clara proud.

Matthew is now ten and becoming more like his pa each day. I am so thankful that Jonah is such a good role model for him to follow in his footsteps. He still follows his pa everywhere when he isn't at school and is learning so much about how to grow into a man that any woman would be proud to call her husband.

Catherine, now nine, no longer worries so much about competing with her brother. I think she finally realizes that it's okay if he is better than her at some things. Although I don't see Catherine in the kitchen like Rose, but more a tomboy who much rather be outside than in. I am eager to see where life will take my Catherine and know that whatever that is, I will be one proud momma and cheer her on.

I can see Mother down below hanging her wash on the line. I could have never dreamed that she would be living right beside me one day, after I left Dahlonega and set out west to Arkansas. I thank God daily for such a blessing.

Mother seems to love it here in the valley and has converted Joseph's old room into a sewing/work room where she loves spending her time making beautiful dresses she has started selling at the dress shop in the village where Dottie now works. It keeps her busy and makes her happy.

Mary sometimes writes her friend Chrissy back home but has become best friends with Rose. Those two are never very far from the other. I am grateful for Mary, because Rose needed a close friendship. They share everything, even their crushes on Nathaniel Anderson and Jerry Ayers.

Mary is now almost sixteen and plans to go one more year to school. I am not sure what her plans will be after that, but I know if Nathaniel ever sees her as she sees him, there will be another wedding in the near future.

Joseph and Peggy love being married. It does my heart good to know that my baby brother is finally in Arkansas and so in love with his wife. He always told me that he would meet her in Arkansas, and that he did.

It amazes me the way our farm has expanded with two more fields being plowed to give Joseph and Mary a good crop and vegetables to sell at the market. Joseph is here bright and early each morning helping Jonah all he can. He is also helping Noel and learning to build furniture. I don't think there is anything my younger brother can't or won't do. Not a lazy bone in his body.

Jonah is such a wonderful man to have done all he has for my family, from building them a place to live, to taking Joseph under his wing and becoming more like a pa to him than a brother-in-law.

Yes, my handsome husband is now forty-four and his dark hair is starting to show signs of white growing through. Of course, I would never point that out, as I know he doesn't need to stress about growing older, but just being the wonderful husband, father and friend he already is.

God truly blessed me when Jonah asked my father for my hand in marriage, for I could not imagine my life or where I would be if that had not taken place.

And even though there was a time I thought he would never love me the way I wanted to be loved, there isn't a doubt in my mind that he loves me now, for he not only tells me daily, but shows me by everything he does.

The valley is growing, and the wagon trails have become more defined.

There is still much land all around us that has yet to be settled, and I am excited to see who our new neighbors will be as the years go on.

I can feel fall in the air as the days seem to get shorter.

I think tonight would be a great night to make a pot of chicken dumplings and invite Mother and Mary to come and eat with us. I bet Mother already has some sort of dessert made.

For now, it's time to put the journal away and go find my handsome husband in the barn to see what he is up to. Yes, I am a truly blessed woman, indeed.

A Letter from Karen:

I have so enjoyed writing *Bountiful Blessings,* the second book in the series of *Traded for One Hundred Acres.*

I absolutely LOVE writing about back in the 1800's. When I was a little girl, my favorite television shows were always set back in the olden days.

I think perhaps I am an old soul, and as much as I love modern day conveniences, the thought of going back to those days of long ago intrigues me.

Trust me, I would not do well in those days, though, because I love electricity, heat with just the control of a switch, cell phones, internet, microwave food, and of course, nice big tubs full of hot water.

I never intended to write another book that continued the story of *Traded for One Hundred Acres,* but because you loved it and asked me to continue the story, well, here we are. I do hope that you love what I have done to the characters and all the new characters I allowed to move into the valley. Don't you just love Joseph and his love for Peggy?

You asked me to bring Savannah's family from Georgia to Arkansas, and I happily obliged. I too thought it was a much-needed reunion.

My daughter, Heather, named the main characters, Savannah and Jonah, and I just fell in love with those names. But there is something you might find interesting:

Alice is named after a sweet elderly lady I used to work for when I was a CNA (Caregiver) and her grandchildren called her Momma Alice. She was one of my biggest fans and would love this series if she had not passed before they were published.

The man mentioned that bought the Bowen farm back in Dahlonega, D.L. Butler, was Alice's husband. He passed away five years before she did, but I did have the pleasure of meeting him and working with him for several months before then. He was a gentle, kind man.

Noel and Marylou Ayers are named after my father's parents, my *real* grandparents, and the names of their children (my aunts and uncles, and my father) are all here--Daniel, Peggy, Jerry (my dad), Powell, Glenda, Ricky and Janice.

Janice was killed in a car accident when she was only four, so it was fun to give her a role in this story, since she did not have much of one in life.

Norman, the barber, was my mother's father, my grandfather, and believe it or not, he was actually a barber and cut hair for the people of the community. I remember when I was a little girl, going into a shop he built right next to the old home place, and sitting in the red swivel leather chair. I remember the smell of shaving creams and lotions.

Katie, Pastor Anderson's wife, is named after my mother's real mom, my grandmother. I do not remember her, as she passed with cancer a year before I was born. But people who knew her said she was a wonderful godly woman and the best cook they had ever seen.

John Barge is named after a man I met once several years ago who allowed me to use his cabin to write *Traded for One Hundred Acres*.

I hated that I had to write the passing of John in *Bountiful Blessings*, but he was an elderly man in the first book, and here ten years have passed. Death is a part of life, and as the years pass here in the valley, so do the characters.

Don't you love the way God sent an angel in the form of John to show Jonah where his son was and save Matthew's life? Jonah would never give up trying to find his boy, so he actually saved two lives. (I so enjoyed writing that part)

When Savannah told of her teacher, Mrs. Rogers, and how she gave her the dream of becoming a teacher someday, I too, had a Mrs. Rogers as a teacher when I was in the fourth grade, and after turning in a short story I had written, she asked to speak to me after class.

I thought I was in trouble and was terrified. But on that day, one shy little girl who thought she did nothing right, was told she had a great imagination and that she should become an author someday and write books that people would enjoy.

That dream lived inside of me for thirty-seven years until *The Secrets of Westingdale* came to life, my very first book.

If you know me, you know I love Jesus, which is why I write Christian Fiction. I have been told more than once that I should write books of other genres, because people aren't much into God anymore.

But you see, He has *always* been there for me, and so I would much rather use the gift of writing, that He gave me, for Him, than try to be famous writing things my own heart isn't into.

Jesus came to this earth, God wrapped in flesh, to die for everyone, not just some. And those that believe shall live forever in eternity with Him.

For God so loved the world, that He gave His only begotten Son, that **WHOSOEVER** *believeth in Him should not perish, but have everlasting life. John 3:16*

*****

This has always been my favorite Bible verse because to me, it says it all. The word **WHOSOEVER** means anyone, everyone, all of us, if we just BELIEVE that Jesus is our Savior.

We can have everlasting life when this life is over. It does not matter what we have done or where we came from. It doesn't matter the color of our skin, our race or nationality. He died for ALL OF US--isn't that great?

If you have never asked Jesus into your heart, and believe that He is the Son of God, God in the flesh, born of a virgin, to live on this earth and die for our sins, and that He rose again after just three days, then humble yourself and ask Him today.

*****

Dear Lord, I believe that You are the Son of God. I believe that You come to this earth to die for my sins. I am asking You today, to fill me with Your Holy presence and save my soul. Forgive me, Lord, and save me from past sins. Today, dear Jesus, wipe the slate clean, and allow me to start again, a new creation in You.

Thank You, Lord Jesus, for becoming my Savior.

Amen

*****

If you have just prayed the prayer of salvation and asked Jesus to become your Lord and Savior, then I'd like to give you this advice: Make sure, if you don't have a Bible, that you go and buy one TODAY. The King James version or the New Revised Version are both good.

If you cannot afford a Bible, then write to me, and I will mail you one free of charge. I advise you to seek a Bible-believing church and get to know the people there. Learn from them and grow deeper in your relationship with Jesus.

*****

If *Bountiful Blessings* touched you in any way, I'd like to hear from you. Please email me at karenyp46@gmail.com I would love to hear your comments.

*****

You can also find me on Twitter, Facebook, Instagram or LinkedIn, As: Karen Ayers, Author, Motivational Speaker. Follow along with me daily as I share inspirational quotes and let you know of upcoming books.

*****

For speaking engagements at Churches, Christian Schools, Women's Conventions, etc., please allow six to eight weeks' notice. It would please me to come and share with you my own testimony of faith.

*****

Look for other books by Karen Ayers at: www.sbpra.com/KarenAyers

The Seasons of Change Series
Sweet Summer Rain
Fall's Undying Promise
Cold Winter's Chill
The Fragrance of Spring

Stand Alone Books:
The Secrets of Westingdale
Amazing Grace, the Ultimate Forgiveness

Imperfect World, Perfect Me (Self-help)

Traded for One Hundred Acres (1832)
Bountiful Blessings (1842)

Review Requested:

We'd like to know if you enjoyed the book.
Please consider leaving a review on the platform
from which you purchased the book.

CPSIA information can be obtained
at www.ICGtesting.com
Printed in the USA
LVHW010815300321
682936LV00009B/88